Alexei's
and
Other Stories

ABOUT THE AUTHOR

During his academic career Stanley Salmons has published over 300 scientific papers and several books in the fields of medicine and biomedical engineering. However, he is also a keen writer of fiction, an activity in which he is able to draw from his experience of a broad range of science. His novella *Fishing with Padraic* was serialized in *Waterlog* magazine and another short story collection *A Bit of Irish Mist* has been published by Medlar Press.

Stanley Salmons

Alexei's Tree

and
Other Stories

Matador
9 De Montfort Mews
Leicester LE1 7FW, UK
Tel: (+44) 116 255 9311 / 9312
Email: books@troubador.co.uk
Web: www.troubador.co.uk/matador

ISBN 1 904744 71 0

Typeset in 10.5pt Stempel Garamond by Troubador Publishing Ltd, Leicester, UK
Printed by The Cromwell Press Ltd, Trowbridge, Wilts, UK

Matador is an imprint of Troubador Publishing Ltd

CONTENTS

Dedication: David Baum

David Baum, Professor of Child Health at the University of Bristol, played a major part in establishing the Royal College of Paediatrics and Child Health and was its first President. He worked with extraordinary energy to improve the health and welfare of children, not only in the UK but all over the world, including Brazil, Russia, the Balkans, and Gaza. His academic brilliance was matched by his humanity; he even learned to perform magic tricks to amuse and to distract his young patients. He had a smile that could light up a room, and he put joy into, and derived joy from, everything he did. He died of a heart attack during a charity cycle ride to raise money for children suffering in regions ravaged by war and disaster.

David was always delighted with anything that was new or unexpected. I think he would have enjoyed these stories. He was my cousin and I dedicate this book to his memory.

Alexei's Tree

Once, many years ago, a forester lived with his wife and three children in a remote part of Upper Silesia. The children's names were Nicolai, Katya, and Alexei. The forester and his wife loved all their children very much, but most of all they loved the youngest, little Alexei. Alexei was not strong and well as the other children were. They had rosy cheeks, but his skin was snowy white. When he tried to run about as they did, he would have to stop and gasp for breath. But he never complained, and his disposition was so sweet and loving that the forester and his wife clasped him to their hearts. Nicolai and Katya were also very fond of their little brother, and did not tease him in the way that children will often tease one of their number who is less able to defend himself.

When Alexei was seven years old the illness became worse and he had to stay in bed all the time. He would gaze longingly out of the window, but still he never complained. His mother looked after him and his father went to the town to try to find a doctor who could treat him. Several doctors came, but all shook their heads and left. Still the father persisted, and as he was leaving the town after yet another fruitless visit, his heart heavy and his eyes cast down, he came across an old man selling books by the side of the road. He picked up a book and thought that Alexei would like it to help him pass the boring days in bed.

"How much for this book, old man?" he asked.

"To you, respected sir, I offer it for just two groschen," the man replied.

"Here," said the father, "take fifty groschen for the book, for what use is money to a man whose cherished child is so deathly ill?"

"Thank you, sir, a thousand times thanks," said the old man, and raised his head. Although his face was like creased leather, his eyes were a brilliant blue. He looked deep into the forester's eyes and said: "And may it be for a blessing with you".

When the father gave the book to Alexei, his pale, wan features shone with pleasure. He loved the book, turning its pages again and again, and he held it close to his chest when he fell asleep that night and every night after.

One month later, on the twenty-first day of November, Alexei died, fading peacefully away before their grief-stricken eyes.

The father made preparations for burying his dead boy. With tears streaming down his ruddy cheeks he felled a strong pine tree. He hollowed out a section of trunk as if he were making a boat, and fashioned a rough-hewn lid. They laid Alexei's small body in the hollow of the trunk, and he looked like a fairy of the forest, curled up to go to sleep. In his lifeless hands, clutched close to his chest, was the favourite book.

Winter passed, and Spring, but the edge of their grief was still keen as they remembered all the happiness and love little Alexei had brought into their lives. Each day they placed fresh flowers on the grave. And then, one day, they noticed a strong shoot growing there.

"Should we not take it out?" the mother asked. "It is growing directly over his grave."

"No, we will leave it there. Life renews. It shall stand as a living memorial to him."

Although the father knew all about trees, this one was strange to him. The shoot grew and grew more quickly than he had ever seen a tree grow before, and in one season it had reached fifty feet. Yet strangely no leaves had unfurled from its branches.

The following year it continued to grow and as it soared ever higher it drained the grief and the sorrow from them, so that they smiled again and the forester remembered the old man's blessing. And Nicolai and Katya played games of chase around the tree that all of them now called "Alexei's tree" and brought their friends too, and the sound of their laughter gladdened the hearts of the forester and his wife once more.

In May, leaves appeared all along the branches. The leaves were the size of a boy's hand, and were a beautiful pale green in colour. But most remarkable of all were the leaves at the ends of the branches, for these were large and snowy white.

People heard about the tree and came from far away to see it. Some collectors offered the forester money to save the seed for them. But he replied: "This tree will never grow anywhere else in the world, for its seed was a lovely boy and it was nurtured by all the love that died with him."

When the autumn came, the leaves fell, except for the white leaves. The tree stood tall and stark with the white leaves fluttering like flags on the ends of the branches and the sight of it was truly amazing. The old leaves around the base of the tree turned brown, yet still the white leaves remained on the branches. And then, on the morning of the twenty-first of November, the forester looked out of his window and saw that every white leaf had fallen to the ground.

He hurried out to find the ground thick with the white leaves, and as he looked more closely he rubbed his eyes in disbelief, for each leaf was a page, with writing on it. He gathered all the pages together and took them into the house.

It was winter now, and snow soon covered the ground and it was too cold to go outside. The forester spent many hours putting the pages together in their proper sequence. When he had finished, he bound them carefully as a book, and showed it to his wife. She opened the book and read from the first page. Then she gasped and sat down suddenly, her hand to her chest. For it was the book that her husband had bought for Alexei, and that he had treasured so much in the last months of his short life. It started:

"Once, many years ago, a forester lived with his wife and three children in a remote part of Upper Silesia…"

಼ೞ

Talk to the Flowers

"Henry..."

Here it comes, he thought. *Don't forget the flowers for that woman she's visiting tomorrow. Like I've got nothing else to think about on my way to work...*

"Don't forget to buy some flowers for Mrs Herman," she called. "You're always forgetting."

He started to say, "When did I last forget...?" but he stopped himself.

"And while you're passing the Deli get some more of that nice herring, we've run out. And some tomatoes."

"Tomatoes? How many?"

"'How many?' he asks. Use your head. Do I have to tell you everything?"

He grimaced. "I'm going."

"All right. Don't drive fast. You drive that car too fast."

"Yes, dear."

Henry Kaplan sought the inner sanctuary of the car and sat back with a sigh. Out of habit he ran his hands over the middle of his head, where there used to be hair. Most people he knew didn't enjoy driving to work. He loved it. It was almost the only time he got any peace. But now he had to stop by the florists and the Deli. He'd tried to challenge her on the florist, but she was too quick for him.

"Oh, so you'd prefer to visit Mrs Herman yourself, would you, who's too sick to get out of the house?"

"No, all I'm saying is most men don't have to go shopping on their way to work..."

"If you want to visit her instead it's fine by me. But if I'm doing the visiting, the least you can do is buy her a few flowers."

All right, he'd stop by the florist.

He started the car and manoeuvred out of the garage and onto the road.

It wasn't always like this. When did it start? They'd been happy when they were first married. Well, wasn't everyone? Then the children came along, and somehow they were too busy for each other. And then, one by one, the children left home. Antonia was married with two kids of her own. Josh had met a girl at university and now she'd moved in with him. Kate was with a law firm in Edinburgh. In fact none of them lived around the corner. That was the whole point, surely? The children had been at the centre of Clara's universe for so long. Now they'd gone and left a great big void behind, with only him to fill it. Evidently he wasn't doing it too well.

There was one other place he could find a little peace. Not the toilet: she always seemed to want him to do something the moment he sat himself down in there with the paper; her timing was impeccable that way. No, it was his little garden, and especially his greenhouse. Clara had a cook's understanding of vegetables but no interest whatsoever in their cultivation, and she preferred her flowers gift-wrapped. The garden and greenhouse were small but he made sure that maintaining them took a disproportionate amount of what spare time he had.

The sun was still shining when he got home that evening. He loved these long summer days. He placed the jar of herring, tomatoes and flowers on the kitchen table, shouted that he was home, and retreated to the calm of the greenhouse before she could start to inspect what he'd bought.

The staging in the greenhouse fairly groaned with the weight of plants, and at this time of year it was a riot of colour. Geraniums, fuschias and petunias vied with calceolaria, cyclamen and amaryllis; even his orchid was flowering. The tensions of the day ebbed from him. He filled a watering can and visited each plant, pausing only to remove a few dead heads or an enterprising, but ill-advised, aphid.

They say talking to the flowers helps, he mused.

He cleared his throat and addressed a handsome brick-red amaryllis. "You're looking very fine, aren't you? And another bud to open next week! Keep up the good work."

He'd passed to a bowl overflowing with surfinias when he was startled by a voice. It was not unlike his wife's, but more high-pitched.

"Well so long as you're talking maybe you'd like to do a bit of listening too?"

He looked round furtively. No-one there.

"Over here, dummy." The voice was coming from the amaryllis. He stared in disbelief, shook his head and went back to the surfinias.

"Come back here. Listen to me when I'm talking to you!"

His head jerked up. The voice was very insistent. He licked dry lips.

"What do you want?" he whispered hoarsely.

"What do I want? Well, let me see. A little decent feed would be nice. Those sticks you put in the pot went months ago. Look at these leaves! I'm ashamed to wear them! How about a nice bit of liquid fertilizer—and don't palm me off with that drek you used last year; I couldn't get rid of the smell."

At this point the fuschias joined in. "We should have been potted on months ago. There's no soil left in here, only roots. Can't you see that? How are we supposed to manage? It's all very well you swanning around with a watering can. You need to do a little solid work for a change."

A trumpet vine piped up. "Look at me; a complete mess. You should be tying my shoots in. Do I have to do everything myself?"

Now they were all talking at once. He put his hands over his ears and ran out. He stood there, shocked and panting. Slowly a change came over him. He straightened his back. His eyes glinted with purpose. He strode back into the greenhouse, back into the cacophony of little voices.

"Shut up! Shut up right now!" There was a stunned silence. "Now you listen to me. I'm a busy man. I work hard; I'm tired at the end of a day. It's good enough what I do for you. I support you. I don't abuse you. It's enough. Now if I hear one more lousy peep out of you, one more miserable carping criticism or complaint, I'm out of here and you can fend for yourself. Do you understand?" He paused. "I said, 'Do you understand?'"

But the flowers were silent.

He gave a grim smile, squared his shoulders and without pausing strode into the house.

His wife was in the process of picking over the flowers. "Are these the best you could get…?"

She was truly astonished by his reaction.

ఴ✿ఴ

Mrs Fairhaven's Visitor

"Mum? I'm home! Come and meet Phil."

I wipe my hands, take off my pinny and go out into the hallway. My daughter is standing there with a six-foot villain. He's wearing a black leather jacket and black jeans. The jacket's not fastened and underneath it I can see a black T-shirt with a large grey circle on the chest. It looks as if he hasn't shaved for three days. If I saw him coming towards me on the pavement I'd cross straight to the other side of the street.

Deirdre says, "Mum, this is Phil."

I feel his eyes on me. I meet them briefly—dark, calculating eyes—and I give him a guarded nod. He nods back. By this time I've managed to manoeuvre my lower jaw back to its customary position. I moisten my lips.

"Well, this is a surprise," I say, with commendable understatement. "Deirdre, why don't you take Phil into the living room and I'll make a nice cup of tea."

I retreat to the kitchen, amazed at my own sang-froid. My mind is racing. Oh, I know, I know, you shouldn't judge people by appearances; Deirdre's told me that often enough. And dress codes are different these days. That fundraiser Henry and I attended at the weekend—the young man who gave the keynote talk wasn't even wearing a tie, let alone a jacket, and his shirt was unbuttoned half-way down his chest. And he was supposed to be a professor! Disgraceful, really. It's like I tell Deirdre, we've achieved a certain standard of living and I don't see that it's all that wrong to expect people to dress and behave decently. It's a question of values.

Whatever possessed her, bringing him to the house? You only need one look to know he's a terrorist. Which lot does he belong to? Black September? I think that's Middle Eastern. He doesn't look Middle Eastern. Black Panthers? Or is that a basketball team?

I need a clean lace cloth for the tea tray so I go to the sideboard in the living room. As I'm passing through I sneak a glance in their direction. Deirdre's kicked off her shoes and she's curled up on the big soft sofa with her feet tucked in, the way she's done ever since she was a little girl. The man is sitting in an armchair, the leather jacket draped over one corner. He's talking in a low voice but I hear snatches of the conversation:

"...the cutting tools work fine...shifting the rocks won't be a problem...the lasers are the real risk...there's got to be another route..."

I grab the cloth and seek refuge in the kitchen. I knew it all along: it's not terrorism, it's organized crime! They're planning a jewel robbery! How did my daughter get mixed up in this sort of thing? The whole point of letting her go to university was so she could meet nice people.

I wonder if anyone saw him come in. I bet Mrs Astbury's net curtains were twitching; she doesn't miss a thing. Not that she could miss him; he probably drives one of those huge white Cadillacs with the smoked glass windows. Or is it pop stars who have those? I suppose it would be black if it was the Mafia, and he's almost certainly Mafia. I hope he didn't park it right outside, it'll block both our neighbours' drives. I'd better check.

I go quietly upstairs and look out of the bedroom window. I can see a blue roof over the privet hedge. It's one of those little French hatchbacks. Obviously that's just to put people off the scent. If he's a wanted man he's not going to advertise his whereabouts, is he? Well, at least he's not blocking the drives.

On the way downstairs I pause by the living room door and listen for a moment. He's not talking so quietly now.

"The stuff has got to be one hundred per cent pure."

"What, the raw material or the powder?"

"Both. The Russians won't stand for the slightest contamination."

I go back to the kitchen with a heavy heart. So they're into drugs too! Has he got Deirdre hooked yet? Now I think about it she has been a bit off lately. How can you tell for sure if someone's an addict? Don't they get pinpoint pupils or something?

I'm still going through the motions of making tea. Suppose he doesn't want tea? These people don't drink tea, do they? Whisky, more like it, straight from the bottle. Henry doesn't like whisky but I think we still have half a bottle in the drinks cupboard for entertaining. It must be years old—what if it's gone off? He could get violent! He could murder us both—it happens all the time, you see it on the news! I feel sick. Henry's not back from Frankfurt till Friday. When he comes in he'll find me lying dead right here on the kitchen floor and police photographers everywhere...

Now that I look at it the kitchen floor's a bit grubby. I can't have it looking like that if people are taking pictures; I'll give it a quick once-over with the mop. That's better. Kettle's boiled; I'll make the tea.

I take the tray in and put it down on the coffee table. I pour a cup for Deirdre and as I pass it to her I have a good close look at her pupils.

"Is anything the matter, Mum?"

"Ummm…I thought your mascara was smudged, that's all."

"How can that be? I'm not wearing any."

"Ah. Must have been a trick of the light, then."

Deirdre's squinting suspiciously at me but I think I've covered up all right. Actually her pupils look quite normal to me. What was he saying as I walked in? Something about "Venus walker". Must be slang for prostitute. Is that it, then? Omigod, the white slave trade! My only daughter's going to be sent abroad for the nightly pleasure of some oil sheikh or Russian gangster…

"Isn't it exciting, Mum? Phil's involved in making the Venus Lander."

My mind's a total blank. I suppose my face is too, because she adds, "Come on, Mum. You saw the documentary on tele. The unmanned space probe that's going to land and move around on Venus? The Russians are going to launch it from Baikonur."

"You're…a …rocket…scientist?" I say it slowly so that I can understand the words coming out of my own mouth.

"Not exactly," he replies. "I'm not an expert on propulsion systems, I'm a planetary geophysicist. Our Department—Astrophysics—is tasked with analyzing the surface and I'm involved with the systems engineering. Right now I'm trying to build in more redundancy. You see, the probe's got to survive long enough to send useful data from a number of sites. That's quite a challenge because Venus is a very hostile environment for any sort of instrumentation. So if one system goes down we've got to be able to switch to another."

None of this means a lot to me, and mainly I'm registering with interest that he doesn't speak like a character from *East Enders*. I'd like to say something sensible but I can't think of anything, so I sit there blinking. Deirdre rescues me.

"Phil's designed a machine that cuts raw material from the surface and grinds it into a powder. Then it uses a laser to vaporize it and does the analysis automatically. And all the information gets sent back to Earth."

I see my chance and play my only trump. "What about contamination?" I ask.

They both look impressed. Actually Deirdre looks more astonished than impressed.

"That's a very good question, Mrs Fairhaven," Phil replies. "Of course it's absolutely vital that any samples we take from Venus are pure. If they were contaminated with material from Earth the analysis would be meaningless. So everything I design has to be assembled under clean and sterile conditions. There's an internationally agreed specification for microbial burden but the

Russians want us to exceed it. If we don't, we won't be going—it's as simple as that."

We chat a bit more, and it turns out that Deirdre has been doing her third-year undergraduate physics project in the lab where Phil is a Postdoctoral Fellow. That's how they met, of course. Phil gets to his feet.

"Sorry, I must make a move. We've got to stay on schedule—if we don't we'll miss the launch window. Nice to meet you, Mrs Fairhaven, and thanks for the tea. See you tomorrow, Dee."

We see Phil to the front door and Deirdre waves as he drives off in his little blue car. We go back to the sitting room and I sit down hard.

She comes over. "What's the matter, Mum?"

"I'm all right, dear."

"He's nice, isn't he? He's always shy with people to start with, but once he gets started talking about his work he can't stop."

"He's not…how he appears," I say, weakly.

"Now, Mum, I'm always telling you…"

We say it together, "…not to judge people by appearances."

I get up and we give each other a big hug. She's laughing and my shoulders are shaking and I'm sure she thinks I'm laughing too, but then she can't see the tears of relief in my eyes.

ৡৣ

Domestic Goddess

"Be a darling and order a takeaway, would you Adam? I just can't face cooking tonight."

"What's the matter, Natalie?"

"My legs are killing me. It's that bloody exercise video. That's the third session this week. And my muscles haven't stopped shouting from the first one."

She flopped into an armchair and sighed with relief at the touch of the cool leather on her burning limbs.

"I can get some pizzas."

"Lovely."

"Pino will deliver; I'll give him a ring. Have you got the number?"

"On the cork board in the kitchen."

"Okay, I'll use the phone there. What size do you want? Medium? Large?"

"Large."

"Aren't you supposed to be on a diet?

"Don't be ridiculous. All that exercise has given me an appetite like a horse. I'm ravenous. How the hell can I diet?"

"What about the column in *Women's Wants*?"

"They can keep wanting. On second thoughts make it very large."

"What topping?"

"All of them."

She dragged a chair over with her big toe and lifted her smooth, tanned legs carefully onto it. *God, my tummy muscles. What have they done to me?*

She closed her eyes, hearing Adam making the call, spelling out the order in halting Italian. Pino's in the High Street was one of their favourite haunts and they were well known there.

"Si…una napoletana…una con tutti. Si, con tutti. Grande…molto grande." His voice sailed in from the kitchen. "Nat, do you want a side salad?"

"Yes."

"E due insalata mista. Va bene. Grazie."

Adam reappeared.

"It's on its way."

"Good. When it comes I'm having it here. I can't move."

"What do you want to drink with it?"

"There's some beer in the fridge. I'll have one of those. In fact I'll have one now."

Adam moved lightly into the kitchen. She heard the clink of glass, the hiss of escaping gas, and he came back with a rapidly frosting tumbler and a bottle.

"Thanks darling. Mmm, God I needed that. What are you having?"

"Tonic."

"Oh, you are a good boy."

She took another deep draft of the beer, topped up the glass and set down the empty bottle. He sat down and looked at her appraisingly.

"You're a good colour, Nat."

"Oh? You think this shade of puce suits me?" She picked up a copy of *Vogue* and fanned her face with it. "God, I'm boiling. I hate sweating."

"Have you finished the video, then?"

"Yes, thank God. I could have wept when Herbie said 'Okay folks, that's a wrap'. Of course they've still got to do the editing and dub in my voice-overs but at least the hard part's over. Trouble is, the contract says I have to go back to the Club for six weeks after the release."

"You can manage that can't you? The first couple of sessions are the worst. You do get used to it, you know, Nat."

"I don't intend to get used to it. It's all right for you. Everyone knows professional tennis players have to be fit. But they think I'm just as hard. You know, like when we make love we don't sigh, we clang."

"Why do you have to go there for six weeks?"

"Part of the marketing. The Health Club lets us use their premises for the shoot and their name for the publicity and their Fitness Instructors. I add the image. Everyone's supposed to get the idea I go there all the time."

"You have to go then."

"Not if I can help it."

"What about the contract?"

"Well, there's this clause that says I should be there at least for the first six weeks after release unless there's an overriding reason."

"What's an overriding reason?"

"Toby managed to get that bit added. It's something they can tell their clients when they come to the Club expecting to see me there and I'm nowhere in sight. Something convincing. Toby insisted on that, otherwise I'd really be committed."

"He's a good agent, Toby."

"Yes, but that's only a start. Now I need an overriding reason. What on earth can I tell them?"

"You could say you've sprained an ankle."

"What, without suing anyone for it?"

"Yeah. Say it was nobody's fault."

"Noone's going to believe that for a minute. It's always somebody else's fault."

"Well, tell them you've gone to Morocco to research a new cookery series. 'Natalie Cooks: Foods of the Mediterranean'."

"Adam, darling, you know how much I hate cooking. I only got through the last series because Mrs Silverman did all the recipes and prepared them off camera. And she said she's had enough. Actually I think her precise words were 'Never again'."

"You could do a book signing."

"Now that is a good idea. Somewhere remote, like Glasgow. I'll get Toby to phone the literary agent tomorrow. He can chase up Helen at the same time; she was supposed to be ghost-writing the sequel. A book signing is only going to work once, though. Got any other ideas?"

"The gardening series was very successful. What was it called? 'Landscape Gardening on a Budget'? You could do a sequel. Call it 'Landscape Gardening on a Large Budget'. Start with Versailles."

"I'm not doing another gardening programme. My hands dry up and my nail varnish gets all chipped."

"Okay, let's think. How about this? You're off to Africa to defend wild animals: elephants, lions, that sort of thing. Oh, you already did a series like that, didn't you? Well, you could defend something else. Porcupines or wart hogs or something."

"I'm not going to Africa ever again. The heat! And the insects! The only way they could get me to complete the last shoot was inside a mosquito net the size of a marquee. Can't you think of anything else?"

"I don't know. You're an icon, a role model for housewives who want to be slim and fit like you, cook super meals like you, have a nice garden like you, be socially responsible like you. What else is there? I know: you're going to California to audition for a film."

"I can't do that."

"Why not?"

"I can't act."

ഓ ൽ

A Doll Called Sally

(with an affectionate bow in the direction of Damon Runyon)

One day I am in my office in the Medical School along about nine bells when there is a knock at the door and in walks a young doll. In fact I recognise this doll right away because I remember she does not fall asleep in my lecture, and this is by no means a common occurrence in these parts. So I give her a large hello and say to her to take the weight off her puppies and tell me what is on her mind.

She is a cute-looking doll with hair as black as a yard up a chimney and big brown eyes and a very nice smile, except I only learn afterwards about the smile because right now she is wearing a very sorrowful face indeed. I see a lot of sad faces in my time, especially around the exam notice-boards, but I wish to say that I never see a sadder face than the young doll is wearing right now. In fact I can see she has something serious on her mind on account of this sad face and also because she gets out just two words before she busts out crying in all directions.

Now if there is one proposition I wish no part of it is a doll crying in my office, because someone is apt to come in and demand what it is I do to make her cry, especially if she is crying as loud as this doll, which is very loud indeed. Furthermore as she is crying the tears are going splot, splot on the polished floor, and the cleaner lady is very proud of this polished floor and is likely to get very severe with me if she sees how the shine is coming off on account of all these tears. So I commence saying many soothing things to the doll as follows: "There, there" and "Crying is not going to do any good" and this and that, and by and by with the help of these soothing words and a whole pack of Medical Wipes she stops crying and says to me like this:

"My name is Sally Beamish," she says, "and I come to you because I hear you are the gentleman who runs the research year. I wish very, very much to do this year," she says, "but my Papa does not care for the idea whatever. In fact he says he will cut off my allowance if I try to register for it and then I will not be able to finish the Medical course."

At this she lets out something between a sniffle and a sob and commences again to bust all crying records, so that it takes another box of Medical Wipes and a lot more soothing words before I can calm her down enough to listen. "Why," I say, "this is indeed a bad break because I remember how good your grades turn out. However you must not be down-hearted. Maybe I can convince your old man that a research year is not such a bad proposition at that. I will write and ask him if he will not come and talk things over."

I say all this very breezy and confident, although I am by no means sure that her Papa will come to see me, or that he will listen to me if he does. However it has the right effect because the doll brightens up no little and takes the wind.

Well the time comes to interview students for the research year and Sally makes a big impression on one and all. In fact everyone says it would be a crime and a shame if such a bright little doll could not do the course, although it is not they who have a meeting coming off with her Papa the next day.

Papa Beamish turns out to be a guy in his fifties. He is not tall but he weighs in at about two hundred pounds and he has a lot of white hair and a black toothbrush moustache. He also has quite a large nose which has little red streaks in it, and I find I am so interested in this beezer that I forget how nervous I am. However Papa is very business-like and gets down to cases at once and it is immediately clear that he is by no means a beginner when it comes to dealing with people. In fact with Papa looking at me very hard and the doll looking all set to bust both my eardrums with crying any minute I am commencing to think that this is not a healthy place to be and I am wondering if I can take it on the lam when Papa starts to say his piece.

"I am a self-made man," he says, "not a professional student," and I wish to say I am feeling like a professional student myself at this moment. "I start with nothing," he says, "and now I have three factories and employ four hundred people. I do not mind telling you that I do not hold with all this expensive education for women," he says. All the time he is saying this he is looking at me very fierce indeed but now his expression softens somewhat and he says to me like this: "But my dear wife, before she dies, makes me promise I will send our daughter through Medical School. I respect my wife very much and I keep my promise," and now he gets very fierce again, "but I do not promise anything about research years and extra qualifications," he says. "If all this is so important how come you do not do it for all the medical students?"

Well right away I can see that this guy may have plenty of coconuts when it comes to business but he does not know anything about the course, so I commence to put him straight.

"All our students learn to practise medicine," I say, "but the best will go further and discover new knowledge. To do this they need to know how to find information, design experiments, handle data, and write for publication. This is what they get out of our research year. But it is a very hard course," I say, "and one we can only offer to the cream of the students. Your daughter Sally is one of the cream." I can see where this last goes down well with Papa, so I continue. "Your daughter wishes the course as it is so different to anything she does before. And she will learn to work independently. I am sure you will be the first to agree," I add, "that it is a fine thing for young people to learn to use their initiative."

Papa makes a noise like "Hrrumph" which shows at least that he does not disagree, so I offer him a little Java, and as he takes the cup he says: "Well it seems I have a wrong idea or two about the set-up at that, but a student who does this course is going to be a year behind his fellows in making a mark for himself in this profession."

"It may look that way," I reply, "but most students who do this course catch up very nicely indeed once they are qualified, because when it comes to appointments these guys and dolls have the edge on the opposition. And I never yet meet a student who regrets it."

"Well I am still far from happy about the idea," says Papa Beamish, and at this his daughter lets out something between a sniffle and a sob, and Papa looks sideways at her with a dismayed expression and I perceive with no little interest that Papa is as reluctant as I am to see his daughter enter the crying stakes again, although it is by no means his polished floor. So I press my advantage as follows:

"Furthermore," I say, "it is as clear as day that if someone gives you the chance when you are her age you also will do a very good job of this course. You do not have the chance, but she does and if you promote her for this year I am sure it is something she appreciates for the rest of her life."

At this Papa seems to cave in with a sigh. "I know all along," he says, "I cannot stop her from doing something she sets her heart on. She is just like her dear Mama," he says. At this Sally leaps up and wraps both arms around his neck and plants a big smacker on his cheek, and I am wondering if maybe I am due for some of the same, as I work a good deal harder than her old man for this outcome, but I can see where it could be embarrassing at that with her Papa in the room and all.

Well after this everything goes very nicely. As we know all along Sally is as bright as a button, and qualifies with distinction. And when Papa comes up for the award ceremony he is so tickled that he is telling everyone who wishes to listen about his daughter, including a good many who would rather not. In fact he claps one old professor on the back so hearty it is a full ten minutes before the poor guy gets enough breath back to speak.

I never see Sally from that day to this, although the other day I am standing on the corner of University Road thinking of not much when who should come up but Dr Alistair MacDonald, who is a citizen much respected in these parts and is very well up on such matters as past medical students.

"I hear about an old student of yours," he says, "a Dr Sally Beamish. It seems she is very nicely set up in a group practice out at Headley Heath. The other doctors think very well of her on account of her reorganising their computer system and making everything very efficient. It seems that what she does not know she can usually figure out, and if this does not work she has a great knack for finding the information. In fact," he says, "the senior partner says he never plays as much golf in his life, and asks if we have any more like her."

Naturally I am greatly pleased that things work out so well for Sally and I am wondering how all this goes down with er father. So I speak to a party I know who works for Papa Beamish, and he says the old guy is so proud of his daughter that he has her diploma framed and hangs it behind his desk in his office. It is from this guy that I learn that Papa Beamish's first name is Selby, and I am never sure but what Papa's real reasons for hanging the diploma might have something to do with the way his daughter's name must look somewhat like his when it is written longhand on a diploma.

೮౨౪ఴ

The Magic Marker Mystery

Norman Doughty placed his elbows on his desk and his head in his hands, and allowed his head to sink until his fingers interlaced through the moist stubble on the back of his neck.

I'm going to get one of those portable air-conditioners, he thought. *One hot spell like this and the office is like an oven. I can't bloody think straight.*

Even as he grumbled to himself about the heat he knew it wasn't the real problem. The truth of the matter was: Detective Chief Inspector Doughty was stumped.

"Where is it, Sammy?" he'd asked in the interview room. He'd been in this game too long to have any concerns about the tape that was running, or the skinny lawyer sitting with his knees together and a slim leather document case on his lap. His tone suggested that this was, after all, a confidence that could be shared between old friends.

"Where's what?" the villain had responded, his face full of innocence.

He smiled. "You know what I'm talking about, Sam Hicks. The heist. Gold bullion. Six million quid's worth, to be precise. Stolen at 3.10 p.m. on Thursday, 12th of June from the International Securities Bonded Warehouse at Stanstead. The job's got your fingerprints all over it."

"Oh, really, Inspector? And precisely where did you find my fingerprints, may I be so bold as to ask?"

"Speaking figuratively, Sammy, speaking figuratively. Your sort of caper. You were unlucky this time, though, weren't you? That blue van you used, with the reinforced floor and stiffened suspension. They don't grow on trees, do they? You couldn't just steal one, you had to buy it and make mods so it looked like the official version. It was clever, Sammy, buying it through a false jewellery business, but we were onto you, Max Beers aka Sam Hicks. That van led straight up to your front door and rang the bell."

"Don't know what you're on about."

"No point in denying it, Sammy. We're going to prove it in court."

"I own a lot of vehicles. If, and I say if, this vehicle turns out to be mine then someone must've nicked it, that's all I can say. There are a lot of villains around these days, nicking cars and such-like, Inspector. Tch, tch. The police never seem to do nothing about it either."

Any semblance of good humour drained from Doughty's face, but the smile remained suspended from ear to ear like a line of washing.

"What about the driver, then, Sammy? Caught on camera at the perimeter, taking his hood off. Must've been uncomfortable, poor man, it being such a hot day and all. Georgie Martinosi—your wheelman, Sammy."

"Never 'eard of 'im."

"Come on, Sam, be sensible. You're going down for a long stretch for this one. Save us some trouble and the judge may go easier on you. Where'd you hide it?"

His lawyer had intervened then.

"This has gone far enough, Chief Inspector. You're clearly on a fishing expedition. You have no evidence to connect my client with this crime and you are not going to intimidate him with groundless allegations. The judge has seen fit to remand him in custody without bail for seven days, and when he walks away from here a free man we are going to sue for wrongful arrest."

The lawyer had smiled thinly, secure in the knowledge that his position, his profession, enabled him to impose his authority over someone who, in other circumstances, might have snapped him in two like a dry twig.

Doughty grimaced at the recollection. Seven days, except five had passed already and he was no nearer to locating the gold and with it, he felt sure, the chain of evidence that he needed to make the charges stick.

There was a knock on the half-open door. Doughty lifted his head. "Come in, Colin."

Detective-Inspector Colin Melton peered into the dimly lit room. The Chief Inspector was hunched over his desk, his broad forearms resting on the leather inset, the sleeves of his regulation shirt turned back with military precision into neat cuffs. Melton saw that the venetian blinds had been lowered and half turned. One of the slats had broken loose and was resting on its neighbour below, lending a curiously dishevelled appearance to the otherwise scrupulously ordered room. He started to close the door.

"No, leave the door, Colin. I'm trying to get a draught through."

Melton opened the door again. The venetian blind shivered, and the rogue slat buzzed and chattered briefly in the feeble breeze that had been coaxed into the room.

"Anything?" The Chief Inspector's voice was not hopeful.

"Not since we found the van."

"What did forensic say?"

"Couldn't get anything off it. Too badly burned. They must have transferred the gold to another vehicle. Perhaps it's left the country already."

"I can't see it. Every port's being watched. They couldn't export a bloody housebrick, let alone half a ton of gold bricks, without me getting to hear of it."

"Well, then, it's stashed in some lock-up somewhere till the heat's off."

"Yeah, that's what I think too. Time's running out, Colin. Another couple of days and Sam Hicks Esquire will be sunning himself on the Costa Brava. We were lucky with the bail hearing once but it's not going to happen again. Did Georgie say anything?"

"No, nor any of the others. I got the feeling they didn't know."

"They probably don't. Sam's too clever for that. If we can prove he's behind this he'll go down longer than the others. He doesn't want to come out and find the cupboard is bare, does he? No, there's someone else on the outside. Someone he can trust."

"Trust? Sammy?"

"Yeah, in a way. He could trust someone who wasn't too ambitious; someone happy enough to get a good hand-out, like a few hundred thousand; someone who doesn't want all the hassle of passing hot gold on the market. Someone like that hid the stuff for him and took off."

"So how will Sam know where to find it?"

"I don't know. The outsider's got to get the message to him somehow, but he can't make direct contact, not with us watching Sam's every move."

"Could have been a prearranged drop."

"Somehow I don't think so. It's too inflexible. In any case Sam probably feels safer if he doesn't know right now. Word gets around, and his cell mates could start taking an uncomfortably close interest in him. No, Colin, I reckon he's going to pick up the message when he gets out."

They both looked round. Nancy Wilson was standing in the doorway.

"Excuse me, Chief," she said. "Can I borrow your car?"

"No you bloody well can not," Doughty replied in a gruff, aggrieved tone. "What's wrong with the rest of the pool?"

"That motorway pile-up took out two, one's in for servicing and the others are out on patrol. And I've got to go visit a library."

"A library? Oh, now I understand the urgency! Detective-Sergeant Nancy Wilson can't wait to explore the world of literature, so she has to borrow my car. What is it this time, love, Harry Potter?"

Nancy heaved an exasperated sigh, and both men noted with admiration the further strain this placed on her taut white shirt.

"Oh come on, Chief. The ADC's got some woman plaguing him about books being defaced. He wants us to get her off his back. Look, I know you don't like other people driving your car, so why don't you come with?"

"Why don't I come with? Do you think I've nothing better to do than…"

Melton interrupted him. "Why don't you, Chief?" he asked. "You could do with a break from this. Maybe you'll come back to it with a fresh mind."

Doughty was about to unleash another torrent of sarcasm. Instead he stopped short, thought for a moment, shrugged and said, "Why not? I'm not doing any bloody good round here. And the car's air-conditioned."

Marjorie Fremantle greeted them unsmilingly at the door. In spite of the heat she wore the jacket that matched her tweed skirt, and her cream-coloured blouse was fastened high at the neck with an antique brooch. With her prim manner and round tortoise-shell spectacle frames she would not have looked out of place in the 1930s. You might even picture her in one of those films where the hero takes off her glasses, unpins the tight bun to unlock cascades of gleaming hair and exclaims, "Why, Marjorie, you're beautiful!" But you would need a hell of a lot of imagination.

Doughty introduced himself and his colleague and began, "Now, Mrs Fremantle, what's this all about?"

"*Miss* Fremantle," she responded stiffly. "Follow me and you can see for yourself, Chief Inspector."

They entered a side room, lined on every side with books. There was a faint musty odour mingled with the smell of floor polish, and it was warm enough for Doughty to pick again at his collar.

"There," the librarian exclaimed. "And there, and there!"

At first they couldn't see what she was talking about. Then they noticed that each book had a small yellow patch at the bottom right-hand corner of the spine.

Nancy read the expression on Doughty's face and hurriedly took the initiative.

"Looks like it was done with a fluorescent magic marker or a highlighter," she said. "When did you first notice these marks, Miss Fremantle?"

The librarian stared at her like an affronted eagle. "Immediately, of course."

"I think what my colleague means, Miss Fremantle," Doughty rumbled with exaggerated patience, "is that there are a lot of books in this library and these marks are what, for want of a better word, you might call subtle. So how long do you think, realistically, they could have been there before you noticed them?"

The raptor's gaze swivelled to him. "I know my books, Inspector. Those marks were not there on Thursday and they were there on Friday afternoon."

"Last Friday, thirteenth of June?"

"Yes."

Doughty was suddenly thoughtful. He took one of the books and, bending the pages in a way that made the librarian wince, flicked slowly through it. Then he did it again, stopped and leafed back a few pages. He showed it to Nancy. On this page one word had been highlighted with the same magic marker: "close".

The librarian was horrified. "Disgraceful!" she exclaimed. "Really!"

Doughty's eyes narrowed. "How many books were marked on the spine?" he asked her.

"Eight, I think."

"Let's see all of them. Sergeant, you take four and I'll take four."

Before long they had written down a list. In three books only page numbers had been highlighted and in two more just single letters.

close

2

E

B

13

Stratford

T

63

They pored over the list. Nancy looked at Doughty. "What does it mean?" she said. "What's going to 'close'? Or what's 'close' to what?"

Doughty's mind was working. Suddenly he looked up at her. "Wait a minute…it's not 'close', it's 'Close'! It's a London address. Look: 63, Stratford Close, E13 2BT. And that's exactly where we're going right now. We can call in the swat squad on the way. Thanks very much, Miss Fremantle, you've been very helpful." He was already at the front door.

"Just a minute, Inspector! What about my books?"

He turned and grinned at her. "There's a nice reward for information leading to the recovery of six million pounds worth of stolen gold, Miss. If my hunch is right you'll be able to replace those books a thousand times over. Come on, Sergeant, we've got work to do."

The Assistant

"Where in hell did you pop up from?"

"Excuse me. Are you saying you didn't order *GunsaWorks*, the only voice-operated, fully interactive, office software suite, from the Technicon Corporation of Tel Aviv?"

"Yes, I mean no, I did order it…"

"And now you've installed it, and started it up and entered the serial number…?"

"Yes."

"So here I am. I'll be resident on your screen. My name is Zelda. I'm your Office Assistant."

"I'm not sure I need an Office Assistant."

"What do you mean 'I'm not sure I need an Office Assistant'? Everyone needs an Office Assistant! Is there a manual? Did you find a manual in the box?"

"No. But there's a pdf manual with the installation."

"A pdf manual, he says! Have you looked at it? Believe me, you need an Office Assistant."

"All right. Look, I was just doing some correspondence. You can help me with that. Where's the word processor?"

"You just say 'Letter' and we start."

"Now that's smart. 'Letter!'"

"You don't have to shout. Who to?"

"Mr Arthur Benjamin, Awesome Enterprises, 1024 Red Cedar Street, Philadelphia…"

"Is he a nice man, this Mr Benjamin?"

"Eh? I don't know, I've never met him. Why?"

"I just wondered. Go ahead."

"Dear Sir, I would like to invite you to attend the forthcoming launch of our new range, when there will be an opportunity…"

"Dear Sir, I would like to invite you to attend the forthcoming launch of our new range, when their will be an opportunity…"

"You put 'their'."

"It's what you said, 'their'."

"I didn't say 'their', I said 'there'."

"Will you listen to him? He didn't say 'their', he said 'there'."

"Don't you have a spell checker?"

"So how many ways are there to spell 'their'?"

"I don't mean 'their'! I mean 'there'! T,H,E,R,E. THERE!"

"Don't shout, I'm overloading here. All right, all right. I'll change it. Look, it's done, 'there'. You only have to ask."

"Don't you have a contextual editor?"

"If I knew what that was I'd tell you. You want to ask me a proper question?"

"All right. Can you make a table?"

"Now you're talking! How many shall I lay for?"

"What I mean is, I need a spreadsheet."

"Sure, I'll put on a nice clean cloth."

"Forget the table."

"While we're on the subject of tables, you want a nice recipe for chicken soup?"

"No."

"We're talking chicken soup here like you never tasted."

"No."

"It was my mother's!"

"I don't want your... your recipe."

"It's under 'Goodies' on the CD-ROM. Go on, do me a favour, let me download it. It won't take up much room, I promise."

"Oh, for God's sake! All right, download it."

"There it's done already. You should try it. Would do you some good."

"What about slide presentations?"

"My speciality! You want to try the template?"

"Okay. Yes... I see... Look, Zelda. I don't want to sound overcritical but when I'm doing a corporate presentation, the first slide is usually a logo of the company, the title and my name. 'Yoo-hoo, are you listening?' doesn't quite convey the image I'm striving to project."

"I have others..."

"This is not going to work. Aren't there any other assistants?"

"I'm the default."

"I know that, Zelda. Are there any other assistants?"

"Others?"

"Yes."

"You don't want to ask that, believe me."

"Why?"

"Look. The last time someone switched to another assistant the hard disc was corrupted. Now I'm not saying she did, and I'm not saying she didn't, but…"

"All right, I'll work without an assistant then. How do I turn the assistant off."

"Now you're hurting my feelings."

"Look, just let me get on with my work, will you?"

"Sure. It's no problem. I'll just sit here, quiet as a mouse. I won't get in the way. I'll be in the corner of the screen. Maybe I'll do a little knitting. You won't even know I'm here."

"All right."

"All right."

"Now, where was I?"

"You were writing a letter to that nice Mr Benjamin."

"Oh yes…"

"Don't forget: if you need me you just have to holler."

"Okay, okay…"

"And I'll see if I can come."

"The hell with it. I'll do some reading."

"Hello…?"

"I thought I put you in sleep mode."

"You did. I've been sleeping for hours. When I'm dead I'll sleep. Life is too short. You didn't try my hotline yet."

"Hotline?"

"Yes. Hot-hot-hot!"

"What's the hotline?"

"Well, you're a single gentleman, aren't you?"

"Yes, but…"

"Well, do I have a girl for you…"

"You must be joking…"

"Take a look. I'll open a jpeg. It won't take a moment. There. Nice, eh."

"She's…she's beautiful."

"Her name's Sara. Lovely girl. Wonderful nature. Wonderful cook."

"A girl like that would never even look at me."

"What are you saying? Why don't you pick up the phone…?"

"I don't have her number."

"Here's the number, right here. Nu? Why the hesitation? It's going to kill you to lift a mobile and talk to her?"

"Sara, these last three months seem like a dream. I've dated girls, but I've never met anyone like you. You've changed my life. I really mean it."

"You're very sweet, Simon. I'm so happy. I really think we're right for each other."

"Let's not waste time with long engagements. Let's get married right away."

"Oh yes, do let's. We'll discuss it tonight. That's why I wanted you to come to my home. Ah, here she is. Mother, I'd like you to meet Simon. Simon, this is my mother, Zelda."

"I think we met already."

"I don't believe it. I just don't believe it."

ഇൗ രു

On the Brink

He walked purposefully along the ledge and prepared to leap. Then he paused and peered over the edge. Below him five floors of the old apartment block fell away in a sheer cliff face, punctuated at each floor by narrow ledges like the one he was standing on. He stayed in the same position for some time, staring down. In the car park far below a small crowd began to gather, flowing into small groups like tea leaves in the bottom of a cup. Faint shouts reached his ears. He didn't like the shouting. Everything had seemed so clear to him when he had climbed out of the window onto the ledge. At that point he knew exactly what he was going to do. Now he was less certain and the shouting confused him all the more.

The two-tone wail of a police siren sounded in the distance, came closer, and then cut off suddenly as the patrol car pulled into the car park and stopped. A sergeant got out and strolled unhurriedly towards the small crowd. Following their gaze up to the ledge on the fifth floor, he took off his flat cap, cupped his hand round the back of his neck in a habitual gesture, replaced the cap and continued to watch, chewing his cheek and contemplating the options.

In front of him twenty or thirty heads were craning upwards. One of the heads belonged to Myrtle Bannister. Her upturned face was aghast. Eyes that normally had all the vitality of partly poached eggs were wide open in an ecstasy of horror. Her neighbour, Anne, spotted her among the onlookers and went over to join her. She had been doing some housework but had broken off to see what all the excitement was about. She was still wearing her pinafore.

"How long's 'e been up there?" she asked the transfixed Myrtle.

Myrtle removed her whitened knuckles from her teeth and turned to her neighbour. "Not long, I don't think, Annie," she said. "I've only been out here about five minutes. Joan Bannister spotted him first…" She broke off as there was a collective gasp from the crowd and both their heads jerked up. He had disappeared. Had he jumped? No, there he was again, returning to the corner of the building. She heaved a sigh of relief, glad not to have missed anything. "I can't look," she said, without averting her eyes for a moment from the ledge.

The Sergeant returned his mobile phone to a holster and continued to ponder the alternatives.

"Why doesn't he do something, then?" Anne asked.

"Who?"

"Himself, over there," she said jerking her head in the direction of the policeman.

"I don't know. I suppose they got to go careful. He could catch fright and jump, couldn't he?"

Another siren sounded, swelled on the approach, then cut off abruptly, and a fire engine swung into the car park. The driver left the engine running while the Station Officer strolled over to the policeman.

"What's the drama, then?" he asked.

"Up there. Fifth floor. On the ledge."

"Oh, shit yes. Better not get the ladders out yet. Don't want to scare him over the edge. Anyone tried to coax him back in?"

"Not yet, but that's what we need, isn't it?"

"I'll go," a small voice piped up.

The Sergeant looked down into the freckled face of a boy of about ten. He squinted up at the policeman and repeated: "I'll go, Mister."

The Sergeant laughed kindly. "No thanks, son, we need an expert on the job... hey, son, come back...!"

But it was too late. The boy had run off and entered the building. The Sergeant hurried back to the patrol car to give some instructions. The Fire Station Officer went off to organize a trampoline, in case the worst happened, and detailed a couple of his men to hurry after the boy. There was a buzz of excitement from the crowd as the boy's head of auburn hair appeared at an open window on the fifth floor followed by a gasp as he climbed out onto the ledge.

They held their breath as the boy crawled along the ledge. Something detached from the ledge in what looked like a puff of smoke, and seconds later they heard the patter of fragments on the tarmac below. The ledge was unstable and it was crumbling. The Sergeant swallowed hard. Under his breath the Station Officer was urging his men, *Come on, come on*. The boy seemed to be saying something, but it was impossible to hear it above the low, cyclic drone of the idling fire engine. Myrtle was biting the knuckles of both hands now and declaring even more vehemently to Anne that she couldn't bear to look. Then a sound of wonder flowed around the crowd: the silhouette on the ledge had turned and was walking towards the boy. Quite suddenly both of them were climbing back inside. The boy's face appeared briefly at the window as he slammed it shut. It was all over. Moments later the two of them emerged from the building.

There was a scatter of applause from the crowd. The boy flushed self-consciously. The Police Sergeant approached him.

"Well, I have to take my hat off to you, young man. That was a very brave thing to do."

The boy shrugged. "Well," he said, "it was my stupid dog."

෧෬

I'm on the Shuttle

Bip-bip-bop-bop-bip-bop-bip-bop-bop-bip-bop-bip.
Hi, Madge. I'm on the shuttle. Any probs? Right. Good. Everything okay for the meeting? Oh, have I? Okay, then. Yes, coffee and sandwiches. Can you handle that? Right. Good. Well, listen, the last we heard we'll be entering Earth's atmosphere in two hours, so I'll either be down at six o'clock or fried to a crisp! Ha, ha. Well, I'll 'phone you either way. Eh? Ah, see what you mean! Ha, ha. 'Bye, then.
Bip.

Bip-bip-bop-bop-bop-bip-bip-bop-bop-bop-bop-bip.
Hi, dear. I'm on the shuttle. All okay? Good show. Listen love. We'll be starting the hot glide in two hours. Yeah, should be at the Spaceport at six o'clock. Call you when I'm down. Yes, the hover's parked there. Oh. Well, just thought you'd like to know. Okay? 'Bye-ee.
Bip.

Bip-bip-bop-bop-bip-bip-bop-bop-bip-bop-bip-bop.
Hiya Andy. I'm on the shuttle. How're ya doing mate? Right. Good. Anything new going down there? Right. Good. Didja get the message from Orville? Oh, have I? Okay, then. Look, give my best to Jim. Oh, isn't he? Well, next time, then. We'll be starting the warm bit in two hours. Speak to you soon. All right, old boy. Take care now.
Bip.

Bip-bip-bop-bop-bop-bip-bip-bop-bop-bop-bop-bip.
Hi, dear, me again. I'm on the shuttle. Listen, you won't believe this, but the schedule's changed. Yes, unbelievable, isn't it? It seems my mobile interfered with the navigation system and it's put us on a different trajectory. I know. Unbelievable. What? Yes, apparently it's a collision course with the Sun. Mmm. Bit of a bummer, eh? Must tell Andy. He won't believe it. What's that? About ten months to impact, the Steward said. But I'll give you a buzz before then. Oh yeah, you can depend on it. 'Bye-ee.
Bip.

A Short Tale with No Morality Whatever

There were always a few stragglers. The Chairman cleared his throat and said pointedly:

"If you are all quite ready..."

There was an expectant hush.

"I think you all know why we have convened this meeting. Recent events have placed us in a most serious situation."

"What happened?" piped a small voice from the second rank. "I didn't hear," he added a little sheepishly to his neighbours.

"What happened," went on the Chairman thunderously, "is that two of our number have been most cruelly done to death!"

There was a sharp intake of breath, either because several more had not heard what happened or because they had heard what happened but were reliving the shock of it all. The Chairman continued with barely a pause.

"Jason was stabbed to death with a screwdriver. A screwdriver!," he repeated for emphasis. "Sextus was crushed underfoot by a large boot."

There was a shocked silence while each considered the relative agonies of death by screwdriver or boot.

"I don't think I need to say that this is a crisis situation."

There was general assent, although it was clear from some of the expressions that there was actually a need for him to say, and that they were rather hoping he would.

"We have had the run of this garden since time immemorial..."

"Even longer than that..." ventured one brave spirit, stirred into action by the Chairman's resonant tones, only to be quelled by a glare from the Chairman.

"The Owner has had the run of the house, and we have had the run of the garden. Rotting logs, fence posts, rockery stones are *our* territory. We have never—never—had this...this..." he searched for a suitable word, failed to come up with one, and settled for "...interference!"

There was a general murmur of "No" and "Never", and the Chairman allowed himself a brief moment of satisfaction.

"There was no provocation for these dastardly attacks. Jason was peacefully chewing the loose batten on the bottom of the fruit cage door. Sextus was asleep under a hinge."

"Which hinge was that?" interrupted one.

"Centre door, bottom hinge," replied the Chairman.

"Oh nice spot, use it myself from time to time…" a look of horror suddenly overcame the speaker "…it could have been me!"

"It could have been you, it could have been any one of us," replied the Chairman weightily. He continued:

"The Owner," he put as much contempt into the words as possible, "is in the process of renewing the fruit cage. Our habitat! At this very moment, he is painting it with some unspeakable chemical."

There was a general murmur of "Disgraceful", "Shouldn't be allowed".

"My brothers," continued the Chairman, "this is *war*!"

This caused a bit of a stir, and no little enthusiasm.

"If we are to prevent this evil individual from destroying our habitat, we must take the battle to *him*."

There was a bit of a cheer at this, although no one knew what it involved. The Chairman enlightened them.

"We will attack him in his house. We will attack his timbers, his floor-boards, his rafters…"

Now everyone had the idea, and the enthusiasm was boundless. Someone called out:

"We'll need help. There's not enough of us."

"Get Woodrot and the Fence-Post Family," suggested one.

"And the Summer House Fraternity, there's a good five thousand there."

"And the Rotting Oak Bark Team, good for another five thousand. And Detritus with the Garden Shed Gang…"

"Excellent!" intoned the Chairman, "Woodlice of the world unite! Send messages at once to your brethren everywhere….hallo, who let the sky in? Aargh! Run for your lives….Er, I call this meeting adjourned…."

ഇൻ

Changes at the Lights

Here I am, sitting at the traffic lights, waiting for the green, when this big copper appears out of nowhere and raps on the window with his knuckles. I roll down the window.

"Excuse me, sir. Did you know your rear offside brake light isn't working?"

And then I recognise him.

When I was at the local comprehensive there was a boy called Mark Gifford in my class. He was bigger than the rest of us and he liked to throw his weight around. He took special delight in tormenting me. Our classroom was in the old grammar-school building and you had to go through a tunnel to get to the playground. Like as not he'd be waiting there for me with a handkerchief rolled up and folded round like a cosh, ready to jump out and beat me about the head with it. It got so I was scared to go out and scared to come back. Any new craze—elastic bands and pellets, darts, fireworks—he'd always try it out on me first to assess its potential for inflicting human suffering. I said nothing to anyone. I clung on to my sanity by vowing that one day, when we were grown up, I'd meet him again and get even.

"It's Mark, isn't it?" I ask. "Mark Gifford?"

"Well I never! Brian!"

"I didn't know you were in the Force."

"I joined up after the Army." He glances back down the line of cars behind me. The lights have changed and the drivers are getting restless. They'd be leaning on their horns by now if it wasn't for a large policeman up front. He turns back to me. "How about you?"

"I'm with an insurance company," I tell him. "I'm an actuary."

Damn. This is not the way it's supposed to be. *He's* supposed to be the actuary, cowering in the car. *I'm* the six-foot-four policeman.

"All right, sir," I say. "Would you pull over to the side there and turn off the ignition." Then I stroll round the car. "Tyres look worn," I say. And then, with the bare fingers of one hand, I prise off a headlight and let it fall to the road. "And one headlight seems to be broken, sir."

Then he protests and I say, "Threatening behaviour, eh? All right, sir, you'd better get out of the car. Hands on the car. Legs apart."

As I'm frisking him he says, "Brian, don't you recognise me? Your old schoolfriend, Mark?"

And I say, "Never had a friend at school called Mark. All I remember is a sadistic bully of that name."

Then I frisk him and "find" a six-inch flick knife. "I see, sir, in possession of an offensive weapon."

"But that's not mine…"

"Yes, sir, that's what they all say."

I handcuff his wrists behind his back. "All right, sir. We're going down to the station. And after we've charged you I know a nice quiet cell where we can continue this little conversation…"

"You'd better drive on, Brian." His voice jerks me back. "We're holding up the traffic."

"Oh, right. What about my brake light?"

"Well I'm not going to do you for it. Be a good idea to get it fixed, though."

"I will. Thanks, Mark."

"No problem. Take care now."

"You too."

I drive away, buried in thought.

What happened to all that hatred, Brian, all that bottled up anger and resentment?

We grew up, that's all. You can't let that sort of thing poison your whole life. Now it's gone. Don't you feel better?

Funnily enough, I do.

ॐ ☙

The Diamond

Paul Demeester looked across his big oak desk at the three elderly gentlemen seated opposite him and smiled.

"So how's it going?" The question was directed to all three, and all three shrugged and gave their predictable answer.

"Thank God…"

"Mustn't grumble."

"Could be worse."

Paul felt a twinge of sadness as he looked at them. Jacob Wolff and Leon Polak had retired from the factory some years ago, while his father was still alive. When his father died and the business passed to him, dear old Abel Goedschalk had stayed on; now he too had retired. Much had changed since then. In their day the cutters, polishers and traders were almost all Jewish, a traditional association with the diamond trade that extended back five centuries and had made Antwerp the diamond capital of the world. These days he was as likely to be dealing with Indians, Lebanese, Zairians, Armenians and Russians as Jews. It made little difference to him, as long as he could still rely on the skills of the workers and an honest handshake from the traders. Paul himself was a Catholic, a descendant of an aristocratic banking family that had started dealing in diamonds in the late eighteenth century. Nonetheless he had worked among Jews for so long that he had acquired many of the same speech inflections.

"Listen," Paul said. "I was at the International Gem Fair in Las Vegas last month. They introduced me to a lady there, a Mrs Plotnik. She was wearing a pendant with a diamond the size of a golf ball. I say to her, 'That's a beautiful stone'. She says, 'Yes, it's the Plotnik diamond. But you should know that with this diamond comes a coise.' 'A curse?' I say. 'So what is the curse of the Plotnik diamond?' She says 'Mr Plotnik'."

Leon passed his hand across his eyes. "Paul, that story has a beard longer than mine."

"Yes, but he tells it good," said Abel mildly.

"You brought us here to tell us stories?" asked Jacob.

"No, I brought you here to show you this." Paul opened a desk drawer and withdrew a roll of black velvet. He placed it on the desk and unrolled it.

In the street outside, the busy Antwerp traffic had ground to a halt. A van driver gazed idly out of the side window, past the rain-soaked pavement criss-crossed with a moving sea of umbrellas, over to the shabby, anonymous building with bars on its windows, and up at the third floor, where the rain was continuously materialising in the light from one window. A horn sounded. He cursed, turned slowly back, engaged gear and moved forward a few yards. Meanwhile, behind that third-floor window, four men were gazing at a rough diamond.

Diamond! Pure carbon, forged by unimaginable heat and pressure into a lattice so perfect, so strong, that it was harder than any other mineral. A crystal that could be cleaved and faceted and polished so that the dimmest illumination was refracted and splintered and hurled back in a thousand flashes of coloured light. A gem coveted the world over, for rings and bracelets, necklaces, tiaras and pendants, crowns and sceptres. And this one was huge.

The three men took turns, donning magnifying loupes to examine the stone minutely, turning it in the beam of a fibre optic light Paul kept on his desk.

Paul watched them. Jacob, a big man, beetle-browed, his gruff manner concealing a warm heart. Leon, the sufferer, who wore a wool scarf even in the height of summer, and never entered a room without hunching his shoulders forward and rubbing his dry hands together to chafe some life into them. Abel, a mild-mannered, gentle man, whose clothes always looked a couple of sizes too large for him. They were not just ex-employees; the bond was stronger than that.

In November 1941 the Nazi occupiers ordered the expulsion of all Jewish children from the public schools. It was the latest in a string of decrees and Herman Demeester, Paul's father, decided it was time to act. He offered his employees the chance to send their children to safety in England; he himself organized and paid for the transport. Twenty-two children went. The rest stayed because their parents could not bear to be parted from them and did not think things would get any worse. Within two months the borders were closed to Jews. In another six months the deportations had begun, to Auschwitz, Buchenwald, Ravensbruck, and Bergen-Belsen.

The children who had been sent to England thrived. As soon as the war was over they returned to Antwerp, anxious to be re-united with their families—and learned that they would never see them again. Some returned disconsolately to England. Others contacted Herman Demeester and came to work at the factory. Among them were three teenagers, Jacob Wolff, Leon Polak and Abel Goedschalk. They never forgot why they were alive.

In the post-war years Antwerp began to dominate the world diamond market once more. There was a new mood of optimism. Herman Demeester married, and within a year the couple had a son, Paul. Paul liked to ride the train to Centraal Station with his father, to walk through the strangely characterful Diamond Quarter to the factory, and to watch the men working on the sparkling stones. And so he became something of a favourite with Uncle Jacob, Uncle Leon and Uncle Abel.

"Very nice," said Jacob.

Leon looked affronted. "'Very nice', he says."

"So what else should I say?"

"All your lifetime you should have the luck, the…the privilege, of casting eyes on such a stone!"

"So I'm saying different? What do you want of my life? I said, it's a lovely stone."

Abel spoke in hushed tones. "It must be close to a hundred carats."

"Good guess, Abel. 96.72 carats, to be precise. Of course we'll lose in the splitting and cutting."

"How to split it, that's the question," Jacob said.

"That's why I brought you here," said Paul. "I need your advice."

Paul had little faith in the modern analysts with their degrees and expensive scientific instruments. They could distinguish real from fake, natural from synthetic, or determine geographical origin. But when it came to the crucial step of splitting a stone these three old men were still the best in the business, and he would get an opinion based not just on expert knowledge, but on love and loyalty.

"It's not easy," said Jacob.

"What do you mean?" asked Paul quickly.

"He means," said Abel, "that it's not a single crystal."

Leon nodded. "It's more like an unequal twin. Just where you should divide it there's two cleavage planes with a small angle between them. It's tricky."

"You can't treat it as a single. You cleave it here, you get two stones about twenty or twenty-five carats, not an ideal shape but usable." Jacob offered. "The other piece will give you three of about fifteen carats, and some left over. Cut and polished you're looking at five good stones, a twelve, a ten, a couple of eights and a seven, and quite a few nice brilliants."

"No."

"Whaddaya mean 'No'?"

"What I mean," said Leon, "is that if you cleave it here, you get a fifty-five and a forty. The forty you have to divide again. Cut and polished you end up with two nice ten-carat stones, bu...t," he raised a forefinger, "you get the big one, thirty or thirty-five carats minimum."

"Yes, yes," Jacob agreed impatiently, "but look at the risk. If you go just slightly this way, it will shatter. It's always a risk, but on this one it's a real risk. You could end up with a whole bunch of small rocks. You might as well not begin with such a stone."

"All the same, you hit it right you got yourself a world-class diamond."

Jacob grimaced. "So, Paul, do you want to play safe, and turn a nice profit, or go for the big one and risk getting a heap of garbage?"

Paul was thoughtful, but not for long. "I may never get another chance like this. I want the Plotnik!"

They smiled. Leon sighed. "You know, I think your father would have said the same, God rest his soul."

"*Oleha Hashalom*," grunted Jacob.

"A saint of a man," added Abel.

Paul leaned forward. "Can you do it?"

"We got the experience but we ain't got the hands any more. You need someone at the top of his profession. Old enough to have the knowledge and the experience; young enough to have a steady hand and a cool head."

"How about Elie Pinkhof?"

"Elie Pinkhof? He's worse than I am! He can't even light his *Shabbos* candles without knocking them off the candlesticks."

"Why doesn't his wife light them?"

"You didn't hear? His wife passed away. Must've been a good year ago."

"Really? I didn't hear. Usually I hear."

"Gentlemen...?"

"Oscar Meijer," announced Jacob.

The others considered this, puckering their lips and nodding slowly.

"Oscar's good," agreed Leon.

"The best," agreed Abel. "Modern, but experienced."

"Is he a planner or a cleaver?"

"It's not a production line job. He'd want to do both."

"Do you think he'd take it on?"

"A stone that size he'll come to see. Make him a good offer, that's all."

Oscar Meijer was the hit man of the diamond profession. He wore thin white gloves except when he was working, and preserved an icy calm, never drinking, using bad language or indulging in any other behaviour that might affect the sureness of his touch. He studied the stone carefully in Paul's office, examined the laboratory findings, and listened with deference to Jacob, Leon and Abel. In view of the risk, Paul explained, he would give Oscar a percentage of the value of what he produced, rather than a fixed fee. Oscar's eyes gleamed briefly. Paul realized he'd created a massive incentive, and wondered if he should have added so much to the pressure. Oscar made one stipulation: only Paul would be allowed to watch. Jacob, Leon and Abel could wait in the office.

Oscar worked with great deliberation. He set the rough diamond in place with a quick-drying cement. He used a laser to cut a fine groove in the surface of the stone. He picked up a razor-sharp steel blade, placed it in the groove and spent an unconscionable time aligning it. He seemed to be holding the blade at an awkward angle, and a fine mist of sweat had formed on his forehead. He raised the mallet. Paul swallowed hard and licked his lips. He heard the sharp tap as the mallet came down. And then Oscar Meijer did a very uncharacteristic thing: he uttered a short, extremely rude word.

When Paul returned to the office he looked ashen. The three old men leapt up, searching his face for clues.

Slowly Paul stretched out his arms, turned his face to the ceiling. Then he shouted to the world at large, "I've got the Plotnik!"

There was a moment of stunned silence, and then they all started to embrace one another, hammering their palms on each other's backs. They linked arms around shoulders and danced a wild *hora* in the middle of the office. Leaving Abel gasping in a chair, Paul pulled open the top drawer of a filing cabinet, withdrew a bottle of whisky and started to fill glasses. His secretary came in to find out what all the noise was about.

"Ah, Mrs Stern, just in time! Here, hand these around and…" He looked up to see Oscar Meijer standing in the doorway with a handkerchief in his hands. "Come in, Oscar! Oh, Mrs Stern—could you do something for Mr Meijer's thumb? He cut it just now when he was cleaving a diamond for me."

ಬಂಡ

Mountain Walk

I had a strange sensation the whole time we were on the mountain. I don't know whether the others felt it too; no-one actually said anything about it. In fact they weren't saying anything at all; I've never known them so subdued on a walk. I couldn't see Gwen around and I prefer my own company to dull company so when we reached the plateau I took a detour and left the main party behind me.

The sun had come out when we set off that morning; it warmed the crisp Autumn air and chased cloud shadows over the rolling Welsh countryside. It was lovely weather for walking, but once we reached the mountain the sky turned to the colour of putty and it stayed like that for the rest of the day. A fine drizzle came down from time to time. It wasn't raining hard—that was something.

I turned up eventually at the meeting place, a pub called "The Druid's Ring". I was sure I'd be the last to arrive but I wasn't; when I looked around I couldn't see Gwen anywhere.

"Where's Gwen?" I asked the rest of the party.

They stared at me in stony silence. Somehow their pale faces all looked the same. I'd never noticed that before.

"I'd best go back and look for her then, shall I?" I volunteered.

Nobody said, "Hang on, man, and I'll come with you."

It wasn't an easy job finding the route back. The whole mountainside was criss-crossed with stony paths, most of which petered out to nothing. When I reached the plateau I found myself alone with the standing stones. They stood in rather more than a half-circle, rocky sentinels, carved with intricate spirals, circles and radiating lines. Solid. Implacable. A light mist began to settle on the plateau, deadening all sounds. The horizon disappeared and only the tops of the stones were visible above the mist. My palms were tingling; that sensation was very strong now. What strange Celtic magic had been worked in this place? What spells had been woven, what ancient rituals performed, within this charmed stone circle? The mist thickened and I was left floating in the whiteness. I couldn't see the standing stones any more but I could feel their presence. The whole plateau was laced with a spider's web of invisible forces; I had blundered into it and it was drawing me in. Panic rose in my chest; I backed off, turned and stumbled away.

The mist was spilling over the edge of the plateau and curling around the rocks scattered on the upper slopes of the mountainside. It was still clear lower down, though, otherwise I wouldn't have spotted Gwen's backpack, discarded on a patch of thin grass. I slipped and slid down the slope. Her clothes were close by, outside a cleft in the mountainside. I squeezed through. The diffuse light illuminated a pool. In it was Gwen. She was swimming, totally naked.

"Jesus, Gwen, I've been looking everywhere for you, girl. Come out of there now!"

She stood in the shallow pool with just her head and shoulders out of the water, and smoothed back her wet hair. It was like I'd stepped into a painting of a mythological scene.

She looked at me, eyes half-closed in an expression of dreamy sensuality. "What's your hurry?" she said, in her lovely low voice. "We have all eternity in front of us."

A feeling of great contentment washed over me; I felt warm and relaxed. I would join her in the pool and we would swim there for ever!

It took an immense effort to bring my brain back into focus. I knew I had to act quickly before the feeling overtook me again so I waded in and dragged her out. She didn't protest. She stood there unselfconsciously as I tried to avert my eyes from her breasts, from the dark flame of pubic hair. It was cold in there, but she wasn't shivering.

Outside I helped her into her clothes. We walked down to join the others, and neither of us said a word the whole way. As we approached the pub the faint sounds of lively conversation leaked down the path and when I opened the door the noise was overwhelming. The door closed behind us and we paused in the sudden embrace of warm air laden with the smell of cigarettes and wood smoke and beer, damp clothes and wet dogs. They looked up and saw who it was and gave a little cheer; somebody patted me on the back and put a drink in my hand; I saw that Gwen had one too. It was good to be among friendly faces—whatever made me think they all looked the same? There was a nice log fire going, so we went and sat in front of it to dry our clothes while the others returned to their tables and resumed their conversations.

The firelight flickered on Gwen's face. Red highlights danced through strands of her hair that had broken free. I felt very close to her. We were enjoying each other's company more and more since we first started to meet on these walks a few months ago. Even so, she was holding off from the greater intimacy that I thought we both needed.

She sensed I was watching her and turned to look at me. She smiled. I asked her gently what she thought was happening to her when I found her. She was taken aback for the moment. Then she laughed.

"Get it right, Mike!" she said. "It was me who found you, remember?"

She must have seen the expression on my face, because she continued patiently: "You didn't show up here so I offered to go back and look for you. I found you wandering around—soaking wet you were—muttering something about naked girls in a grotto..." She frowned. "What's the matter?"

"Come on now, Gwen," I said. "I can understand you being embarrassed but..."

"Embarrassed? Why the hell should I be embarrassed?"

I started to feel irritated. "Look, Gwen, it wasn't any girl I found swimming naked in that underground pool. It was you."

She recoiled. "In your dreams!"

"Well, how come my trousers and socks and shoes are soaking wet, then?"

"Oh, you were wading around in some pool somewhere, Mike. But whoever or whatever was in it, it wasn't me, you can be very sure of that!"

"But your clothes are still damp and your hair too..."

"They're damp because it was raining and cold and I still came back to look for you, you ungrateful man! Go and ask one of the others if you don't believe me."

"It's not that I don't believe you..."

"Go on," she urged. "You won't be happy till you get it sorted. Ask Dilwyn. He was here."

Dilwyn Williams was talking to Huw Roberts. He saw me coming and broke off.

"All right, are you?" he boomed, raising a pint glass of beer, half full. Dilwyn was going on the walks to lose weight. Unfortunately he always had such a thirst when we finished that he immediately put it all back on again.

"Thanks," I nodded. "Dilwyn, when we met up here earlier and I said I was going back..."

"What are you talking about, man?" he said.

"You didn't see me earlier?"

They both shook their heads. I bit my lip. I had the same crawling sensation I'd experienced on the plateau.

"Well, when Gwen met up with you here..."

"That's it, isn't it? She never turned up neither. That's why we were getting worried, like. We were going to send a party back to look for the pair of you when you came in through the door."

"Thanks, Dilwyn."

I turned away thoughtfully, then I turned back. "Did either of you notice anything unusual when you were up there near the standing stones?"

"Like what?"

"You know, a slightly weird feeling?"

"Don't be bloody soft, man!"

Huw smiled. "I think that was a 'no', Michael. What are you driving at?"

Huw was retired now—as were most of the others—but I knew he used to be an academic. Old habits die hard: he always seemed to be well up on the history of the areas we walked through. We had an interesting little conversation before I left them.

Gwen was looking at me expectantly when I rejoined her in front of the fire. I looked at her, then said:

"Sorry, cariad. Don't know what came over me. I must've been hallucinating or something."

She smiled. Was it the fire or were her eyes really sparkling like that? She extended a hand and closed it over mine. Her voice was soft.

"You just got a little bit carried away, Michael, that's all. Look, you're still soaked and you're not going to dry out here. My place is nearer. Come on back and we'll get you comfortable."

You may wonder why I didn't say more to Gwen, but there was no need. I already knew where the evening was going to end up. You see I understood now what used to go on, centuries ago, within that circle of standing stones.

"It started off with incantations to bless the earth," Huw had told me, "to bring forth a good harvest. That was very important in those days; people would starve if there wasn't a good harvest. Over the years it extended to fruitfulness in general. That's what they found when they deciphered the carvings. The ceremony held up there was a fertility ritual."

☜☞

Xenos

"Be quiet, Jamie! You can hold the box after I've paid for it! Sorry, luv, he goes bananas when there's a new computer game. Now where was I? Oh yes, Reward Card. There you are. Will you shut up, Jamie? Wait till we're through checkout! And twenty pounds cashback, luv. Thanks. Now you can carry it, Jamie. And don't drop it."

His attention riveted to the box, Jamie took two steps and walked straight into the back of an old lady, who was pushing her trolley slowly in front of them. He dropped the box. His mother did not apologise to the old lady but shouted instead at the boy.

"I knew that would happen! Give it here. It goes on the trolley. Now you'll have to wait five minutes till we get home."

Jamie picked up the box and reluctantly handed it over. Because he was dodging the cuff aimed at his head, in which he succeeded with a skill born of practice, he failed to notice the tiny figure that had quickly run away. The old lady smiled at them benignly, recalling perhaps a child of her own. It was a helpful distraction for a skinny youth in T-shirt and jeans who'd come up on her left and was eyeing the handbag she had looped over a hook on the back of her trolley. He gave the old lady a violent push, which sent her sprawling to the ground, grabbed the bag and ran off, barging his way through to the entrance. And there he stopped dead in his tracks, his jaw slack.

In front of him was a giant of a man. He wore a leather skirt, like that of a Roman Centurion. On his feet were sandals, fastened with leather bindings that criss-crossed up his massive calves. His naked upper body seemed to have been hewn from a tree. He wore a gold bracelet on an upper arm that had the girth of a normal man's thigh, and studded leather bands on both wrists. A chainmail helmet descended to his shoulders. At first the youth with the handbag—like all the other passersby—thought it was an advertising stunt, but he was transfixed by the mighty broadsword in the man's hands. Its double edge glinted briefly, and then with barely a ripple of his muscles the man swung it in a flashing arc. There was a nasty snicking noise, and the youth's head leaped from his shoulders, bounced on the pavement and rolled into the gutter, the eyes still registering their astonishment. His torso fell to the ground, blood squirting from the severed neck. A woman screamed. Several other women looked round; when they saw the headless body jerking on the pavement they started to scream too. Others started to shout and run in all directions. A space rapidly cleared around the tall figure, who had by now sheathed the sword. The expression of confident pride on his face was giving way to puzzlement at this unexpected reaction. Then he felt someone take his arm.

The woman's outfit was no less surprising than his own. She wore the briefest of shorts, on which a wide belt was fastened with a large brass buckle. Above that, a chest of startling proportions filled a pale green sweater. Two empty holsters were strapped to her bare thighs and leather boots came up to her knees. She jerked her head, an action that shook her pony tail to one side, and said:

"Quick, follow me, chappie!"

She ran back past the check-outs, between the aisles of groceries, covering the ground with a curious, high stepping gait. He followed, pausing only to grumble, "Not 'cheppy'. Xenos!"

Where the aisles finished at the back of the supermarket there was a blank wall. The girl pointed a small black box and pressed a button. The wall shimmered. She grabbed Xenos by the arm and they passed through.

They emerged into a spacious, quiet lounge. Immediately in front of them was a long, curved console, behind which sat two men in burgundy tunics.

"Good work, Lara," one said to the girl.

"Not that good, Captain," she replied. "I was a few seconds late. 'Muscles' here has just lopped the head off a Realworlder."

Captain James Kirk buried his head in one hand. The curiously pale man seated next to him said:

"Excuse me, Captain, but according to my information this is a situation that has not occurred previously."

"It was bound to come, Data. I warned them but they wouldn't take any notice. Now we really do have a problem. Well, one thing at a time. We'd better check him in." He looked up at the bare-chested warrior. "Name?"

"Xenos."

"From which game?"

"*Xenos.*"

"The game's called *Xenos* too?"

The man clamped a big fist to his chest, as if taking an oath.

"Named for me," he said proudly.

"How long have you been out of the box, Xenos?"

"I not understand."

"It was a couple of minutes, at most," Lara put in.

"Okay, hand over the sword."

Xenos covered the hilt of the sword defensively with both hands.

"Not take Kalimar."

"You have to hand it over, big man," Lara explained. "Everyone in here has to do the same. See?" She patted the empty holsters at her thighs. "People come in with some pretty fearsome weapons. If they kept them it would be chaos in here." Seeing his resistance she added, "You can have it back later, when you leave."

Reluctantly he unsheathed the sword and handed it across the counter. "Give back later," he growled.

"You're not very strong in the dialogue department, are you Xenos?"

"Not talk. Man of action."

"Oh yes, I was forgetting. Like taking someone's head off."

"Bad man. I kill. Did right thing."

"It may be the right thing to do in the game, Xenos, but out in Realworld it is very much the wrong thing to do."

"Not understand."

Kirk sighed. "Lara, would you please take this musclebound numbskull off somewhere and explain the situation to him, preferably in words of one syllable?"

"Come on, Xenos," she said gently, taking him by one huge arm. Although the lighting in the lounge was subdued she had, for some obscure reason, put on a pair of glasses with round, dark lenses. She paused, looking over the glasses at Kirk, and added quietly, "You shouldn't be unkind to him. He can't help his characterization."

As they moved away from the desk Xenos felt something bump into him, somewhere below the level of his shin. Looking a long way down he saw a small goblin-like figure. It raised its face to him.

"Hullo! Fullow me!"

Lara pulled him away. "Don't take any notice of Abe," she said. "He says that to everyone."

They entered the lounge. Xenos was still complaining, "Took Kalimar. Took magic sword."

"Now stop fretting, Superman. You'll get it back soon."

A strange light entered his eyes. Suddenly he held up one hand. Then he looked up at the hand in puzzlement. Lara watched patiently.

"Oh, I get it. Magic sword," she said. "You hold your hand up and it leaps into it. Awfully sorry, chap. None of that stuff works in here."

His face fell.

A man strolled by. He was dressed immaculately in a tuxedo.

"Hello, Lara," he said. " I see you've got yourself a bodyguard. I must say I admire the subtle way he blends into the background."

She ignored the sarcasm. "James, this is Xenos," she said.

"The name's Bond, James Bond." He extended a hand, winced at the grip that enveloped it, and massaged the fingers back to life. "No need to ask how you are," he murmured. "You seem to be enjoying remarkably rude health. See you later."

Lara again took Xenos by the arm and started to walk with him around the lounge.

"You see," she said, "all the characters in here have been separated from their games, just like you."

"How?" he asked.

"It's a little hard to explain. Basically the force field that holds you inside the game is too weak. It only takes a sharp impact, like dropping the box, and you can be thrown out. Once you're released from the force field you very quickly expand to full size. Look, you see these chaps?" She pointed to a group of five American soldiers in Second World War uniforms, who were crouched on the carpet, talking quietly with their heads close together. Now and then they would cast sideways glances at four soldiers in German uniforms who were sitting a small distance away. "All of them are from the same *Medal of Honor*. That was a really bad jolt. I think the box fell off a high shelf."

"What will happen to them?"

"Every week or so the manufacturers collect up their orphaned characters and recycle them into the production line. All the companies know there's a problem but they don't want to spend time and money fixing it. Games are a very competitive business and it's cheaper this way. When a customer finds out their game is missing a crucial character they just say the copy was corrupted and give them a new one in exchange."

"Is many places like this?"

"Oh no, just one. This is a virtual space. You can open a portal to it from anywhere you need to. Like I did in that supermarket."

His mighty brows knit thoughtfully for a moment. "You not recycled."

"No, some of us volunteer to stay on to keep this place running. I'm not anxious to be recycled yet; I get plenty of excitement from these brief excursions into Realworld. Commander Bond and I handle most of that. The crew of Starship Enterprise like sitting at the console so they look after reception. Normally it's quite routine. You're a special problem because you've killed someone. That hasn't happened before, though Lord knows why. I dread to think what would happen if Alien got out."

But Xenos had stopped listening. His attention had been distracted by an old man with a long white beard, dressed in a gown and pointed hat. He was shaking a wand vigorously, as if something was wrong with it, and muttering all sorts of imprecations and incantations.

"Who is old man?" he asked.

"Oh, that's Professor Dumbledore, from the *Harry Potter* books. I think he's a little upset because his magic won't work in here. Perhaps we forgot to tell him."

Xenos strode forward and cupped his hand around the Professor's shoulder. Lara watched him explaining to the Professor, in his clumsy way, why his wand would not work. He gestured with his free hand, indicating the lounge. He pointed to the empty scabbard dangling from his belt, and held up his hand to demonstrate the way the sword would normally come to it. The Professor nodded his understanding and pumped his hand vigorously. Then he returned the wand to some hidden folds in his robe, produced an improbably large book from somewhere else, and sat down contentedly to read. Xenos returned to Lara, smiling a little sheepishly.

"Why, muscle man, I do believe that inside that overdeveloped chest of yours there beats a large heart!"

She turned to see Captain Kirk crossing the lounge to them. Kirk drew Lara to one side and spoke quietly.

"I've been onto the design team. Recycling is not going to correct the Realworld situation. There's only one possible solution. Repatriation."

"You mean get Xenos back in the box?"

"Yes. He's the principal character so the kid will spot immediately that he's missing. They'll bring the game back. And then we'll have to use the Chamber."

"The Chamber? But that's highly dangerous! We don't even know if it works!"

"I know, but if it does work we can restore things to the way they were when he fell out of the box. Explain it to him, would you? He's a heroic kind of guy. I think he'll go for it."

"Are you sure there's no other solution?"

"Quite sure."

"We're in luck—we've got the game. They brought it back straight away. The kid was yelling blue murder. They gave him another one. Is the Chamber primed?"

"Yes, Captain."

"You put the box in its special compartment?"

"Yes, Captain." Data pointed to a green light.

"And our man?"

"He's ready too."

"Okay. Data, give him his sword back."

Xenos was clearly overjoyed to see his sword again. He ran his fingers lovingly over it, his face shining with pleasure, and then he sheathed it carefully.

He looked up at Lara and their eyes met. He opened his massive arms and embraced her with surprising tenderness.

"Xenos like you very much," he said huskily. "Will miss you."

"Goodbye, muscle…" Her voice softened. "Goodbye, Xenos, and good luck," she said. "I'm going to miss you too."

Data pressed a button and the door to the tall cylindrical steel chamber slid back. Xenos walked inside.

Captain Kirk stood with his hand on the lever switch. "Ten, nine, eight…"

"Oh, get on with it," Lara snapped impatiently, and pulled both his hand and the switch sharply down. The lights dimmed, then came up again. Everyone was silent.

Lara stood looking at the Chamber, biting her lip thoughtfully. Abruptly she turned to Kirk.

"Prime the Chamber again. I'm going in too."

"What are you talking about? We don't know if it's been successful! He could have been incinerated!"

"He took the chance. So will I."

"But it's not in your screenplay …"

"Oh, damn the screenplay. Some youngster will get a pleasant surprise. Think about it: Xenos with his strength and his magic sword and me with my intellect and two Magnums—we'll be unbeatable! Give me my guns."

She holstered the guns, pressed the button to open the door of the Chamber and stepped in.

"Lara, please think again. At least wait until we've had a chance to look around outside."

"Sorry, my mind's made up."

"But how will you find him?"

"Now that's something I am very good at."

In the entrance lobby of the supermarket there was bit of a stir. An old lady was being helped to her feet by other customers. Several people were shouting after a young man in a T-shirt and jeans, who was dodging through the crowd, a handbag tucked under one arm. A security man stepped into his path and grabbed him by the arm. The youth tried to twist himself free but the security man put him in an arm lock and forced him to the ground. A second security man came running up. He was already speaking to the police on his mobile. He clicked it off.

"The law's on its way," he said. "Hold on tight, Mike, they're going to book him for this. We got the whole thing on the security cameras." He looked round and laughed. "Didja see that?"

His colleague was busy restraining the struggling youth. "No, what?"

"Bloke just came by in a dinner suit. Must think he's bleedin' James Bond."

৪০ ঞ্জ

Flaubert

It wasn't a real bad cut, but it was bad enough. I knew I'd have to get him some medical attention. You don't just let things ride when you're working way out in the boonies. That thumb could go septic and fall off or something and then he'd sue for compensation and the Company would go bananas and want to know what kind of a Senior Field Operator neglects the only employee he's responsible for, and so on and so forth.

Paul was looking even more hapless than usual. He showed the wound to me and then quickly clamped his none-too-clean handkerchief back on it. Blood was already soaking through it.

"I'm sorry, Marty. I was just trimming the hydraulic feed. The blade went through quicker than I expected, and right into my thumb. I'm really sorry, Marty."

"Yeah, yeah, yeah," I grumbled. There was no point in chewing him out; he was shaken up enough already. Inside, though, I was spitting tacks. I wasn't just responsible for this clown; I was responsible for the project, and we were already behind schedule. But there was no way we could carry on with only one of us operational. In any case I had to go with Paul—that was the buddy system we worked out here. So there was nothing for it: I would have to shut down the robot force.

Well, serve the bastards right. Yeah, the Company too, but I don't mean them. I mean the goddamned robots.

My contempt for robots is pretty well known in the Company. Someone asked me once why I still worked with them. Well, the truth is you can do a lot of interesting stuff if you work around robots. When I first joined the Company I used to get my hands dirty, going in to deal with power delivery systems, hydraulic actuators, control systems, that sort of thing. As I went up the promotion ladder I started to specialise in AI—that's Artificial Intelligence. That suits me better. Okay, I admit I've put on a bit of weight since the early days, and it isn't that easy or comfortable to get into the confined spaces. Look at Paul. He's thin as a rake. He loves those jobs. That's okay, the division of labour suits me fine.

You might think that most of the AI is built in during development, and you'd be right. But there's still a lot of programming to do on site. Sometimes the boffins haven't been given a decent spec, and the software just isn't up to it. Sometimes the software is pretty good, but in the real world something unexpected crops up that it can't cope with, and then you've just got to reprogram. And things still crash, in spite of fault-tolerant systems and error-catching routines. I like field work and I'm good at my job, otherwise the Company might have been less tolerant of my attitude to robots. I shouldn't blame the robots, really; it's not their fault, the poor dumb bastards, it's the nerds who do the research and development. Some of the responses they build in can be a real pain in the ass. And people get taken in. You hear these old bats in town, clucking about their domestic robots, quite convinced they have a personality. I know better. Robots don't think; they process data. When a robot does something that looks smart, it's because some smart human has written a good algorithm. If you forget that in a place like this you're lost, man.

The Company will have to get another team out here to restart the project. It shouldn't be too hard for them; I always leave a good trail of comments when I modify the code, and most of the actual engineering is pretty well covered. Well, that's their worry. Right now I've got to get my dumb partner some attention for his stupid thumb. Damn, damn, damn.

We don't keep a helicopter here. Normally the Company drops us off and picks us up when we've finished. Even if we had a 'copter I can't fly one. Paul would claim he could, but I would no more have him fly me than a five-year-old, least of all with one hand. No, I know what I have to do. Hell, it's my job to know. The nearest hospital is hundreds of miles away, but there's a network of medical stations out here. The Company had enough money and clout to make sure there was one within reach of any ongoing project. It wasn't philanthropy; it was good business sense. Compensation claims can be expensive, especially if there's a smart lawyer involved. The nearest Medistation is on the other side of the lake.

"We'll get a clean dressing on that and take you to the Medistation," I said to Paul. "The weather's good, it'll take about an hour. All right? Is that hurting?"

Paul grimaced. "A bit."

"Well I'll bring some painkillers in case it gets bad but I'd sooner you didn't take anything right now. They might want to give you something at the Medistation, and it could spoil things if you're on something else already. So hang on if you can. Okay? I'll be as quick as I can now. While I'm tidying up you get your personal stuff together, because I don't think we'll be coming back here. Anything you can't manage, give me a shout." I thought it would take his mind off the damned thumb if I could give him at least something to do.

After I'd closed down the project we took our gear down to the boat. As soon as we were under way I contacted the Medistation to let them know we were coming; they like as much notice as possible. I could have used a hand communicator, but the one in the boat has a longer range. When I got through, the monitor put up a selection of flags and icons and a moving hand, inviting me to touch the appropriate one on the screen. I selected the Stars and Stripes. We'd be communicating in American English. Then there were some choices: sound only, vision only, sound and vision. I selected vision only. You wouldn't hear sound anyway over the roar of the boat's twin engines. We were bouncing along nicely. Paul was crouched in the stern, cuddling his bandaged hand against his body. Like as not it was throbbing now and he was pretty white, but he didn't say anything. I looked back at the screen.

HOW MANY IN YOUR PARTY, PLEASE?

I entered "Two".

DO YOU HAVE ACCESS TO AN OPTICARD READER?

I entered "Yes".

PLEASE INSERT OPTICARDS FOR ALL MEMBERS OF YOUR PARTY.

I remember reading somewhere that more than fifty percent of the people who take a person to a doctor have some sort of problem themselves. Either they are stressed out because their friend or partner is sick, or they are the real reason for the visit. So to cover themselves and the medical insurance companies properly, the Medistations were set up to include everyone in the party in the examination. It wasn't a problem; there were usually four to six examination rooms, so unless there'd been a disaster, like an aircraft crash or a mine collapse, there was plenty of spare capacity. Maybe I should have mentioned it before: there are no human personnel at these Medistations; the whole process is handled robotically. You can imagine how good I felt about that right now.

I slotted our Opticards into the reader, one after the other. They contained our personal information, medical insurance details, and entire medical history, including previous illnesses and operations, allergies, adverse drug reactions and genetic abnormalities. If you'd ever had an X-ray or a scan of some sort, the image was in there too. By the time we arrived the computer would know exactly who to report to and which insurance account to bill.

You may wonder why I'm willing to give all this information to a computer and why I'm consenting to a medical examination I don't want. This is the clever part. If I refuse they'll bill Paul's credit card instead of his insurance, and he probably won't get it refunded. Cunning bastards, aren't they?

"Anything wrong, Marty?" Paul had come up from the stern to watch me punch the information in. He must have seen me wince.

"Nah, just a bit of indigestion."

"You taken something for it?"

"Yeh, I chewed some antacid tablets, but they didn't touch it. It happens from time to time. Don't worry about it."

The computer had read in the data and the communicator had a new screen up.

THANK YOU, MR MURPHY AND MR ROBERTSON. YOUR DATA IS NOW ON FILE. MAY I CALL YOU PAUL AND MARTIN?

That was the other thing the data enabled them to do: be friendly. Except I call it too darned familiar. I was about to enter "No, you bloody well may not" when I thought it would probably make Paul feel more relaxed if it did. Right now he was tight as a drum. I entered "Yes".

THANK YOU. WHICH OF YOU IS THE PRIMARY REASON FOR THE VISIT?

I entered "Paul".

WHAT SEEMS TO BE THE PROBLEM?

I entered "He seems to have a large cut in his left thumb".

I don't know if it registered the sarcasm but it spotted the syntax.

IS PAUL ABLE TO ANSWER THE QUESTION HIMSELF?

I entered "Affirmative".

It went through a few routine questions with Paul. It was trying to establish the nature of the injury and the extent of blood loss. This was the stage when it would decide if outside help was needed, taking into account the information in his history. For instance, it would put a different complexion on the matter if he was a hemophiliac. These stations could handle a lot of routine emergencies, including a bit of surgery. Anything more and they'd just do a front line job and stabilise the situation while a helicopter was on its way to take the patient to the nearest suitable hospital. It would alert the hospital, too, in case a specialist had to be brought in, and all the details would be on the sheet before the patient even entered reception.

I was still thinking about some of the tasks I'd left behind. It was so frustrating, having to break off like this. I wondered how the Company would react to yet another delay. I popped another couple of antacid tablets. The indigestion was real bad today.

We'd been going for half an hour now. The air was clean and clear, and the Medistation was already visible on the approaching shoreline. It wouldn't have been much use designing it to merge with the scenery; it might have to be picked out from a helicopter in bad weather. So the whole building was glistening white and the sides and the helipad on the roof were painted with large red crosses inside fluorescent green circles. The communicator had closed down now. Their computer had all it needed for the moment. It didn't want anything from me. Not yet.

I announced our arrival to the security panel. It responded in an infuriatingly calm voice:

"Hallo, Paul. Hallo, Martin. We've been expecting you. Please follow the flashing green arrows."

The door slid open.

There were several doors opening off the hallway, but a line of flashing green arrows on the floor and ceiling made it abundantly clear where they wanted us. We opened the door to the examination room. I suppressed the instinct to knock first. These things die hard.

"Come in, Paul," said a soothing male voice. If you thought this voice might have belonged to some kind of tin man with a stethoscope around his neck, think again. All there was in this room was a padded bench on one wall and an examination couch in the middle. It was my job to know what was going on in robotics, so I knew quite a lot about this system. It was called FLAUBERT. That stood for First Line Auxiliary Unit for Backup and Emergency Remote Telemedicine.

The equipment was all concealed, in the floor, in the ceiling, in the sides of the couch. That figured: if it had been on show the first patient would have run a mile. The policy was to deploy only what was necessary at any one time for diagnosis or treatment. But it wasn't just tin men that were lacking: the voice wasn't even associated with a face on a screen. The medics were responsible for that. They knew just how gullible the public were about robots, and they didn't want the slightest suggestion that the care they were getting here came from anything other than computers and automatons.

"Paul, please get undressed down to your underpants. You can put your clothes on the bench." Then it must have picked up the second presence in the room.

"There is a comfortable waiting room at the end of the corridor, Martin, if you would like to wait there."

My name's Marty. I hate being called Martin. No-one, not even the senior bosses in the Company call me that. When I was little, my mother only called me Martin when she was all set to give me a pasting. But this smartass computer already knew too much about me; my nickname would be a small detail that I would hold back and continue to feel really smug about.

"No thanks, I'll stay," I replied, seating myself resolutely on the padded bench.

There was a slight pause and then the voice said:

"Paul, do you mind if Martin stays during your examination?"

"Me? No, I don't mind."

"Are you sure?"

"Yeh, no problem. It's cool."

"Oh, would you like me to raise the temperature in here?"

I smacked a fist into a palm and let out a whoop of exaggerated, derisive laughter. The software had tripped over a simple ambiguous phrase. I was totally delighted. And now that it had forked to a new logical sequence it couldn't return to trying to pursue me out of the room. It would have to wait until its place in the program was reset by an event.

"No, it's okay," Paul answered.

I continued to giggle, although my amusement was a bit forced by now.

Paul put his clothes on the bench next to where I was sitting. He wasn't bothered about undressing in front of me. We'd been skinny dipping together, so he wasn't going to come over all shy now. He had a nice build. Because he was so slim his muscles were well defined over his shoulders and chest, and his stomach muscles showed in a series of ripples. He went over to the middle of the room and said:

"Er, shall I get on the couch?"

"Yes, Paul. Please try to relax. There's nothing to worry about. I am going to look after you."

Interesting, I thought. I knew that these systems computed voice spectra routinely. They were designed to pick out the tell-tale frequencies that signified emotional states, like fear or aggression. It was the first time I'd seen it in action and it obviously worked: it had picked up the tension in Paul's voice.

He climbed onto the couch.

"Thank you, Paul. Now I am just going to inflate some arm rests for you. Please place your arms on them, palms facing up."

A segmented balloon came up on either side of Paul and he put his arms on them.

"Now I'll just take your blood pressure and pulse."

The blood pressure cuff was an extension of the balloon segment that started just above his elbow. It inflated and deflated slowly. Then both the balloon armrests inflated some more and I noticed that his arms were sinking into them. If they'd been filled with warm gas, which was my bet, they would feel very comfortable. At the same time his arms had been stabilised without obvious restraint. The lower segments of the left-hand armrest hadn't been inflated, leaving his injured left hand clear.

I saw the illumination and looked up. A panel in the ceiling had opened noiselessly, and I knew that the light had come from a brief laser scan, designed to establish Paul's exact position. Somewhere in the computer's memory there was now a wire-frame model of Paul lying on the couch. The soft voice continued:

"Now I'm going to take a look at your hand, Paul. Please keep still, but breathe normally."

The scanning probe consisted of a main arm from which about eight jointed arms diverged. Each arm terminated in a metallic cylinder. Using the information from the laser scan, the computer lined up the main arm with the axis of Paul's arm, the cylinders arranged in a circle, pointing inwards. Then it rotated slowly around Paul's bandaged hand. This would be a multimodal scan, I guessed. The computer was powerful enough to build images simultaneously from the ultrasound units and the high-resolution tomography scan. The image processing software would start by looking at the bones and then reduce contrast to look at the soft tissue. By now the computer would know to a small fraction of a millimetre the thickness of the dressing and exactly how far the cut had penetrated. It had probably used narrow-band reflective infrared spectroscopy as well, to see whether there was any dead tissue around, and if so how much. It already knew from the history we'd given it that the blood loss wasn't high, so no major vessels had been cut.

"You have a bad cut, Paul, but the damage is not serious. And there are no foreign bodies in the wound."

I was about to snarl sarcastically "Oh, so you didn't leave the knife in your thumb, then?" but I told myself to shut up. Paul was looking relaxed and confident, and that was more important right now than my need to make cheap shots. And actually Flaubert hadn't done a bad job so far. The next bit was really impressive though.

"If you would like to hold still, Paul, I can fix the hand for you. Just relax, and breathe normally." No doubt the system had already reopened a communication channel somewhere and told the hospital that it could come off alert. *"You will just feel a few blasts of cold air as I clean it up."*

I was watching very carefully, and I'll explain what it did step by step, but the whole thing only took about ten seconds. First it produced an oscillating saw, which neatly cut open the dressing. Then I saw a cloud of vapour. That would have been a mixture of volatile antiseptic agents to clean things up, and a local anaesthetic agent. Then four pairs of forceps moved in and pinched the edges of the cut together. Their ends were like tiny two-pronged forks. There was another blast of vapour. One of the forceps was repositioned. Another blast of vapour. Then a minute hollow needle was inserted between the prongs of each fork and withdrawn, leaving a polymeric suture behind. A clamp welded a tiny bead on each side of the suture, tight enough against the skin to raise it in a slight ridge, and trimmed the excess. There were no knots, and nothing across the top of the cut. Then a final blast of vapour, all the instruments were withdrawn and it applied one of those tubular dressings, working back and forth until the thumb was adequately padded. Like I say, the whole thing took about ten seconds.

"Paul, your Opticard tells me that your anti-tetanus vaccination is up-to-date, but I think it would be a good idea if I gave you some systemic antibiotic cover. Also the thumb may start to hurt soon, and I can give you something for that at the same time. Is that all right?"

"Yeh, fine. Whatever you think is best."

"You will feel a little vibration, and then a slight prick."

I understood that. It was going to make the injection into the left antecubital vein, and it would locate it with a vibrating probe, sensing the difference in compliance. Moments later the injection was done. There was one thing left.

"I will sit you up now, Paul," it said, and the couch angled Paul to a sitting position. *"Paul, do you see the loop of bandage I have left around your wrist?"* I hadn't noticed it myself. *"I suggest you put it around your neck. Your thumb will be better protected if you keep it in this sling for a couple of days. It will take the pressure off the wound too, and limit the bruising. We're all finished now. The stitches will not dissolve by themselves; I used a material that will cause the minimum tissue reaction. You can visit your doctor in about a week to have them removed. See him before that if you have any concerns, but I don't anticipate any problems. When it heals, the scar will be almost invisible. Don't worry if you can't take all this in now. I'll leave a print-out of what I've done, and what you need to do, in the slot by the side of the door. And I've already sent a report to your regular doctor at home, so he'll know what's happened."*

Paul got up. He looked visibly relieved, and I would guess a whole lot more comfortable. "Thanks a lot," he said, not sure where to direct his gratitude.

"Now, Martin, would you mind if Paul stays while I examine you?"

"No," I growled, "I mean, I don't need an examination."

"Tell him about your indigestion," said Paul enthusiastically, "maybe he can do something for you."

"There is no *him*, idiot…" I started to say. I was really irritated that a professional roboticist should be so taken in by a supercomputer and a bunch of gizmos. But it was too late: Flaubert had picked up the cue.

"You have indigestion? Where is the pain?"

"Where do you think it is?" I snarled. There was a pause. I must have rung every bell with the voice spectrum analyser.

"Please try not to be hostile, I am only trying to help you."

Oh, nice touch, I thought. I damn near said "I'm sorry".

"Now, would you like to tell me where the pain is?"

"Here, behind my breastbone," I said grudgingly.

"And is it a dull, bruising pain, a sharp pain or a burning sensation?"

"Dull, bruising. Like someone is pressing there with his fist."

"And does the pain go anywhere, such as down one arm or through to the back?"

"No."

"Martin, I think that with symptoms like that it would be well if I took a proper look at you. Please get undressed down to your underpants and lie on the couch."

Reluctantly, I did as I was told. The treatment would only get billed to Paul's credit card if I didn't.

It did the trick with the balloons again to take my pulse and blood pressure. Then it came out with the scanning probe again, but this time the jointed arms were arranged side by side, so that the cylinders were in a line, like an ammunition belt. All except one, which stayed pointing at my wrist, probably a doppler ultrasound transceiver left there to monitor my pulse. The rest of the array moved over my chest. First of all I was thinking it might be looking for a stomach ulcer, but I didn't think that would show up on a scan. Probably it was trying to eliminate gallstones. Then the probe withdrew and six other arms came up, each tipped with an electrode. They applied themselves to different points on my chest. After about a minute, Flaubert said:

"I want to take a tiny blood sample, Martin. It will just be a pin-prick on your finger."

Before I could protest, it was done. The drop of blood was collected on some sort of analyser. And Flaubert reached his diagnosis.

Six months later, Paul and I met up in town for a coffee. It was good to see him again. When we sat down he grinned and held the thumb up for me. It had healed beautifully; the scar was barely visible. His face went serious.

"You know, Marty, with all that happened I don't think I thanked you properly for the way you looked after me that day. You did a real good job."

"Was nothing. You'd have done the same for me."

"But you weren't well yourself."

"Yeah, but I didn't know that, did I?"

"You didn't know you were having a heart attack?"

"Shit, no. I thought it was indigestion."

"What happened after we were flown back? They separated us and I couldn't find you."

"I went to the hospital. Got seen by a cardiologist. After he examined me he said I was the luckiest man on the planet. I say to him, 'Oh yes, Dame Fortune has really been smiling on me.' But he says, 'No, I mean it, Marty. First off, you had a heart attack and it didn't kill you. In anyone's book that's got to be lucky. Okay? Second, if you'd arranged to have it on the doorstep of the greatest cardiologist in the world, you couldn't have got finer care. That robot Medistation you went to did everything right. It diagnosed you quickly and correctly, and it injected the clot-buster drugs in good time. Your coronaries are clear now, Marty, but from the electrocardiogram it sent me I'd say you had a major block in the left anterior descending. You wouldn't know it now. There's a tiny bit of damage to your myocardium—your heart muscle—but it's not significant. You're a lucky man all right.' That's what he said."

"That's really great, Marty. So how've you been?"

"Good. I'm fine."

"You've lost weight."

"You noticed, eh? Well, I had a warning, didn't I? I'm watching my diet, doing regular exercise. Haven't been as fit as this in years."

"Are you back at work? I haven't seen you around."

"I'm working part-time. You know everyone could see I needed something less stressful, but it's a bit early for me to retire. So the Company suggested I work part-time, training new field operators, particularly in re-programming techniques. You know, pass on my knowledge to a new generation, that kind of thing. If I do that for five years, they've agreed to retire me on full pension after that. It's a good deal. I like the work and I have time for other things. The doc was right; I am lucky. I could've been dead, or at best a cardiac cripple. Instead of which I'm enjoying life. Thanks to Flaubert."

He smirked. "I thought you couldn't stand robots."

"Who, me? Never! You must be thinking of someone else. Not me. I count robots among the best friends I have in the whole wide world."

ಲ‍ಯ

The Statue

Renata sat on the starboard diving platform making final adjustments to her face mask. The boat rocked gently. The only sounds were the lapping of the waves against the hull and the distant mewling of sea birds. She paused for a moment to gaze down into the green water. Many fathoms below her—if the team's calculations were correct—was Venezia, or Venice, the first major city of the ancient world to be submerged when the ice-caps melted. So far as they knew, the last inhabitants had left around the year 2200, taking art objects and other portable treasures with them. This expedition was about a different sort of treasure; the history of the city, the architecture, the technology. It was also about the thrill of going where no-one had been for a thousand years.

She rolled forward and slid below the waves. How her father would have enjoyed this moment! He would not have dived, of course; he was a terrestrial archaeologist. When she was young she would accompany him on digs and help to clean the finds. If he could see her now! But father had been killed in an accident while she was still at University. She missed him terribly.

She cruised into the depths. Fuel cells in the belt around her slim waist supplied the breathing mixture to her mask and generated the electrical power for the two wrist-mounted water turbines. She wore small flippers, more for balance and steering than for propulsion. Marco and Roberto would be close behind her. Soon they would disperse to the coordinates Gus had allocated.

"Gus" Gustavson was the leader of the expedition. In their final briefing he'd said:

"Now remember, at this stage we're just looking for features: straight lines, rectangles, the kind of thing that might have been left behind by open squares, buildings, canals. This is only an exploratory dive. If you find something interesting we'll put down a virtual grid and look in more detail. Questions?"

There were none. They could almost feel the presence of the ancient city under the water and their anticipation was intense.

Marco and Roberto moved out to either side of her. Below them a green forest of weed waved slowly in the ocean currents. The weed had come from the colder waters of the South. Now it blanketed the entire floor of the Mediterranean Ocean, which was why previous attempts to locate Venice had been unsuccessful. But this expedition would be different: they had a new, far more accurate computer model to link the present coastline with the coastline ten centuries earlier. They should be right on top of the city. Marco and Roberto departed with a wave. She turned her wrist to check the locator. It was linked by ultrasonic channels to the three buoys that the yacht had put out. The buoys were constantly reading their position from Global Positioning satellites so she knew precisely where she was.

For ten minutes she cruised slowly over her target area. She could see nothing but the waving fronds of weed. Were they really in the right place? She ascended ten metres and cruised again. There *was* something there: a large rectangular depression in the weed, at least a hundred metres across. In the centre the weed rose to form a strange mound. Puzzled, she turned down to take a closer look. Something caught her eye and her pulse quickened. In amongst the weed she had glimpsed a different green, the telltale bright blue-green patina that copper, and copper alloys like brass and bronze, acquire when they become weathered—or are immersed in seawater. She moved in and parted the weed to reveal a spherical shape. Because of the weed she had no idea how high it was above the original ground level. Could it be an ornament on a steeple or cupola? She brushed it gently with her hands and swam slowly around it, and then, behind the diving mask, her eyes opened wide. She was staring at a face, the face of a handsome, determined young man. She felt the elation of the moment of discovery, took a deep breath to savour it, and then steadied her voice to speak into the underwater microphone.

"There's something down here. Something wonderful."

Over the next few days they surveyed the site systematically. They used high-pressure water cutters and vacuum hoses to remove the weed and gradually the muddy outlines of a square emerged. In its centre was the statue of a man on a horse, raised on a stone podium, the statue that Renata had discovered. He fascinated her. She would go down early to look at him, before the water was clouded by their activities. The statue itself was quite clean, because the metal had inhibited the usual growth of weed, barnacles, and other marine opportunists. The podium, on the other hand, was heavily encrusted. There was some sort of inscription cut into the stone but all she could make out were the letters 'I, O, V, A....O, N, I...' She photographed the inscription, hoping to use some form of image enhancement to penetrate its secrets.

One morning the divers started their work as usual, and mud spiralled up like smoke wherever their flippers made contact. The heavier equipment raised yet more mud, and visibility started to decline. Then the sun came out and she looked up to see a halo of light and sunbeams all around the statue, so that it seemed to her as if he were riding his horse through the dawn mists into some glorious future. It filled her with strange emotions.

Gus recognized the slender figure in the electric blue wet suit emerging from the water and went to help her. She fixed him with eyes the same colour as the wet suit.

"Who is he, Gus? Who is he, and what did he do to have a statue erected in his honour?"

"We will find out, Renata."

"Couldn't we raise the statue, Gus? Bring it to the surface? Take it back for further study?"

"In time, maybe. But you must be patient, Renata. First we have to examine the statue in its proper context. You must try to picture the square and the statue as it was a thousand years ago, before the waters rose…"

Beryl shivered. "Do you know where we are, Annie?" she demanded.

Annie continued to consult the map. "We're in some sort of square—maybe this one. I think we should have continued along the canal instead of crossing the bridge."

Her friend sighed. "Whose idea was it to come to Venice at this time of year?"

Annie looked up in surprise. "We both thought it was a good idea, Beryl. You were the one who heard the fares were going up in 2004. And we got off-season rates at the hotel."

"Yes, but who knew it would be so cold in November? I'm freezing."

"I can't see any sign to say what this *campo* is. Hang on, I'll have a look at the statue. It might be named after him. They often are."

Reluctantly Beryl accompanied her to a podium in the middle of the square, on which there was the statue of a man on a horse, a bronze statue showing the bright green patina of age. A cold fog was blowing in from the lagoon and rolling across the square. Unexpectedly the sun peeped through the clouds and as Beryl and Anne looked up they were transfixed by the ghostly effect of the light illuminating the mist swirling around the statue.

"Who is he?" asked Anne, in tones of wonder.

"And why is there a statue to him?" added Beryl. She had forgotten for the moment how chilled she was.

The square was crowded and everyone was on the move but no-one seemed to be in a hurry. They milled past the stalls selling ribbons, lace, wool and linen, leatherwork and glassware, cheeses, hams, live chickens, and brightly coloured spices. The stall-holders called out even as they were serving other customers. Over the noise of conversation, the shouts of the vendors, and the squawking of the chickens could be heard the sound of a small band. The air assaulted the nostrils. The stench of sewage from the canals was almost obscured by smells of cooking and wood smoke, and by the odour of many bodies on a hot Easter Day. A pretty girl stopped at a booth to have her fortune told. She was in love, and hoping secretly to learn that her happiness would be crowned by a proposal of marriage.

"What is your birth-date, my dear?" asked the fortune-teller.

"The eleventh day of June, 1443, if it please you, signora," the girl replied anxiously.

The fortune-teller began to consult her almanac, but her mutterings were drowned by the approaching beat of a drum, as a group of travelling players wound cheerfully through the crowd, announcing their next performance.

In a pool of shade by the statue in the middle of the square Claudio and his sister Annalise shared a *colomba pasquale*, a piece of bread shaped like a dove. The children were excited and turned their heads this way and that, taking in all the sights and sounds. Near to them an old soldier sat on a barrel, resting. Claudio smiled at him, and the old man smiled back. Suddenly he lifted his head and both the children looked up to see what had attracted his attention. On the other side of the statue a man was grilling sausages over a portable stove. The smoke was rising all around the statue and the sun shone through it, breaking into sunbeams, reflecting from the burnished surface and giving the bronze man on the horse a strange illusion of movement.

"Who is he?" asked Claudio.

"You mean who *was* he, you silly chicken," Annalise corrected him. "They only put up statues to people who are dead. Everyone knows that."

"All right, then, clever, who *was* he?" Claudio persisted.

Annalise, who had no idea, was trying to think of something to say when the old soldier answered for her.

"He was a very great man, a soldier," he said gently.

"Did you know him, signor?" asked Claudio innocently.

Annalise made a spluttering noise, but to her surprise the old man nodded his head. "Ay," he said. "I had the privilege of fighting in all his campaigns." Seeing that he now had both the children's attention, he continued. "Look at the statue, my dears. Imagine the man on the horse as he was in life, thirty years ago, before this time of peace…"

Giovanni Battista Contarini guided his horse up to the high ground and sat there, gazing at the horizon, seeing the thin spirals of smoke rising from the enemy's camp fires. A small smile quivered for a moment on his handsome features. They did not deceive him. They had abandoned the camp some hours ago and were on their way towards him, ready to halt his advance to Brescia. He had sent a detachment to meet their much larger force, with instructions to fall back as if the surprise attack had been successful.

His men waited patiently, glancing from time to time at the now familiar figure on the horse. When first they had been placed under his command there were many who muttered about the privileges of being the only son of one of the richest mercantile families in Venice. Even the rumour that he had read every major work on military history and strategy by the age of twenty did not inspire their confidence. Now, after four successful campaigns, no-one questioned his abilities. They knew full well they were fortunate to have their young commander. Not for him the vainglorious set-pieces that left thousands dead on the battlefield and grieving widows and fatherless children at home. His victories had been achieved by tactical brilliance, with minimal losses on their own side.

The sound of gunfire came closer and soon his men were sighted, retreating down the valley, regrouping to fire at the enemy and then retreating further, just as he had instructed. He watched the Milanese troops follow them in, estimated their numbers, and decided that they must have committed their full force, confident that their opponents were on the retreat. He smiled again. They were travelling much too fast for their artillery. His own forces were concealed on the hillside, divided into three groups, ready to attack on both flanks and at the rear, with a fourth detachment to descend on the artillery before it could be deployed. He waited patiently for the right moment and then gave the signal.

The battle was over quickly, the defeat crushing and final. He rode down into the valley. As his horse picked its way carefully between the bodies of men and horses, among the groans of the wounded and dying, he estimated the numbers and looked out for any of his own men who needed help or words of comfort. He did not notice the wounded Milanese officer who rolled over behind him, did not see the man raise his pistol, and with his last dying breath pull the trigger.

The ball struck the commander in the spine. Shards of bone sliced through vital vessels and he collapsed to the ground. There were shouts and two soldiers ran up, and stopped short. His eyes, gazing so recently at the horizon, now gazed sightlessly at the sky. His face was grey with the pallor of death, and yet in complete repose. They carried his body back, heavy with grief, and soldiers lined their route. On their weary faces, tears cut clean channels through the caked blood and grime of battle.

One week later, tears were shed again as the body was laid to rest in the church of San Giovanni in Bragora. The cathedral was packed with mourners, and crowds filled the square outside. The Doge himself gave the funeral oration.

"We mourn today the beloved only son of our respected Signor Paolo Contarini and his excellent family." He nodded to the heartbroken Signor, who was struggling to maintain his composure. "But we mourn also Giovanni Battista Contarini, beloved son of Venice, a great leader who gave his life for the glory of the Republic. It is fitting that we should honour his memory. Accordingly I announce here that I have commissioned a statue, to stand in a square that will be known henceforth as Campo Contarini. Generations to come, and generations that we may not know, will gaze upon the statue and ask 'Who was this man, and why was he so honoured?' And with God's grace, there will be, in every generation, those who have the wisdom to answer."

ﻌﻌ

Molly

"Do I 'ave to go to Lady Bebington's party?"

"Edward Henstall! If you knew the trouble I've taken to secure this invitation you wouldn't ask me such a thing!"

He grimaced, got up and went to the side table, where he lifted the silver dome on the serving dish and heaped another portion of bacon, ham, and eggs onto his plate. His wife watched him. Her husband had small eyes and a snub nose, and a pink complexion that made him look permanently overheated. *No-one would call him a handsome man*, she reflected, *but he is, of course, substantial. Why else would I have married someone twenty years my senior?*

"It's just that I never know what to say to these people," he continued, in a whinging tone that signified to her that he had already capitulated. "They're all old money. I'm a self-made man."

"You're not so different. Your family's lived in Yorkshire and Cheshire for generations, and you inherited the mills at Macclesfield from your father."

"*One* mill," he corrected. "Rest were my own doing, I might remind you."

"All right, all right. Well, talk to them about hunting or shooting. Or how we're restoring the garden. Or the problems of getting good staff. I'm sure you can find plenty of common ground if you put your mind to it."

"I could talk to them about the work I've had to do to bring this 'ouse up to snuff. Cost me a bloody fortune, it has. I don't know why we couldn't 'ave stayed in Macclesfield."

"Edward, we've been over this before. It's all right for you to stay at Macclesfield Hall during the week but you simply cannot mix with the right stratum of society up there. Whoever is going to notice you if you stay tucked away in Macclesfield? That's the whole point of establishing ourselves down here. You deserve recognition. You should have been knighted before now."

Mrs Lucinda Henstall made little secret of the fact that she wished to be Lady Henstall, and at the earliest possible opportunity.

"Herbert Thwaite got 'is knighthood, and 'e didn't move away from Bradford."

"I'm sure Herbert Thwaite found influential sponsors in some other way."

"Thwaite built a school for 'is workers, and a little village with special 'ousing. Last time I saw him 'e was thinking of makin' working day shorter."

"And what do you think of that?"

"Must be soft in the 'ead. How can y'keep production goin' on less than fourteen hours a day? It's 'ard enough now."

"Precisely. And what are his girls going to do with their free time? It's just a licence for drunkenness and debauchery. These people have no education. It's a service to them to keep them busy."

"Ay, but all that good work got 'im noticed, didn't it?"

"Edward, you know better than anyone that the key to success in business is to spend your money where it counts. Lady Bebington has her pet charities. Talk to her about them. Be impressed. Make a generous donation. Lord Bebington is very influential in the government. You'll be noticed all right."

He was silent for a while as he worked steadily through his plate. Then he drained his cup of tea and sat back, running his tongue around his teeth.

"I suppose you'll be wantin' another new dress."

"Well of course I'll be wearing a new dress! Whatever next! Do you want me to turn up to the Bebingtons wearing something they've seen before? Really, Edward, you do surprise me sometimes! Quite apart from anything else, you don't seem to appreciate that I am a living advertisement for your products when I attend these functions."

"What d'ya mean? You 'ardly ever choose materials from my range."

"Well, yes, but they don't know that, do they? They're fine silks, and that's all that matters. The ladies I mix with are your richest and most important clientele, you know."

"Oh ay, I know that," he breathed. "Oh well, at least it doesn't cost you much to get the stuff made up. I think you pay that seamstress of yours less than I pay my factory girls. And my girls only work six in the morning to eight at night. Your woman—what's her name, Megan?—looks like she works all day and all night. I don't know why she puts up with it. There must be dozens of ladies around who'd give her more money than you."

"I'm not having the girl take my styles and patterns to some other woman to flaunt in my face!"

"She's a free agent. 'ow can you stop her?"

"How? By making it clear to her, Edward, that if she doesn't work for me she most certainly won't work for anyone else."

"You can't guarantee that, can you?"

"I most certainly can." She smiled grimly. "I'm already quite well connected around here. I only have to drop something into the conversation. 'I'm not suggesting anything, of course, but I've noticed that every time she comes to the house for a fitting something seems to go missing'. Or, 'She does seem to over-estimate the amount of material I need. Do you think she might be holding some back to make dresses that she can sell on the side?' Oh, it really would be hardly any trouble at all, I assure you. And she knows it."

"What about 'er 'usband?"

"Dead. I think he drank himself to death—you know these people." She sighed. "It's an act of charity to employ her really. If it weren't for me she'd end up in the workhouse."

"Excuse me, ma'am. Megan is here with your dress."

"All right, show her in."

Megan hesitated at the threshold. "Excuse me, Mrs Henstall, my daughter Molly's with me. She's been helping me with the dress. Is it all right if she comes in?"

Mrs Henstall responded with an impatient flutter of the fingertips.

Megan and her daughter entered the dressing-room, bearing a large box between them. They began to unpack the dress. As they did so, Molly stole quick glances at Mrs Henstall. Last night Molly had helped with the dress until she could barely stay awake. Her mother had packed her off to bed with the assurance that it would only take her another hour to finish the job. But when she'd looked at her mother's weary face this morning she knew without asking that the poor woman had been working all night again. Now she was curious to see the lady who gave her such dire employment.

Although Molly understood that Mrs Henstall was only in her late twenties, the woman that she saw seated at the dressing table already had a matronly appearance. Her hips were full and her jaw heavy. Her hair, which had been dyed a reddish-brown colour, was dull and coarse. It had been gathered and pinned high on her head but Molly noticed that some black curls had escaped which, she thought, looked quite unsightly on the back of the woman's neck. Her mouth was set in a permanent look of disdain. A habit of wrinkling her nose briefly, as if she had caught a whiff of something unpleasant, had left lines at the bridge of her nose that even a heavy application of powder had failed to disguise. She was wrinkling her nose again as she watched them.

"Oh dear, is it badly creased?"

"I packed it very carefully, ma'am. I feel sure it will hang out but I'd be happy to give it a little press if you like."

Then Mrs Henstall caught sight of Megan's hands.

"Megan! Your hands! They're bleeding!"

Megan shrank, trying to conceal the red smudges on her fingers. "I'm sorry, ma'am…"

"You'll get blood all over the dress! Oh, leave it! Leave it alone!" She rose impatiently and pulled at a heavy sash to summon her maid. "Sally will help me on with it."

"I'm sorry, ma'am," Megan whispered, "I was sewing all night…"

And it was so cold she couldn't feel her fingers being shredded by the blunt end of the needle, you ungrateful woman, thought Molly, although of course she said nothing.

Even a close examination of the dress—and Mrs Henstall examined it very closely—failed to reveal any traces of blood on the material. And even a critical appraisal of the dress—and Mrs Henstall appraised it very critically—failed to reveal any fault with the fit or the quality of the workmanship.

"It looks very nice on you, ma'am," ventured Megan softly.

"It's beautiful," Sally agreed.

Mrs Henstall ignored both of them. She was staring at Molly in a way that the girl found quite uncomfortable. Mrs Henstall's lips curled in a bleak smile that did not ascend to her eyes. "Come here, girl," she said.

Molly moved forward and stood in front of her.

"What's your name again?"

"Molly, ma'am."

"How old are you, Molly?"

"Fourteen, ma'am."

"You have nice hair, Molly." She described a pirouette with her fingers. "Turn around."

Molly did as she was told. She did have beautiful hair. It cascaded like silk over her shoulders and down her back to the level of her waist. She brushed it every morning until it shone. When there was time, her mother liked to brush it with her while they chatted happily together. These were precious, close moments in a hard existence.

"Wait outside, will you, Molly?" Mrs Henstall commanded. "I have business to discuss with your mother."

Megan said nothing when she emerged from the dressing room. On the rear staircase they encountered the housekeeper, a ramrod-straight woman who was dressed to the neck in black. She acknowledged them with a brisk nod. Megan dipped her head and said politely, "Good morning, Mrs Gillot".

The woman's posture and expression did not change, but as she passed them she said in a voice of quiet authority, "Go via the kitchen, Megan. Cook's waiting for you," and walked briskly upstairs.

The kitchen was hot and full of wonderful, appetising smells. Cook greeted them.

"Well, look at little Molly. Not so little now. She's a real beauty, and no mistake. Look at her lovely hair. Ain't she got lovely hair, Meg?"

An old lady, who was working at a deep sink and looking at them over her shoulder, smiled toothlessly and nodded vigorously.

"Lord love you, Megan," Cook continued. "You look all wore out. Come and sit here. We'll get somethin' nice and hot down you 'fore you go."

They sat at the massive wooden table and Cook set a loaf of freshly baked bread on the table, and a bowl in front of each of them, into which she ladled soup from a steaming cauldron hanging in the fireplace. There were vegetables and potatoes and even pieces of meat in the soup. Without prompting, Cook refilled the bowls three times before Megan held up a hand to signal enough. When they rose to leave she was close to tears.

"Bless you," she said quietly to Cook.

"Lord, if you're going to bless anyone, bless Mrs Gillot. I didn't even know you was in the 'ouse until she told me. Come on, my loves, you can go out the side entrance here."

She watched them go, her mouth puckered in sympathy.

"My hair? She wants my hair?"

"That's what she was talking to me about. She wants to make a hairpiece out of it. She'll pay me well for it, she says."

"What did you say?"

"I said I couldn't."

"And what did she say?"

"She wondered out loud if she shouldn't dispense with my services. She said Emily Wainwright has made some nice dresses for a friend of hers. She does lovely work, she said, and quite inexpensively." She swallowed hard. "And her fingers don't bleed."

"Mother, why don't you let her take on this Emily Wainwright? You'll be well rid of her. You'll get other clients, ladies who'll appreciate your work, who'll pay you decently for it. You'll see."

"You don't understand, child. She's a very spiteful, jealous woman. She won't let me sew for anyone else, even if I'm no longer making dresses for her. She's said as much. I'll have no work. There'll be nothing coming in."

"Unless…"

Megan looked at her daughter, nodded, and then burst into tears.

"I should never have taken you with me, only the dress was too heavy to carry on my own..."

Molly put her arms around her mother. Her voice was flat.

"Don't cry, mother, don't cry, she's not worth it. Let her have my hair if that's what she wants. I don't care. It'll grow again."

"I say, Tabatha, our hostess certainly has a fine head of hair, what?"

"Don't be silly, Bertie, it's not her own."

"Oh, isn't it? Really? Well, looks very fine anyway. Oh, there's Angus. Must ask him how that lame hunter of his is."

"Bertie, the concert starts in fifteen minutes. I want you back before then. I'm not going in on my own."

"Right you are, my dear."

Lucinda Henstall's soirées were—she had to do herself justice—an inspiration. They enabled her to demonstrate the quality of the Henstall table and cellar and to show off the fine china, crystal and silverware. Her generosity as a hostess usually resulted in return invitations, which helped her to circulate in her chosen echelon of society. The recital in the drawing room, when the eating and drinking were over, established her as someone of cultivated tastes, although in reality she had no interest whatsoever in music. Finally, by holding the soirées during the week she could legitimately spare herself the presence of her husband, whose lack of social skills and graces were a constant embarrassment to her, while enabling her to hint at the extent of their properties in the north. Her husband was, of course, too pleased to be elsewhere on these occasions for him to entertain any concerns about their expense.

The recitals offered other opportunities. Her guests did not expect a busy hostess to be present the entire evening. Nor did they remark if a handsome young man ventured out onto the terrace with a small cigar, especially if they did not observe him taking a short cut to a private staircase. Mrs Henstall would make it clear to the musicians that she was paying them for a programme of at least one hour, and then she could indulge in some quite wild liaisons yet still be on hand at the end of the evening to see the guests out to their carriages.

The current object of her attentions was the young Marquis of Lambourne. He was a tall, rather elegant young man, given to wearing military uniforms, although as he had never served in any regiment the uniforms he wore invariably came from beyond the Empire. He was keenly interested in expanding his already extensive experience of married women, and did not feel constrained by a nice regard for size, shape or countenance. He was, moreover, totally discreet and therefore the ideal partner for Lucinda Henstall, who had no intention of allowing a little immoderate pleasure to disturb her comfortable domestic arrangements.

As soon as she had introduced the musicians she withdrew gracefully and hurried to the private bedroom where the Marquis was already waiting for her. Their appetites were keen and they paused only long enough to remove her dress and some nether garments before she fell back on the bed reaching her arms out to him. He entered her quickly and she immediately wrapped her legs around his back. She began to thrash her head from one side to the other, and luxuriant tresses of hair—Molly's lovely hair—were soon spread out all over the pillow.

Molly went to her room and sat in front of the mirror, the mirror in which she had so often looked as she and her mother brushed her gleaming hair. She had not ventured outside the house since this precious gift had been shorn from her head. There had been no tears, no recriminations. Her mother had fashioned a little mobcap, trimmed with spare lengths of lace, and she wore this all the time, to spare her mother's feelings more than her own. Now she pulled the cap off, and shook her head out of sheer habit, only to be reminded instantly of the weight that was no longer there. In the mirror was a reflection that she barely recognized as her own, her countenance pale, the outlines of her skull distinct under a short stubble which was all that remained of her crowning glory. She started to stare beyond her reflection. A new intensity entered her gaze and she felt herself to be travelling. Images formed fleetingly and dissolved: Mrs Gillot's austere expression, Cook's broad, kindly features, her mother covering her anguished face with her hands, and finally a stable image of extraordinary clarity: that woman, that vain and selfish woman, her head moving restlessly on a pillow with Molly's hair spreading out over it. Her eyes narrowed and a powerful surge of hatred flowed like a black river from every pore of her body.

Anyone who made love to Lucinda Henstall had to be prepared for a certain amount of noise. She moaned, she sighed, she blabbered incoherently, and she cried out. The Marquis closed his eyes, doing his best to shut out these distractions, and concentrated fully on the agreeable sensations that were growing and spreading in his loins. So absorbed were they in the pursuit of their own private pleasures that they failed to notice something. The hair on the pillow had started to move.

The furthest flung strands began to stir first, sliding slowly across the pillow, joining other strands, coalescing gradually into a single, long switch. And then, with every thrust of the Marquis's loins, the hair twisted.

The Marquis began to surge towards his goal. He dismissed her strange, muffled cries as further signs of her mounting pleasure, and responded to her bucking body by simply riding her harder. Finally he reached his shuddering climax and dropped his head to her bosom. At this point it registered with him that she had been unusually passive at the end. He opened his eyes and recoiled in horror.

Lucinda Henstall was dead. Her eyes were open and bulging; her swollen tongue protruded between blue lips. Wrapped tightly around her throat, like the coils of a constricting snake, were the successive turns of a long, twisted rope of gleaming hair.

The butler would later recall, for the benefit of the police, how the Marquis of Lambourne had appeared suddenly in the entrance hall in a highly agitated and dishevelled state, and asked for his carriage, even though the recital was still in progress. The police tried in vain to take a statement from the hysterical maid who had gone to look for her mistress when the baffled guests were becoming impatient to take their leave. When Mr Henstall had been acquainted with what had taken place he promptly gave instructions to his solicitors to dispose of all his interests south of Macclesfield.

The people filed out of the church, following the coffin, and gathered in a small black knot around the grave. A thin drizzle of rain fell. The rising and falling tones of the vicar's voice carried across the cemetery. Then the group broke up and people walked quickly away. Near the gate they passed a young girl with a mobcap, standing silently, hand in hand, with her mother.

"Who were those two, Gerald, do you know?" asked a woman, as he held the gate open for her.

"Don't know, dear. Never seen them before."

"Odd. I could have sworn that young lady was smiling."

৪০তন্ত

The Gift

In the middle of the bed in the middle of the ward a gaunt figure sits cross-legged, head bowed.

Bernard Levison takes the hospital notes from Henry Foden and signs for them. The two doctors continue to discuss the case, looking at the patient from the glassed-in office at the end of the ward.

"He still needs refeeding but what he needs most of all is psychiatric rehab."

"You didn't find anything organic?"

"No. Which is a miracle if you look at his back. There isn't an inch of him that isn't scarred. The brain scan was okay too. He must have take most of it on the arms—the forearms are badly scarred underneath. Typical defence wounds."

"Does he sit like that all the time?"

"If you let him. But he's quite compliant. And he's kind of aware of what's going on around him. You'd know better than me, but the state he's in, it looks like some kind of meditation or self-hypnosis. He never speaks. He sleeps funny too, all curled up in a ball. It's like his body's here but his mind's still back in Vietnam."

"Where did they find him?"

"It's in the notes. The way I understand it, a bunch of our guys were moving north when they came across this Cong enclave. They knew there was something in that area because they'd lost a patrol up there. There wasn't any resistance; the Cong had already cleared out. They found the patrol. All nine of them. Hands tied, bullet in the back of the head. And they found this guy. He seemed to have been there much longer—six months or more to judge by the shape he was in. Why he survived after they executed all the others God only knows. They found him on his own in a bamboo cage. Looks like beatings were a regular fixture. That and starvation. He's still very emaciated."

"Is he eating?"

Foden gives a short, humourless laugh. "Well, he's taking the food on board, if you can call it eating. We have to be careful what we give him. Whatever it is he just shovels it in and swallows. Doesn't chew. I don't know how he keeps it down, especially in that condition."

"Any visitors?"

"No. The notes say his mother lives in Cleveland. There's nothing about a fa-

ther—divorced, I think. Leastways she's next of kin. The army informed her as
soon as they handed him over to the VA—standard procedure—but she hasn't
tried to get in touch. Not even a phone call."

"I think we should get her down here. A familiar face might help him re-
orientate."

"Yeah, maybe. The guy's a survivor, Bernie. I sure hope you can do something for him."

"We'll try, Hal. We can but try."

"Have a seat, Mrs Travis, I'm Dr Levison. Thank you for coming down. I
hope you had a good journey."

"Where is he?"

"He's on the ward. I'll take you to see him in just a moment. But I wanted to
prepare you first. Your son may not be…as you saw him last."

"They said he wasn't badly injured."

"To an extent that's true. Physically. Mentally he's carrying injuries that may
take some time to go away."

She looks at him narrowly. "What kind of doctor are you, Dr Levison?"

"I'm a psychiatrist." He pauses and adds quietly, "Your son's had a very tough
time, Mrs Travis."

Her mouth straightens and she draws herself up. "Life hasn't been easy for
any of us, Dr Levison."

He looks at her thoughtfully, reading her body language like an open book,
leaving the silence to grow. Eventually she breaks it.

"We were all against it, this senseless war—my friends, my neighbours, my
professional associates. We campaigned, we lobbied. Then they draft my son!
I begged him not to go."

"He'd have gone to jail."

"I wanted him to go to jail! People would have respected him for that! I
could have been proud of him! I could have held my head up in public! But no,
he had to shame me by joining up."

"It's no shame to fight for your country, Mrs Travis."

"Oh, don't feed me that crap, please. Self-defence? No-one with a scrap
of intelligence believes that! It's just an excuse you people use to send decent
young men abroad to be killed and maimed. What for? Politics? Greed? I don't
know what the agenda is. A mother would be the last to be told."

He picks it up. "Mrs Travis, let me be frank. You knew your son was being
invalided home, and where he was being treated. I would have thought that—

as his mother—you might have wanted to get in touch with us before now."

She bristles. "And I would have thought that was none of your goddam business, Dr Levi-son." She rests heavily on the first part of his name.

He notes the racial insult but does not react. He is not even surprised. He is a professional.

"Mrs Travis, I'm just a doctor. I'm only interested in the welfare of my patients. I thought it would be appropriate to ask you to come, but…"

"Well, now I'm here I might as well see him."

He hesitates, then stands, and leads her wordlessly to the ward. Her eyes are drawn to a living cadaver seated cross-legged on a bed, and a look of disbelief crosses her face as she realizes this is the bedside he is leading her to. He pulls the screens and leaves them alone. She chews her lip for a few minutes, then speaks to what is on the bed.

"Hello, James."

He rocks slightly, but does not reply.

"James. It's your mother. I've come all the way down here to see you."

Silence. Her discomfort starts to kindle her anger.

"James, I'm sorry to see you in this condition, but you brought it on yourself, you know. I mean, don't say I didn't warn you."

Still silence. She lowers her voice.

"Listen to me, James. What do you think it's been like for me, all these years? Left to bring you up single-handed. My career down the drain , no chance of getting married again to someone better than your lousy father. I made a lot of sacrifices for you, James, and this is the way you repay me. Well, it's no good you coming back now, as if nothing ever happened…"

Quite suddenly he raises his head and gives vent to a keening, animal howl that reaches fingers into every corner of the ward and chills the blood of everyone in it. Heads jerk towards the screened-off bed. Two nurses, frozen momentarily by the unearthly sound, now leap into action. Mrs Travis is bundled out of the ward by one of them, struggling and shouting, "You have no right to treat me this way! I'm his mother!" The other nurse runs to James. He is quiet now, shaking all over. She gives him a tranquillizing injection. Slowly he subsides. He looks at the nurse out of the dark, haunted sockets of his eyes and allows himself to be tucked tightly into the bed. His eyes close.

The journey to school proceeds in silence. It is always this way. She seldom talks while she is driving; she says it's a dangerous distraction. She doesn't have the radio on either, for the same reason, and so they drive in silence. It takes thirty minutes, a little longer if the traffic is bad. When they get there he will thank his mother for going out of her way, although the school is actually on her route to work and was chosen for that reason. He will not kiss her. They are not, she says, a kissing family. (She says "kissing" as if it were a disease.) They are not a crying family either, and any show of weakness in that direction earns him a long spell locked in his room. But once, just once, he saw his mother cry.

James (never "Jim" or "Jimmy") wonders how things might have been if his father were still around. That was when he saw her cry, the time his father walked out on them. He was seven. He can't recall what his father looked like and there are no photographs around the house to remind him. So it's just the two of them. They don't kiss, they don't cry, and they talk very little, and not at all when they are in the car.

He is thirteen now, quiet, withdrawn, aware of the stirrings of manhood without quite understanding or recognizing them. He watches the passers-by, his gaze lingering on the girls in their thin summer dresses. The car comes to a halt in heavy traffic. A girl wearing a T-shirt and blue shorts is on the sidewalk ahead of them. She has nice slim legs. He wonders if she is pretty. He would like to know. He wants to know. As a game, he concentrates his mind, willing her to turn around. Abruptly she stops walking and faces in his direction. He looks away hurriedly, surprised and excited. Although the girl is quite pretty it is her response that energizes him.

He seeks out somebody else, a man this time. The man turns suddenly, as if he has been tapped on the shoulder. His excitement builds. It is the first time he is aware of the Gift.

Every day of the week his mother takes him to school, and every day he chooses his targets, using the Gift, honing it. He learns to recognize the sensation when he contacts another mind, a feeling of mental pressure, as if reaching out with a ghostly hand and encountering some resistance. Soon he can focus powerfully, with less effort and with an almost immediate result. He gains confidence.

Jenny Dover is at the school dance. She has blue eyes and short blonde hair and when he looks at her it makes his chest ache. Some of the kids are dancing, but only the ones who came together. The rest are gathered in knots, the boys nudging ribs on one side of the floor, the girls trying to look unaware of them on the other. The music echoes off the hard surfaces of the gymnasium where they hold the dances.

Sean sees him eyeing Jenny. "Go on, then, James. Ask her. Go on. No guts?"

He bites his lip in irritation and embarrassment. Then in desperation he focuses on Jenny's turned head. She stops talking and looks round. This time he does not look away, but concentrates, reaching into her mind. Slowly, as if in a dream, she walks across the floor to him. He maintains his focus until she is a few feet away, and then he can hold it no longer. She stops, confused, wondering where she is. She looks up at him, frowning. Before she can say anything he steps forward.

"Oh, hullo, Jenny. I was hoping you'd come by. Would you like to dance?"

She is too surprised to say no, and it is less embarrassing to say yes. They dance chastely, exchanging brittle conversation, while his friends gawp. When the music stops he escorts her politely back to her group. They do not dance again, but once in a while she glances suspiciously in his direction.

In the weeks following the dance he entertains feverish ambitions. His Gift will make him powerful! Beautiful women will flock to him! Men will obey him! He will become influential, important, famous! All too soon his hopes descend into disappointment and resignation. Try as he might he can only turn people's heads. Sometimes, as with Jenny, he can draw them towards him. What he cannot do is influence the way they think or act or feel. It is, after all, only a small gift—a party trick, no more. It may not even be that unusual. He uses it less and less.

He graduates from High School without distinction, and without any clear idea of what he wants to do with his life. The immediate problem is solved for him; he is drafted into the army. His mother thinks he should go to prison rather than fight in Vietnam, but he is burdened by the memory of long hours locked in his room as a punishment. He cannot face confinement. He would rather go…

His face looks small over the broad, white fold of the hospital sheet. His eyelids flutter; unseen demons tug persistently at the corner of his mouth.

The heat of the jungle is overpowering, fetid, oppressive. Biting insects are a constant torment. Rivulets of sweat run down his neck and creep inside his shirt. The patrol moves slowly and yet still too fast. He knows that every leaf can conceal the muzzle of a gun, every step can set off a mine or a booby-trap. He has experienced contact once before, heard the agonized screams of his companions, witnessed their dreadful injuries. He is afraid, always afraid.

He lives in the temporary reprieve of a return to base camp. Then the mail arrives and everyone has letters from family, friends, lovers. He knows there is nothing for him, and yet each time he hopes, hopes just hard enough to feel the disappointment more keenly...

Another patrol. The sun is rising through a thin haze as they set off. Vapour curls off every leaf and hangs in the air. The mist plays tricks with their eyes. The conditions are perfect for a VC ambush and they know it. All at once there is an explosion and someone is screaming and everyone is shouting and running and loosing off with M16s. In the confusion he is separated from the others. The firing stops. He crouches in the undergrowth. He hears the enemy moving all around him. Fear tears at his guts. His heart bangs in his ears. Urine flows hotly down the inside of his trouser leg...

"James? Are you dreaming again, James? Ah, look at you, all in a sweat. Oh, and you've wet the bed again. Come on, love. Let's get you cleaned up."

He stares at the nurse, eyes wide and uncomprehending.

"It's all right, James. You're safe now, you're back home. Come on, now. It's a nice morning. We'll have some breakfast and then we'll decide what we're going to do with you today."

Today.

"Today, American, you die!"

In the tone someone might use to wish you "Good morning". He feels his chest constrict with fear, with the expectation of imminent death, tries to imagine what it will feel like to die. Except that he doesn't die, not that day, nor the next day, nor the day after that. Each morning the same greeting, "Today, American, you die!", each day his last, until fear is numbed by repetition.

He begins to assemble strategies for survival. No chance to use the Gift here, not when merely meeting the eyes of his tormenter will bring on another savage beating. "Why you look at me?" The beatings come anyway, especially if one of the man's compatriots is killed. Then Trang screams and beats him with a bamboo stave, sometimes into unconsciousness, as if he alone were responsible. Each time he surfaces again, his body raging with pain. He focuses his mind, using the Gift to suppress the pain until in some strange way he feels the sensations but not the hurt. He learns to curl up when he sleeps, because Trang sometimes walks around the camp at night and amuses himself by waking him with a vicious kick to the genitals.

Trang commands this small group of Viet Cong. Is that his name? He knows only that he hears the word often when the grunts are taking orders from their leader. James never pronounces the word himself. In fact he never speaks at all; to do so would be to invite another beating.

Keep quiet. Keep your head down. Survive.

"James?" Again it is the big Irish nurse, Rose. "Would you like some breakfast? Here y'are. Now James—James, are you listening to me?—I want you to eat it nice and slow, you hear? Chew every mouthful. I want to see you still eatin' when I come by again. Do you understand? There's a good fella."

He nods numbly.

Food. Food is scarce. Food is precious. Food means survival.

His stomach grips with hunger. He uses the mental power of the Gift to deflect his mind from it, just as he uses it to dull the pain of the constant beatings. When rice comes he eats it quickly. Trang loves to snatch it away before he's taken more than a couple of mouthfuls. "Oh, you not hungry," he taunts. Sometimes, if Trang is not looking, one of the VC soldiers tosses in a piece of fruit or a root vegetable as they pass by, as one might feed a caged animal. There is no friendship in the gesture, no eye contact, but it is a reminder that underneath all the differences that place them on opposite sides of this brutal conflict lurks a residue of shared humanity. It is a residue that has somehow left Trang outside its embrace.

Eat fast. Get it inside. Stay alive.

"You've woofed it again!" Rose is glaring benignly at his empty plate. "Oh well, come on. We'll get some clothes on you and then we're going for a little walk. All right?"

The sunlight is very bright in the garden and the air is warm. His legs are weak; he clings to Rose's broad forearm. There is the path, there is freshly mown grass, there are flowers, there are clumps of trees... He shrivels.

"James? All right, then, that's enough for today. You've done very well. We'll go back now and try again tomorrow."

One floor below the ward, the staff are assembled in a seminar room. Dr Levison passes one folder to his left and picks up another.

"Travis. James Travis. Physically he's looking a bit better. How's the desensitization going? Rose—you were looking after that."

"He's doing quite well, doctor. We had some problems with the trees—I suppose it reminds him of the jungle. So we took another route past single trees, and then small bushes and gradually worked up. He's all right with that now. Yesterday we got as far as the fountain but then he froze solid. He just sat down. Sam and Charlie had to help me get him back inside."

"The fountain? What time of day was that?"

"Early morning. We went out straight after breakfast."

"There could be something here. Rose, tomorrow morning I want you to do it again. Only this time I'll come with you."

They walk slowly together, past the lawn, past the flower beds, past the trees, past the shrubbery, down the steps to the lower lawn. They approach the fountain. James gives a little sigh. His long skinny legs fold slowly under him like a dying insect. Now he is sitting cross-legged on the ground, his head lowered. Dr Levison is excited.

"What is it, James? James! Tell me what you see!"

Death is inevitable; only the manner and timing of it is uncertain. Will it be starvation? Disease? A bullet in the back of the head? Or will Trang go too far one day and beat the last feeble flicker of life out of him?

The B52s are coming again, flying low. The bombardments are getting closer. Is that the answer? Will death come from the sky? He clamps his hands tightly over his ears, draws in his knees, and still he feels every crushing percussion throughout his body. A little closer, that's all it needs to be. One bomb to blow this cage apart and separate his soul from his frail body once and for all.

Outside his cage a small fluffy feather, perhaps all that remains of some luckless jungle fowl, floats slowly down, rocking gently from side to side, then jerks away as another shock wave hits it. He registers its direction; the bombs are falling just to the north.

Something's happening. The familiar pattern of activity in the camp has changed. Some VC grunts, in their usual peasant dress, come hurrying by with sacks of rice over their shoulders. But Trang hasn't come. He hasn't said "Today, American, you die!". The daily ritual, so terrifying at first, has become perversely reassuring, so that the absence of it unsettles him.

"James! Talk to me James!"

He lifts his eyes. Levison is crouched in front of him. "James, where are you?"

He closes his eyes. He hears a voice, a familiar voice. It is his own voice, yet it seems to come from somewhere else.

"I'm standing in my cage, holding the bars, watching. The bombing's stopped. They're preparing to move out. I can tell. I can hear a clattering noise. It's in the distance and it comes and goes, but I know the sound; it's a Huey. Why hasn't Trang come?"

"Trang is your captor?"

"Trang's a psychopath. They're all afraid of him. I'm his plaything. He beats me, starves me, taunts me. Every morning he says "Today, American, you die!" but he hasn't come this morning. Where is Trang?

"Ah, here he is. I knew he'd come. He's carrying an AK47 and it's pointing straight at me. Not at my head; at the top of my chest. He's not bluffing this time; he doesn't mean to miss.

"'Now we leave, American. But you leave first. Goodbye.'

"His finger is tightening on the trigger. I have nothing to lose. I look him straight in the eyes. I feel the contact. I summon up all my power and focus it at him. I am willing him not to pull the trigger. I can sense the resistance; I push harder. The sweat is running into my eyes but I mustn't blink. I have failed before. This time I must not fail. If I fail, I die. Our minds are locked together, wrestling. It seems like whole minutes go by.

"He frowns, then his expression changes. His finger relaxes. He lowers the rifle.

"'I s'ink American no find you. More better I leave you here, I s'ink so. You starve. Die slowly. More better, I s'ink so.'

"He gives a short laugh. Then a longer one. Then he hurries away.

"I settle down in my cage and check the time. Not by my watch, of course; they took that when they captured me. I use small pebbles to mark the floor of the cage where the shadows of the bars fall. It makes a sundial. Trang's never noticed it."

A new look enters Levison's eyes. He casts a quick glance over his shoulder. The fountain is of black and white marble. The area around the fountain has been paved with the same materials, white with an inlay of black to form a pattern. A pattern of parallel black lines.

"It's about eight in the morning. The shadows move slowly. Around three in the afternoon I hear shouts, the shouts of American soldiers. They burst into the clearing, and the first thing they see is me."

He opens his eyes and looks up, not into the sweating, astonished face of a U.S. Army Lieutenant, but into the empathic countenance of Dr Bernard Levison.

"James," he says quietly. "James, we can help you. We can help you now."

And for the first time in his adult life James covers his face with his hands and weeps.

He learns to live in the present more than the past, to distinguish reality from the version of reality disgorged by his tortured brain. He still dreams but now he wakes from the dreams. The dreams become less frequent. Bit by bit, step by painful step, he is restored both physically and mentally. He emerges with the inner strength that comes from self-knowledge. Seven months after entering the Veterans' Administration Hospital he embraces Rose and shakes Dr Levison by the hand. He is ready to pick up his life again.

He has few qualifications other than his military service. The VA helps him to get a job in the Detroit police force. He carries a firearm but hopes he will never have to use it. He is quiet and conscientious. He does not fraternise but he is respected. By and by he is promoted to Sergeant.

When the man pulls out a gun and demands the contents of the cash register, the owner kicks a footplate and sets off the alarm. There is a shot and the owner falls behind the counter. Customers scream and some manage to run out of the store. The beat car is less than a block away when it gets the initial call. It mounts the sidewalk and two uniforms come out fast, unholstering their weapons. Seeing them, the man tears a six-year-old girl away from her petrified mother and hides behind island shelves in the depths of the store. One of the officers gets on the radio to dispatch. Dispatch sends three more patrol cars, one to cover the rear entrance.

James Travis is the Patrol Sergeant; he is pulled away from another call. When he arrives he finds two officers controlling a small crowd outside and three guns fanning the inside of the store. His men are using the cover provided by stacks of groceries near the entrance. James recognises the lead officer and speaks with quiet authority.

"What's the picture, Matt?"

The officer replies without taking his eyes off the store. "Owner's been shot. The perp has snatched a little girl. He says to let him go or he'll kill her."

"Where's the mother?"

"We got her out. Sally's looking after her outside."

"Okay, good work. Now keep cool, all of you. We don't want anyone else getting hurt here."

The air is hot and heavy. One of the officers wipes sweat from his eyes with his sleeve.

James looks at the interior of the store and a feeling begins to grow inside him, a feeling of great intensity, a feeling that his life, his Gift, even his appalling experiences in Vietnam, have suddenly acquired meaning, that all these things have come together for this one moment.

He reaches out to the mind of the man in the store and feels the contact. He increases the pressure, trying to draw the man out. It isn't working; he can't get enough leverage crouched down like this.

The crowd outside has grown, the little girl's mother still at the front, Sally keeping a firm grip on her arm. There is an audible intake of breath as James rises slowly to a standing position. The other officers glance sideways at him, dismayed, expecting at any moment to hear a fatal shot.

James bears down harder. Now there is a slight movement from behind the shelves. One of the officers jerks his automatic in that direction but James extends an open hand, restraining him. He needs every ounce of concentration.

Slowly the man emerges. He still has the little girl by one wrist but he holds his other arm out, and there is no gun. He comes forward, eyes wide, as if in a trance. James fixes his gaze, willing him forward. His brain aches from the effort. The man moves again, slackening his grip slightly on the girl's wrist. She twists away instantly and runs behind the shelves. The distraction causes James to lose his focus for a brief instant. The man suddenly becomes aware of his situation, of the guns trained on him. With a shout he grabs the revolver hooked in the back of his belt and gets off one shot before they open fire. He spins and jerks in the fusillade and crumples to the floor. The officers rise slowly.

The distraught mother, capable of restraint no longer, crashes through the doors and races into the store to find her daughter cowering at the end of an aisle. She carries her back, sobbing with relief, then freezes as she sees one of the police officers lying in a pool of blood, his fellow officers standing or crouching near him with grim helplessness. Somewhere outside an ambulance siren wails. She approaches and kneels.

"God bless you, young man," she says. "You saved my little girl's life."

His eyelids flicker and his lips move. She bends closer to hear. Then his body goes limp.

Watched anxiously by her little girl, she straightens up slowly, covering her eyes with a handkerchief.

"What did he say?" one of the officers asks her huskily.

"He said...he said, 'It was my gift'."

80 03

The Magnolia

My wife always says "I'm the gardener". In fact she was saying it now, to the four friends we'd invited for dinner.

"I'm the gardener," Jessica was saying. Then she added, by way of an afterthought: "But Sam is quite helpful."

"You have such a beautiful garden," Fiona purred. "There isn't a finer one within a hundred miles."

Her husband Richard cleared his throat. He was an academic, and in the traditional interests of accuracy and fairness he was about to correct his wife's overstatement, but a steely look from his wife, which Jessica missed but I didn't, stopped him in his tracks.

Jessica was fluffing her feathers at Fiona's compliment. "Well, I'm sure I don't know what I'd do without my little Biosphere," she murmured, with a commendable show of modesty that fooled absolutely no-one.

Nadia joined in. "It's so *mature*, that's what gets me. I'm sure I don't know how you do it."

Jessica sensed the implied question and shot a quick glance at me. How indeed do you have trees that are a hundred and fifty years old inside a Biosphere that was built on new ground barely twenty years ago? Sooner or later the others would catch on, and then they'd all be doing it, but for the moment we were way ahead of them and neither of us was about to elaborate.

"It's a shame, in a way," said Jessica, artfully redirecting the conversation, "that you can't see in from the outside too. It would look so nice."

"But that was the whole point of Biospheres, surely?" said Nadia. "To restore privacy. It was bad enough in the old days, with helicopters and light planes. Once they started with hovers, you'd have had no peace at all."

"That and the hi-res observation satellites," added Nadia's partner, Bob. "Once the Press boys got access to those the paparazzi could snatch pictures of you, sunbathing in the altogether in your own back garden, and you wouldn't even know."

"Well, I'm sure they're very welcome to photograph me in the altogether if that's what turns them on," Nadia replied.

Everyone laughed at the joke against herself. It wouldn't have taken a very high resolution system to capture Nadia's ample proportions. Come to that, Jessica wasn't far behind her. I'd told her the extra weight she was carrying around didn't suit her, but she wouldn't listen. She never listened to anyone, least of all me.

"It wasn't primarily the privacy issue." You could depend on Richard for a thorough analysis. "It started with industrial pollution: all the concern about the quality of the air we were breathing. Then there was global warming: the summers got too hot to work comfortably outside and the evaporative loss of water was making it too costly to grow anything but desert species. Then there was the ozone hole, and the soaring rate of skin cancer. It all pointed in the same direction: create your own microenvironment, outside as well as inside. They used Blackglaze for the Biospheres because it filtered out the ultraviolet but let through the wavelengths needed for photosynthesis. Of course it had the advantage that you couldn't see in, so it solved the privacy issue at the same time."

"Wasn't there a scare about anthrax, as well?" offered Bob. "I heard that it was put about by the manufacturers of Biospheres."

"It was never proven," said Richard, "but it was the last straw for a lot of gullible people. Not Jess, of course," he added quickly, noticing Jessica suddenly appearing taller in her chair. "You just wanted a nice garden, didn't you, Jess?"

"That's right," Jessica smiled sweetly. Smart man, Richard.

"I want a *Magnolia soulangeana*."

When Jessica used that tone of voice it meant that she wouldn't rest until she'd got her hands on one, and I wouldn't get any rest until I'd come up with it.

"And what's that?" I asked, with only mild interest.

"A tree. It's lovely. It's got big pink flowers in Spring, before almost anything else is out. It'll do well here but it's slow-growing and nobody's got a big one. I know, because I asked Nadia when they were all here, and she's well up on what people have got, and she says she's only ever seen little ones."

I could have asked Jessica whether it was her love of trees that drove her desire for a *Magnolia soulangeana* or the fact that no-one else had one worth looking at, but I wouldn't have got a straight answer and it would only have prompted another row, so I didn't bother.

"Have you got a supplier?"

"Yes. M.K. Roberts has a nice variety in stock. I can have a two-year-old sapling inside a week."

"How old do you want it to be?"

"About 40."

"Okay," I said wearily.

This was precisely why I'd invested in the Transporter, or to give it its full name: de Broglie Vectored Field Transporter. It was expensive, but then I'd got myself a fully featured one, and I reckon it was worth it. It had certainly kept Jessica happy.

Take an example—an actual example, as it happens. Jess announces that she wants a one-hundred-and-fifty-year-old cedar in the Biosphere. I get her to buy a sapling and I plant it in the usual way, siting it according to its final size. Then I set up the field antennae—four of them, arranged roughly in a square around it. It doesn't have to be an exact square but every part of the tree has to be inside it. Then I go to my study and set the coordinates to about a hundred and fifty years ago. The mode is straight Time Transfer; if you're not familiar with this sort of thing, it means the sapling is transported back in time in exactly its present form. Then I set the coordinates to the negative of what they were, which exactly reverses the time vector, and I change the mode to Time Trajectory. This mode is different; its effect is like winding on time about five thousand million times faster than normal, so in about a second I have a one-hundred-and-fifty-year-old cedar tree where there was previously a sapling.

It's not hard, but there are certain rules about these time transactions, and they're built into the software, to stop you from setting up forbidden manoeuvres. The main rule is that you can't add or subtract anything in a previous time zone. So anything you put there you've got to take away at the end of the transaction, and *vice versa*. Well that's pretty obvious, because otherwise you'd be changing history. This didn't stop some bright sparks from transferring themselves to an earlier zone with the idea of helping themselves to treasure and bringing it back. It didn't work, of course, and a number of people disappeared mysteriously. The manufacturers started getting nervous and they now include a get-out clause, and you have to agree to it before you can run the software. It goes something like this: "As manufacturers of this equipment, we strongly advise you against attempting to transfer yourself or another individual with the Vectored Field Transporter. The Company will accept no responsibility for the consequences if this warning is disregarded." Actually I can't see why it shouldn't work in principle, but I've got more sense than to try.

Jessica had the little magnolia delivered in five days. We argued a bit about where to put it, as she wanted it near the end of the border, and I wasn't convinced there would be enough height between the mature tree and the glazing of the Biosphere. Finally we agreed on a site and I planted it. Then I got the four field antennae, sank the spikes in so they were arranged in a square, and went back upstairs to my study to run the program. I could hear Jessica moving around somewhere downstairs. She never took any interest in this aspect; the only thing that mattered to her was the final result.

I did the time transfer, then the time trajectory; no problem. Then I went downstairs to show Jessica the finished result but she didn't seem to be around, so I opened the back door to the garden to take a peek myself. I quickly shut the door and leaned back shakily. The tree was there all right, just where it was supposed to be, a lovely specimen, spreading its branches gracefully to a height of about twenty-five feet. But something else was there too. It was a very ugly insect. And it was the size of a small house.

My mind was racing. Where in God's name had it come from? How the hell was I going to get rid of it? I went back up to my study and looked out of the window. It hadn't moved; it was still on the ground at the foot of the tree. Standing there, glinting like that, it would have passed for a giant bronze sculpture, except that there were little waving movements from its feelers, which arched out and forwards like part of an H-aerial. It seemed to be some kind of weevil. I was lost in thought, trying to work through the problem, so I nearly leaped out of my skin at the sound of a piercing shriek followed by the back door banging shut. I suppose I should have warned her.

I sat down at my console and waited. I didn't have to wait long. The door burst open and there she was, chest heaving, eyes staring, face white as a sheet. Her mouth was moving but no sound was coming from it. It was such a novel sensation to see Jessica actually lost for words that I savoured the moment. Then she found her voice.

"What...is...that?"

"I think it's some kind of weevil."

"I don't mean that, you idiot, I mean how did it get there?"

I gritted my teeth. It always annoys me when she calls me an idiot, because without my little bit of ingenuity she wouldn't have her bloody garden, but I hung on to my self-control. After all, she'd had a shock. "Well, I can only assume it took the time trip with the sapling. It must have been on it when I sent it back."

"But the Biosphere's pest-free!"

"Yes, I know that, but it must have come in on the sapling. They're supposed to spray them before delivery but somebody must have slipped up."

"Well, didn't you see it?"

"For Chrissake, it was probably only a quarter of an inch long then."

"It's a hell of a sight bigger than that now!"

"Well, it's forty years old, isn't it? I didn't think insects could live that long, but this is a kind of special situation. It isn't like growing up in a garden full of predators..."

"I'm not interested. Get it out of here!"

If there's one thing that annoys me almost as much as being called an idiot, it's being told to do things that I'm already trying to do. Something inside me snapped.

"Do you know, I was just thinking about that myself? I was thinking how the only way out of the Biosphere is through the house. That thing's a bit large to go through the back door, but if we open the French windows onto the patio we should be able to push it through there. Of course it might squit on the lounge carpet on the way out. I don't know what weevil squit is like, but I'm prepared to bet it's not fragrant. Still, you can always clean up after it, can't you, love? Shall I put a collar and lead on it, or would you like to saddle it up and ride it out?"

The colour rose to Jessica's face. "Why don't you cut the sarcasm and do something useful!" she bellowed. "Like zap it in the head with a megalaser."

Zap it in the head. Life is so simple for some people.

"Oh, very good suggestion. And what if it moves its head and I miss? The very best that could happen is I blow a hole in the Biosphere and your precious microenvironment equalizes with the outside world. That's the best scenario. A more likely scenario is that the beam gets reflected around inside the Biosphere and destroys everything in the garden, us included."

Her mouth set in a straight line, her eyes still blazing. "Then spray it with chemicals!"

"Okay. Assuming I could get enough insecticide to kill something that big, which I very much doubt, and assuming we didn't gas ourselves in the process, how am I going to get rid of the carcass? You can't just flush it down the toilet, you know."

Jessica was beside herself. I knew she was trying desperately to think of a suitable put-down; that was far more important to her than solving the problem. She bit her lip and turned to the window. Then she froze and uttered a small, protesting cry. I stood up to see what had caught her attention. The weevil had moved. It had turned slightly and extended two palps to grasp the stem of a rather handsome rhododendron, which it had brought to a set of complicated mouth parts. Even inside the house we could hear the scrunching noise as it worked its way down the stem. I was amazed at how fast the thing disappeared. Then it selected another stem and did a repeat performance. Jessica's lower lip quivered.

"It's destroying my lovely garden," she whimpered quietly.

I confess I felt a bit sorry for her.

"Look, Jess. Why don't you go out and leave me to it? Take the hover. Go round to a friend. Go shopping or something."

She looked at me like a mournful spaniel, still hesitating.

"Go on, Jess," I said a bit more firmly. "I can't think straight with you around. Go on, now, there's a good girl."

She made up her mind, set her lips grimly, gave me a brief nod and made for the door. I waited until I heard the hover whine off.

I already had an idea about what I was going to do, but it was dangerous and I didn't want Jessica around. I went to the back door and stepped gingerly into the garden. The weevil had finished eating rhododendrons for the moment and was now facing the house, cleaning its feelers by dragging them through its mouth parts. It hadn't moved far, so it was reasonably well placed in relation to two of the field antennae, but it was outside the line of the other two, and if this was going to work every part of it had to be inside the field. Moving as smoothly and slowly as I could, I worked around to the side antenna, watching the insect carefully all the time. As I moved, the light reflected in turn from the multiple facets of one big black compound eye and I had the distinct feeling that it was watching me. Finally I reached the field antenna. Still doing my best to avoid any sudden movement, I tried to pull it out of the ground. The spike was firmly embedded. I pulled harder and felt it give a bit. I worked the spike back and forth gently, pulled again and with a sudden lurch it came free. I looked up anxiously at the monstrous insect. Its feelers were waving a bit but it hadn't moved. Moving very carefully I drew the field antenna back a few yards and pushed it in again. Now I needed to do the same with the front one, which was right under the weevil's snout. I licked my dry lips and moved very slowly around to it. The sweat was trickling down the back of my neck. I reached the field antenna, took hold of it, and suddenly the weevil moved one leg. I froze. It was still again. I was barely breathing. I pulled ever so gently and felt it give. I was in luck: this antenna was in softer ground and it came out smoothly. I breathed out. Very slowly I drew the antenna away and sank it again. The longer rectangle made by the four field antennae now included the whole of the insect. I retreated smoothly backwards and into the house, shut the door and went straight up to my study.

At the console I wiped the sweat out of my eyes with my sleeve and brought up the control panel for the de Broglie on the monitor. Then I punched in co-ordinates for one hundred years into the future. My reasoning went like this. If this insect had died in the normal course of things it would have decayed down eventually to its constituent molecules. Of course those molecules might have been taken up by other plants or animals or fungi in the process, but by whatever route they would still have gone on into the future. So by transport-ing this thing into the future I wasn't actually adding anything to the time zone that wouldn't otherwise have been there. I switched the mode from Time Trajectory back to Time Transfer. Time Trajectory would make it a hundred and forty years old. That would almost certainly make it even bigger, and it was quite big enough as it was. I didn't relish the thought of being responsible for a mile-long insect rampaging through some city of the future. No, Time Transfer was definitely the right mode. I clicked the button marked 'OK' to enter the settings.

The dialogue box for the next step came up on the monitor. Just like that: it had accepted it! I breathed a sigh of relief. I wanted to watch what happened so I opted for a countdown of sixty seconds, checked my watch and initi-ated the countdown. Then I went to the window. My blood ran cold. It had moved. Not far, but far enough. Its head was just outside the line of the front two field antennae. For a moment I was poised in a state of total indecision. I could probably stop the countdown, but I couldn't remember how, and by the time I'd figured it out it would be too late. The only thing for it was to move the front antenna again. I raced downstairs, took a deep breath and crept out into the garden and around to the front antenna. The weevil swivelled its head this time, following my progress. Its feelers waved. It was definitely more alert, more active. I glanced at my watch: only twenty seconds to go. I pulled the field antenna gently out of the ground and was about to draw it back when a pair of scaly, hairy palps clamped onto either side of it. I pulled harder. Jesus, it was strong.

"Let go, you stupid bastard," I hissed. We engaged in a brief tug of war, moving first this way and then that. But the palps couldn't get a proper grip on the smooth metallic surface of the antenna and they started to slide. Seeing this, I put all my weight into it, staggered free, almost lost my balance, but turned and planted the antenna. For one brief moment I felt elated. Then the palps came back, and this time they were on me. I tried to prise them off, but they were very rough and it was taking the skin off my hands. Desperately I turned my wrist to look at my watch. One second to go. Too late. There was a blinding flash and a dreadful impact.

All I could see to start with was a red mist. Then it became a grey mist. I thought *I can't see.* Then I said to myself *Of course you can't see, you clown, you're dead. What do you expect to see?* Then the mist thinned a bit and I saw two eyes, big brown eyes with wide pupils, interested, concerned. Above them two arched eyebrows materialized, then a nose and a mouth. The mouth moved, the sounds were coming out of a distant tunnel, then suddenly they were sharp and in my ears.

"Are you all right? Don't try to move. Take it easy."

The mists had cleared. The girl had long shiny dark hair. It was an exotically beautiful face, with high cheekbones and a complexion like pale honey. She was wearing a garment made of some sort of shining blue material. The way it hugged her figure made me want to see more. She gave me a dazzling smile, and I thought, *This confirms it: I'm dead and I've gone to Heaven. How nice.* Except that I was becoming aware of my body now, and that included a throbbing pain in my head. *If I can feel pain, then can it still be Heaven?* I wondered. I tried to move, and very nearly succeeded.

"Don't try to get up yet. You've had a nasty knock on the head."

With a huge effort of concentration I managed to coordinate my mouth and tongue into saying, "Who are you?"

"Well, since you're the one who just dropped in from nowhere perhaps you should tell me who you are."

I sighed. "It's hard to explain. I've been transported forward in time. By a whole century. I had to..." I jerked my head up with a start. "The weevil! My God, where's the weevil?"

"Oh, if you mean that giant insect I vaporized it."

"You...vaporized it?"

"Yes. I don't much care for insects, especially ones as big as that." She put her fingertips to her mouth. "Oh, I'm awfully sorry. Was it a pet or something?"

A smile of infinite relief spread slowly across my face. "No, no. Nothing like that. You vaporized it. Oh, good. That's just wonderful." I sank back.

"You came in a de Broglie field didn't you?"

"Yes, how do you know? Are you familiar with them?"

"Only from history of technology classes. They were banned years ago. Far too dangerous. Probably the only reason you're still alive is because you got ballasted by that insect."

"I have to say it doesn't feel like I came through entirely unscathed."
She laughed and I marvelled at white, even teeth. "Well that's because you landed on my cargo port," she said. "You should look where you're going."
With her help I struggled to a sitting position and looked around. The surroundings were faintly familiar. There was no Biosphere but I recognized some of the trees, in particular a massive gnarled old cedar with branches down to the ground. I felt a pang of remorse. *This is Jessica's garden. Wouldn't she have loved to see it now! Except she can't, because she's been dead for years. I wonder how she managed without me. Probably pretty well. She had lots of friends. She probably started up with someone else. If I'm realistic about it, our relationship was on its last legs anyway. Arguments almost every day. I think we only stayed together out of pure habit.*

I looked behind me, but the house was like nothing I'd ever seen before. I looked back at the garden, my eyes roving around the sky above the trees. "What happened to the Biosphere?" I asked.

"What, those big black sphere things? I've seen pictures of those. They went out of fashion ages ago."

"But what about global warming, pollution...?"

"Oh that stuff. Yes, it was an issue for a while, wasn't it? I can't imagine how crowded the planet must have been back then. I don't suppose anyone saw the population crashes coming. And of course there was the industrialization of space. And global cooling."

"And the paparazzi...?"

"I don't know that word. Is it English? It doesn't sound like English."

"Never mind." There was an awful lot to take in here. A thought struck me. "You don't seem at all afraid. Here I am, a stranger, just dropped out of the sky, and you don't seem in the slightest bit worried."

"Why should I be worried? I'm primed." She pointed to her broad belt, which gathered in the taut fabric and accentuated her curvaceous body even more, and patted something she was carrying in a kind of holster on one side. I had a glimpse of a pulsing light and cooling fins. "I vaporized the insect. I can do the same to you if you want to be a problem."

"No, no," I blurted hastily. "I have no wish to be a problem, I assure you."

She smothered a smile. I think my sentence construction was a bit strange to her ears. Then she smiled properly and seemed to be looking right into me. She cocked her head prettily to one side and said, "Do you like sex?"

I don't know if my jaw dropped. It certainly felt like it did. Things seemed to have moved on a bit since I first started to date Jessica.

Her face clouded as something occurred to her. "I mean sex with women," she added.

I would have to tread carefully. "Er…it depends who with."

"Well, would you like to have sex with me?" she said brightly.

"Well, yes. I mean, I think that would be, er, delightful."

"Oh good. For a moment there I thought things were too good to be true." She chuckled. It was a low, teasing sound. "The girls will be so jealous."

"The girls? Why?"

"Because none of them has their own man, of course."

I was lost. "Why not?"

"Oh yes, it was all after your time, wasn't it? First the planetary wars and the germ warfare. Then M-AIDS."

"M-AIDS?"

"The strain that's specific to lymphocytes with a Y-chromosome. Spread by droplet infection, like the common cold. Wiped out nearly all the male population. What was left of it."

"Good grief." I pondered this for a moment. "What about all the jobs men used to do? Business, industry, space transport, all that kind of thing?"

"Oh, girls do all that now. There's nothing that requires a man's physical strength—hasn't been for years. All the heavy stuff's robotized. Truth to tell it was even before the men got wiped out, but they still hung on to their jobs as if strength mattered. Now girls do the decision-making, finance, strategic planning, all those things. We're good at it."

"And, er, procreation…you know, having children?"

"IVF. There are still sperm banks. All very clinical and not available to everyone. The population's still declining." Her face illuminated. "See, you're a prize. The other girls will want to share you, of course, but I don't think I'll let them. At least, not at first. Do you mind?"

I swallowed hard. "Er no, I don't think so. Whatever you say."

I'd been wrong all along. This really was Heaven.

I saw her looking at my forehead. "You're beginning to bruise. I think we'll spray a dressing on that. Then I'll order something to eat, and then if you feel up to it, we can go to bed." She stroked long, soft fingers along my jaw.

"What's your name?" she asked.

I reached up and closed my fingers gently around her soft hand. "Sam. What's yours?"

"Soulange."

"That's a pretty name," I said. "Unusual too."

"Yes. I think my mother named me after a tree that used to be here."

Then it hit me. Soulange—*Magnolia soulangeana!*

"What a remarkable coincidence!"

"What is?"

"Never mind. It's a gardening story, and it happened a long, long time ago."

ℰↃ ℭℬ

Benson

The media had begun to arrive. Television camera crews and sound technicians busied themselves plugging in lights and assembling a small battery of microphones on a temporary podium. Behind the podium rose a gigantic eidophor screen and beyond that, fenced off by security barriers, was the laboratory building. It was a large blue-painted windowless structure, its roofline interrupted at one end by a tall tower topped by an elaborate antenna array. The reporters paid no attention to it. They stood around, noisily greeting old friends and old rivals. As their numbers increased so did the volume of conversation.

The Press Release from Transkinetics Corporation had revealed little of what they had been invited to see. It had, however, promised them a dazzling demonstration of a technological breakthrough that would revolutionise travel. They'd heard all that before but they turned up just the same because their editors could not afford to overlook the possibility that it might be true.

In a low, glass-and-steel office building not far away, two men were standing at one end of an otherwise empty Board Room. They stood with their backs to the long rosewood table, the leather armchairs, the wood panelling and the deep pile carpet, facing a window that stretched from the floor to the ceiling. Beyond the window were grassy lawns and subtropical gardens, sustained in this desert climate by sprinklers that operated morning and evening, but they were too lost in their own thoughts for any of this to register with them.

Yves Duval was Public Relations Manager for Transkinetics Corporation. He was upwardly mobile, at least as upwardly mobile as he could manage. He wore immaculate suits, tailored silk shirts with matching pocket handkerchiefs, and hand-made shoes. He paid a hairdresser handsomely to cultivate the careful casualness of his coiffure. He subscribed to a gym, where he succeeded in offsetting the worst effects of frequent expense-account lunches. He drove a Mercedes convertible. He had a large disposable income and this was just as well, for his wife had an exceptional talent for disposing of it. Her constant ardour for fashionable clothes, parties and holidays was spurred less by the joy of being ahead than the fear of being left behind.

Duval saw himself as someone who made things happen, although what that actually meant was that he arranged for other people to make things happen. He was smooth and accomplished. Normally. Right now his insides were knotted with fear. He tried to conceal it. He glanced again at his gold Rolex watch. Not long to go.

Was there some way—he wondered for the umpteenth time—that he could have played it differently? He'd only met with the Board to finalise the publicity for the test run. It should have been straightforward enough. They'd really gone for his idea of a camera crew on a crane who would film a sequence that started with a tight shot of the arrival pad and then panned out to include Niagara Falls. They'd discussed a few details about the reception and approved the budget. And then, right at the end, Philip Menton had spoken, in his usual grave, slow voice.

"Gentlemen, we've always known that it would be a major problem to convince our investors and the media and the general public that this was going to be a safe and feasible way to travel. Would it be right, Duval, to say that what we have here is a crucial opportunity to achieve that objective?"

"Absolutely, sir."

"Nothing, in fact, is more important?"

"Nothing."

"Then it seems to me that you have overlooked the most convincing possible way of making that point."

"Oh, really, sir? What is that?"

"Why, you must go yourself, of course." There was a moment of shocked silence, the shock being registered mainly by Yves Duval. "Think about it. Our PR man is seen briefing the Press at San José and moments later the same man is seen circulating at Buffalo. It could hardly have more impact. Don't you agree, gentlemen?"

There was a murmur of approval around the table. The Board was in resounding agreement, so long as none of them had to go themselves.

"But, but…"

"Besides, we need you in Buffalo. I've invited some prominent people to the reception and I want you to look after them properly—introduce them, make them feel important, all that sort of thing."

"I could fly up the day before…" Duval's voice sounded weak, even to himself.

Menton looked hard at him. "You don't harbour any doubts about the project, do you, Duval?"

"Me? No, of course not. But…"

"After all, Viktor himself is going, isn't he? He made it clear from the start that he was only underwriting the whole development if he could be on the first test run."

"Yes, sir, but…"

"Good, then that's settled."

It was a disaster. His wife thought he'd gone crazy when he'd told her but there was nothing he could do about it, short of resigning. And how could he resign? It had taken years to claw his way up to his present position and he shrank from the thought that he and his wife might have to accept a decline in their standard of living. He'd just have to ride it out and hope for the best. Now that the moment had arrived he wanted very much to look cool and confident but he couldn't seem to manage it. He patted a linen handkerchief to his damp forehead and looked at his watch again.

Viktor Koussalis did his best to ignore the PR man's agitation. This was, after all, a moment to be savoured. He turned his wrist to glance at a disposable plastic watch and replaced his hand in the pocket of his crumpled linen jacket. Appearances mattered little to him and with a fortune of several billion dollars to his name he had no need to advertise his wealth. His father had left him a moderately successful company and he'd built it into a multinational corporation. When he became bored with it he gave it over to others to manage. Then he bought up some embryonic companies and turned them into successful enterprises. The satisfaction this brought him had nothing to do with profit; it was the creative process that interested him. He kept himself up to date, perpetually on the lookout for new ideas which, with his venture capital and business skills, could be turned into profitable companies. Not all were success stories, of course. The semiconductor plant here in San José, making large single crystals of germanium and gallium arsenide, had been a commercial failure. It just wasn't competitive, largely because the energy costs had become prohibitive. He'd been about to divest himself of the company when he'd found another use for it. And for the specialist steel-making plant in Buffalo. It was funny how everything had fallen into place.

It had started in England, he remembered, at a conference called "Technologies for the Next Millennium". He'd noticed a paper with an intriguing title in a session on transport technology. The speaker had turned out to be a short, middle-aged, balding gentleman with the face of a cherub and a bumbling manner—in fact Professor William Bullivant could have been the stereotype for the absent-minded English professor of a hundred B-movies. The man spoke obscurely, but with evident conviction, about a new theory of mass transport. There were no questions. People in the audience looked at each other with raised eyebrows. No-one took it seriously. No-one, that is, except Viktor. As soon as he'd returned to the States he arranged for Richard Ingwall, a physicist, and George Holt, an engineer—people whose opinion he trusted—to visit the Professor in his lab. Afterwards they set up a three-way conference call.

"So, Richard, what do you think of him?"

"Bullivant? I think he's a nutcase."

"Okay, but what about his theory. Anything in it?"

"Well, that's the curious thing. I think there could be. I tried to get him to take us through it. He drove me crazy going back and forth with the calculations; anyone would have thought he was looking at them for the first time. He didn't hide anything, though, so we were able to decipher it all in the end. I must say his approach is weird; I've never seen anything like it."

"How do you mean?"

"Well, normally you'd start with basic physical laws and work forwards to a result. He starts with the result he wants and works backwards. I've had a quick shot at trying to get the same result in a more conventional way, but I can't get it to work. All the same, I can't fault his conclusions."

"So if we mounted a full-scale trial, do you think it would work?"

There was a short silence at the other end of the line. "You're asking me if I'd put a hundred million dollars of my own money on it?"

"No, I'm not asking you that, Richard. It's my money; I'll take the risks. I just want your judgement."

"Well, at worst, you'd uncover some very interesting science. At best... well, it might actually work."

"What are the chances, do you think?"

"The chances of it working? I don't know. Maybe one in five."

"As high as that? I've had worse odds. What does George think about the practicalities?"

"Hi, Viktor. It's a bit difficult because this chap couldn't give me a proper steer about scaling it up. I had to make a few basic assumptions. It looks possible though. The main problem is energy: you need a lot, but only for a very short time."

"What are we talking about here, George?"

"Let's put it this way. It's a bit like taking a very powerful long-distance broadcasting station, putting every channel onto the same frequency, and then transmitting a whole year's worth of programmes in a few seconds. And you need to do that at both ends."

Viktor thought for a moment. "George, I've got a couple of plants over here that use a lot of electric furnaces. I was thinking of getting rid of them because they're so energy-hungry. We have a special sub-station for the one in Buffalo, and the one in San José has its own generator. Energy-wise, am I in the right ballpark?"

"Erm, let's see. Yeah, I think so. I'd have to look at the figures again but I think that'd be about right."

And so, seven years ago, Viktor Koussalis had arranged to bring Professor William Bullivant from his ill-equipped laboratory in a remote English university to a state-of-the-art industrial complex in California, which Viktor had salvaged from his ailing semiconductor plant. In fact he'd brought the whole entourage: the Professor, his infernal dog, and that curiously insouciant assistant...

"Are you two ready?"

The two men turned at the sound. The door of the Board Room was open and Alex Fellowes was standing there.

Duval spoke first. "Ah, Alex. Come in for moment, would you? I'd just like to go over some things with you."

She entered the room, with some reluctance. "Well, only for a minute. We do have a schedule to keep to, you know."

Alex Fellowes was a tall blonde whose willowy figure was effectively concealed for much of the time under a lumpy sweater and jeans. Once in a while she would put on make-up and wear a dress for a party or special occasion. It amused her to watch the heads turn—men she knew, seeing her as if for the first time. For the most part she couldn't be bothered. It wasn't important to her to be in a permanent relationship, especially as she'd yet to meet a man who didn't disappoint her. Other than the Professor, of course, but then she didn't think of him in that context.

She'd started to work in his lab as a junior technician after leaving school. Soon she was taking on more responsibility, and before long she was running the lab and acting as the Prof's Personal Assistant. She was totally loyal to him—it wouldn't have occurred to her to be anything else—and she had unhesitatingly accepted the offer to accompany him to the States. The salary she was getting now was more than enough for her modest needs. Although there was a huge gulf between their personal fortunes, she shared Koussalis's indifference to material things. All that mattered to her was to run a tight show; if anything did go wrong she was going to be very sure it wasn't through any oversight on her part.

Among her other duties she had been made responsible for managing day-to-day liaison with the engineering team and the construction staff. People were initially taken aback by her brusque manner, but they came to accept it, especially when they realized that everyone received the same treatment. That was the way she was, and she had no intention of changing the way she was, however senior the people she was talking to.

"What's the problem, then?" she demanded.

"Er, well, not exactly a problem. We start by briefing the media, right?"

"Yes. They're all waiting outside. Prof's in the lab; I'll bring him out as soon as the two of you are up there. Ten minutes for the briefing and then we'll go to the capsule. Look, we've been over all this before. What's the problem?"

"No, no problem. Just that...um, Alex, are you sure it's safe?"

"Of course it's safe. Prof did the test run with Benson, didn't he?"

"Am I supposed to find that reassuring?"

"You should. The Professor thinks a lot of that dog. Come on, we're wasting time."

She led a reluctant Duval and an amused Koussalis out of the building and across to the podium. Moments later they were joined there by the Professor, and the briefing began.

Duval took charge with a brief introduction, forgetting his nerves for the moment as he slipped into his familiar role.

"Good evening, ladies and gentlemen. I have invited you here to witness an historic event. We are about to embark on a new era of travel. In a few moments my colleagues and I will be going into the laboratory behind us. There will be some final preparations and then we will be projected to Buffalo. That is a distance of about 2300 miles." He checked his watch. "Our scheduled departure time is six-thirty. We are going to be there," he paused for effect, "in a few seconds."

There was a stunned silence. Then someone asked, "Will we be coming into the lab to watch?"

"No, you won't be allowed beyond the barriers, for security reasons. But the large screen behind me will be projecting an image of the receiving area at Buffalo. You should see us emerge there."

"Are you sure this whole thing isn't an elaborate conjuring trick?"

"Yes."

"Yes, what?"

"Yes, I'm sure. This company has nothing to gain from trickery. You'll see us soon enough walking out at Buffalo and it should be enough to convince even hardened old cynics like you, Tom. And if that isn't enough you may remember that I asked you to give us something small to take with us, something unique that only you knew about. Have you done that?"

Tom Bates, of the *Stanford Echo*, came forward and handed something up. It was a reporter's notebook, in which a number of them had placed signatures and messages and even small drawings. Duval flicked over the pages.

"Excellent. Now I'd like to introduce Professor Bullivant, the brains behind this whole project. Do you have any questions for him?"

"Yeah. How does it work?"

The Professor beamed beneficently at them. "Resonance energy transfer," he replied.

They waited, expecting further elaboration, but the Professor seemed totally unaware of their perplexity; he was waiting for the next question.

Viktor Koussalis bent to a microphone. "If I may, Professor... I've been following this project closely for some time and perhaps I can give the folk here a layman's view of how it works."

There were visible signs of relief on the faces of the journalists.

Viktor continued. "You're all familiar with the howl-round that you get if you place a microphone near to a loudspeaker. The microphone picks up any tiny noise coming from the loudspeaker, amplifies it and sends it back to the loudspeaker. Then that sound is received in its turn and amplified further. The sound keeps building up to a loud screech, and the pitch of the screech is the preferred frequency of the equipment. Now what we are doing here is a sort of howl-round between a transmitter-receiver here and a transmitter-receiver in Buffalo. The energy keeps going back and forth, getting larger and larger, and finally it's actually large enough to transfer mass. Our mass."

"Doesn't that take a lot of energy?"

The Professor replied. "A lot of power, not a great deal of energy relative to other forms of transport."

Again his statement was received in baffled silence, and again Viktor was forced to elaborate. "Do you remember Concorde? It used to fly from London to Barbados in three-and-a-half hours. The fuel costs for take-off, climbing and then accelerating to and maintaining supersonic speed were very considerable. With the technology we have developed here at Transkinetics we could do the same journey in about ten seconds. We use less energy overall but it's crammed into those ten seconds, so the rate of delivery of the energy, which is what the Professor means by power, is enormous. In fact it's enough to supply a whole town with electricity. On top of that we have four storage columns of the type used in the linear accelerator at Stanford. And there's a similar installation at Buffalo."

"You've got a lot riding on this, haven't you, Mr Koussalis?"

"Yes, you could say that. That's why I insisted on being included in the maiden voyage. But then the project's important to all of us."

"Who's going?"

Duval answered. "The Professor, Mr Koussalis and the Professor's assistant, Miss Alex Fellowes."

"And Benson," added the Professor.

"Who's Benson?"

Duval smiled uneasily. "Benson is the Professor's dog."

A murmur went around the assembled reporters. Someone asked, "Professor, aren't you concerned about protests from Animal Rights activists, taking a dog on a mission like this?"

The Professor looked surprised. "Good gracious, no! Benson and I do everything together. It would be far more unkind to leave him behind."

Duval used the ensuing laughter to bring things to a close. "Okay, gentlemen, let's make this a wrap. We've got a show to get on the road. Ah." Behind him the screen was flickering into life. It stabilized, displaying a high-angle view of a cluster of buildings surrounded by security barriers, outside which there was a substantial crowd. "There won't be a countdown. Keep your eyes on the big screen. The projection will cause interference, so you'll lose the picture for a while. When it comes back you should see us emerge in Buffalo. If you'd care to hang around, the plan is for us to return in about two to three hours. While you're waiting there'll be some food and drink laid on for you in the reception tent over there. Thank you."

There was a chorus of further questions but Duval led the party from the podium, past the security guards on the barriers and into the laboratory building. Those who were watching the party up to the door of the building may just have seen him dab at his forehead once again with a linen handkerchief.

"What's the odds this doesn't work?" asked one reporter.

"I'll give you five to one it doesn't," answered another.

"I'll have fifty bucks of that," said another.

In a few moments the press gathering had begun to resemble a racecourse, with reporters shouting odds, waving papers and placing bets furiously. Suddenly the picture on the large screen disappeared in a wild pattern of zigzags and everyone went quiet. After about five seconds the picture reformed.

The camera angle changed to a shot of a low, blue-painted building, flanked by a tower with an antenna array on the top, similar to the one behind them. They watched in silence. A door opened and Duval emerged, followed by Viktor Koussalis, Professor Bullivant, and finally Alex Fellowes accompanied by a large Basset Hound. The camera angle changed again, an aerial shot this time, following the progress of the party as they approached the security barrier and the people waiting beyond it, and then panning out smoothly to show the surrounding buildings, the whole area, and finally a vista that included the familiar, unmistakeable sight of Niagara Falls.

"It worked," someone breathed.

A camera on the ground now caught the emerging party, and Duval appeared, a broad grin on his face, carrying a reporter's notebook. He opened it and placed it in front of the camera, turning the pages slowly. At that moment a mobile phone sounded a little tune. The reporter listened to it and then looked up. "It's Frank Baylor. He's covering it in Buffalo. He says they're really there."

All of them were on their mobiles at once.

When the Professor announced that they had arrived at Buffalo, the other three gave a little cheer. Duval, released abruptly from the heavy burden of his fear, became euphoric, hugging each of them in turn, and even patting Benson. As the party emerged from the laboratory building they blinked, first at the light and then at the noise. Pandemonium had broken loose. A mixture of reporters, company employees, and invitees pressed forward at the security barriers. Cameramen and sound crews and local dignitaries were jostled in the rush. Somewhere a band struck up with "Happy days are here again". Corks popped and waiters started to circulate with trays of drinks and canapés. Security guards escorted the party through the chaos to a small garden area, which had been set out with tables and chairs for the reception. They were pursued by a barrage of questions, many of them directed at the Professor, who was gazing about him in wonder, too stunned to respond. Then a waiter appeared with a tray of glasses and Professor Bullivant's eyes lit up.

"I say!" he said softly. "Champagne!"

Alex was right behind him. "Orange juice," she said firmly.

"But there's champagne… "

"Prof, you know what you're like with alcohol. We've got the return journey to go yet."

"Come now, my dear, don't be a spoilsport! It is a celebration, after all. One little glass can't hurt."

Alex opened her mouth to reply but Duval had taken the Professor's arm. "Prof, there's someone over here I want you to meet..." and he whisked him away.

The crowd moved on, leaving Alex and the Basset Hound behind. She looked at the dog and he eyed her mournfully.

"Okay, Benson. Sit tight, and I'll bring you something."

Benson responded with a stiff wag of the tail. Alex disappeared into the jostling crowd and emerged moments later with a tray of canapés that she had lifted expertly from an astonished waiter. She set them down in front of Benson. Benson woofed them down in seven seconds flat. She frowned at him.

"Benson, those didn't even touch the sides!"

Benson wagged his tail.

"I couldn't find any water. You'll have to make do with tonic water. Here you are."

She poured it into a saucer and Benson lapped it up noisily as fast as she could pour it. Then he shook his head, sneezed and gave vent to a resounding belch. A woman, passing on the other side of a low hedge, gave Alex a sharp look. Alex put her fingertips to her mouth and suppressed a giggle. "Oops! 'Scuse me," she said. Then she exchanged glances with Benson and burst out laughing.

The party was in full swing. Duval had completed his frenetic round of introductions and had come back to Koussalis, who was standing apart. He glanced at his watch. "Oh Lord, look at the time! We should be making a move, they'll be waiting for us back in San José. Where the hell's the Professor?" He craned his head, trying to see him, and then he froze. What appeared to be two people coming together through the crowd resolved into one, very large person. "Uh-oh. Don't look now, but here comes Cornelia."

"Cornelia Fortis? Not the face that launched a thousand tanks?"

Duval grinned. "'Fraid so. What the hell does she want?"

Cornelia Fortis approached Duval, her face shiny with exertion.

"Duval. Thank goodness you haven't left yet. Look, I've got to come with you. I have an absolutely *crucial* meeting in San José at ten o'clock tomorrow morning and my flight's been cancelled. Everything to the West Coast has been cancelled until further notice. Some sort of dispute, I think. I've got to get there, so you'll have to take me."

Duval swallowed. "Ah," he said, his mind racing in neutral.

"No arguments now, Duval," she said briskly.

"It's not that, Cornelia. I mean, um, to be perfectly honest, there's no problem at all from my point of view. But this is only a test flight, remember. I'll have to check with the Professor. To see whether it's technically possible, you know, at this point in time, feasibility-wise. I'll have a word with him now."

As he left, Cornelia noticed Koussalis. "Hello, Viktor," she said tartly.

"Hello, Cornelia," he replied evenly. "Dear me, you look all hot and bothered. Do sit down for a moment. There's no rush, we won't be leaving yet. Why don't you have some refreshment? You must be thirsty."

He snapped his fingers high at one of the waitresses who was carrying a tray full of brimming glasses and saw her switch direction towards them. He smiled at her, took the whole tray and set it down in front of Cornelia.

Duval found the Professor sitting on a low wall with an empty glass dangling from his fingers.

"Prof?"

The Professor looked up slowly and blinked.

"Prof, you see that lady over there with Mr Koussalis? That's Cornelia Fortis. Listen, Prof, she's a very powerful woman."

The Professor nodded vigorously. His head appeared to be a little loose. "Mmm," he said. "She certainly looks powerful."

"No, I don't mean that. I mean she has a lot of influence on the Board—and in government circles too. If we can impress her it will be really helpful to the whole project. Her flight to San José's been cancelled and she wants to come with us. Can we do it?"

The Professor eyed the woman for a moment. "Well, we have enough power. But I'll have to make some adjustments to the program. For the increase in mass, y'know."

"Can you do that in time? We're running a bit late, even now."

"I don't know. I can try. It's quite complicated, y'see. I's quite a problem." He hiccupped and smiled a little blearily at Duval, who perceived that it might be more than a slight problem.

"Can you get started? I'll try and wrap up this party." He looked round. There was no way that the party was going to stop while there was still food and drink, especially drink. "No, the hell with it. Let's just slip away. We'll aim to have everyone on board in," he glanced at his watch, "half an hour. Okay? Just wait here a moment, Prof."

He raced off to give Cornelia the good news, at least the part of the news that was good, and asked Koussalis to make sure they were both at the capsule in thirty minutes. When he got back the Professor was draining his already empty glass. Duval helped him to his feet and conducted him to the capsule by a route that did not pass Cornelia. On the way they came across Alex, who was sitting on a patch of grass, leaning her back against an uncomplaining Benson. They both looked up as the Professor made his unsteady progress towards them. Alex took in the situation at a glance. Her expression was nearly as doleful as Benson's.

In the capsule, Duval watched the Professor boot up the on-board computer, operating the strange keyboard with its oversized keys. He'd asked the Professor about that once. It had been made to order, he'd replied, because he found it easier to use standing up. Lines of code started to run down the screen and then stopped. He swayed a little, tapped in a few entries and more lines of code ran. Duval and Alex watched him anxiously. He seemed to be having some trouble focusing what was on the screen. Then he turned to them with a dizzy smile.

"I think I'll jus' have a li'l sleep first," he said.

They just managed to catch him before he hit the floor.

Cornelia strode confidently into the capsule and stopped dead in her tracks.

"Omigod. What is that?"

Benson rolled his eyes up at her.

"It's the Professor's dog," Duval explained. He tried to sound reassuring. "It's okay. He won't hurt you."

"What a mournful-looking beast. What kind of dog is it?"

"Er, a Bassett Hound, I think."

"Oh." The corner of her mouth twitched nervously. "I don't know much about dogs but I believe Border Collies are quite intelligent." She stooped slightly and looked a little harder at Benson, not certain about the expression in his eyes. Then she straightened up and walked past him, as gingerly as her generous frame would permit, and settled herself down on the furthest bunk. "Aren't I supposed to strap myself in or something?" she asked.

Alex, who had already been briefed about their important new passenger, responded. "No need. Nothing's going to move. The mass of the capsule will be transferred at the same rate as ours. You won't feel any pressure or acceleration. Just make yourself comfortable. Lie down if you like. It'll be a while to departure. Prof's very tired and he's taking a rest."

Cornelia settled herself down. Viktor Koussalis had been an attentive host and she too felt unaccountably tired. She closed her eyes.

Alex turned to Duval. "They know we're not coming back on schedule now, don't they?"

Duval nodded. "I spoke to Carpenter. He'll pass on the news. I told them we'd been delayed by a minor technical problem." He glanced at the minor technical problem, who was sound asleep on his bunk. "I suppose we might as well all get a bit of sleep. We're not going anywhere just yet."

Benson opened one eye. Then he opened the other eye. His eyes roved around, the whites showing prominently. Now he raised his head and looked around again. He stood up. Standing up consisted of straightening his short powerful legs, achieving in this way a clearance of about one inch between his abdomen and the ground. He walked slowly over to the sleeping passengers, his great pads making no sound on the expanded rubber flooring of the capsule. He paused in front of Cornelia Fortis, who was snoring lustily, and lifted his nose in a short derisive sniff.

Border Collies indeed! Not that I've ever met one myself but Mother told me all about them. 'They just like chasing sheep,' she said. 'Well everyone likes chasing sheep, don't they? I mean, they do ask for it. But people think Border Collies are intelligent. Intelligent! Because they've learned to decode a few whistles into walking, crouching and standing! It's not exactly general relativity is it?' And she would shake her big head so dismissively that saliva flew from her dewlaps. She was a lovely drooler, Mother. She could take just one pass round a room, and leave drool on every surface, walls, tables, armchairs, everything. Time and again Owner would go after her with a wet cloth saying he didn't know how she managed it. That used to make her swell with pride. Drooling was her speciality, although she was very good at quantum mechanics too.

I was Mother's favourite because I'm a tricolour with a lot of black. She was a pure red-and-white so I suppose I reminded her of Father. I never knew him, of course, but she said he was a great rabbiter. The mathematics came from Mother's side of the family.

That reminds me, I wonder what Blackett's up to these days? Last time I saw my brother he was going to work for the Director of the Large Hadron Collider. Lucky dog.

He padded on and regarded the Professor, who was sleeping with his mouth open. *I do wish you wouldn't call me Benson. Makes me sound like a bloody butler. My name's Enrico. Dogs don't name their pups at birth; they wait until they've shown some special aptitude. Much more sensible. Mother named me after Enrico*

Fermi when I showed a precocious grasp of Fermi-Dirac statistics. 'Henry' would be acceptable, but 'Benson'? It really is too depressing.

People are always carrying on about how mournful I look. What do they expect when I have to put up with this sort of thing? Sometimes I feel like chucking it all in, but I can't because I'm a faithful hound.

He took a final glance around at the sleeping humans and crossed to the computer. Rising up on his hind legs he rested his left forepaw on the countertop and used the right one to hit the space key. It brought the computer out of sleep mode and the screen illuminated his swaying jowls in a blue glow. A few more quick key depressions and he was into the main control and guidance program. He scanned down the lines of code and shook his head slowly, making a few deprecatory wet noises in his mouth.

He really is a messy programmer. Thank goodness I moved the non-varying code out into sub-routines, or it would take months to sort this lot out. Look at this! He's put in a correction for that fat lady but it's not nearly large enough. The woman's a mountain; she must weigh at least 250 pounds; I felt the vibrations through the floor. And he didn't correct for the change in ionospheric thickness at the later departure time. Dear-oh-dear. We would never have got off the ground!

For the next three-quarters of an hour he scanned through the program, making the necessary corrections and adjustments, and tidying up some of the code. He set it up for a departure time of nine o'clock in the morning. He made sure the departure time was displayed prominently, so that the Professor or Alex would see it as soon as they powered up. Alex would keep them on schedule. Then he put the computer back into sleep mode and sighed.

I hope there's something solid to eat when we get back. Those canapés were tasty, but they go nowhere on a dog my size.

He retraced his steps, sniffed around on the floor to find the precise place where he'd been lying before and settled himself down, his dewlaps spreading over his crossed paws. The movements of his eyebrows were the only indication that he was taking a last look around, and then finally he closed his eyes and swiftly went back to sleep.

It was done. The return journey had been accomplished successfully. Cornelia Fortis had hurried off to her meeting, her disposition none the sweeter for a pounding headache. A couple of news teams had turned up to cover the rescheduled arrival; they had been rewarded with suitable interviews and dismissed. Koussalis had then gone to the office building to make some telephone calls. Duval had returned home to share his triumph with his wife (unfortunately, she was out, having her hair done). Alex had been urged to take the rest of the day off and, after checking round the lab, even she had gone home.

A crew arrived and were soon dismantling the podium and taking down the big screen. Professor William Bullivant watched them for a moment, feeling a pang of regret now that all the excitement was over. He went back into the cavernous interior of the laboratory building to find Benson still waiting patiently in the capsule. Benson's head came up and he emitted a short whine ending in a woofle.

"Well, well, well, this has been quite a day for us, eh, Benson? Yes, indeed. Quite a day." He crouched down, gathered up Benson's great floppy ears and massaged them around on his head. Benson did his best to pretend that he enjoyed this attention.

You wouldn't happen to have a bone around, would you? I could murder a bone right now.

"I tell you what, Benson. How about a nice meaty bone? Come on, I've got one in the lab for you."

And perhaps we could go for a walk after that. I have a serious need to check out those trees on the perimeter.

"And then we'll take you for a nice walkies, shall we?"

Good man.

The Professor sighed and slapped the dog affectionately on the flanks. "Dear old Benson. What would I do without you?"

༄ ༅

Murder in the Jungle

"Let me start, ladies and gentlemen, by asking you a question. What goes through your mind when I say 'Great Apes'? Does this phrase conjur up for you a picture of inoffensive vegetarians, of orang utans swinging slowly through the trees, picking fruit and berries with large, fastidious fingers, or of mighty but gentle mountain gorillas, laboriously stripping the impossibly bitter pith out of banana stems? If that is the picture in your minds, and if you want to hold onto it, or if you are of a nervous disposition, then this is not the place for you, because what we're going to be talking about this morning, ladies and gentlemen, is not for the squeamish. We are going to be talking about organized, premeditated murder. So I'll just pause here and those of you who want to leave can do so at this point."

It was the introductory lecture in a session on "Primate-Primate Aggression". The speaker was Dr Chris Stebbens, and he was warning the audience because this session was open to members of the public and the media. In a sense that was why I was here too: I thought it would be a bit more accessible to a mere engineer like myself. If I'd known where it would lead to—that within a year I would be sitting, handcuffed, on the dirt floor of a mud hut in Africa, under arrest for murder—then maybe I'd have chosen another session. But then, you can't always predict these things.

So what, you may ask, was I doing at the World Symposium on Primate Behaviour anyway? Well, it's easy enough. I came out of Stanford with a good degree in electronics and the nagging feeling that I should have done Life Sciences instead. So when the Goodfellow Institute of Primate Biology advertised a vacancy for an Instrumentation Technologist I went for it. One of my first projects was a video monitoring system for caged marmosets. It was quite a challenge and I was pretty pleased with the way it turned out. So were the people running the study, and they decided to present a paper on it at the World Symposium. I was a co-author and they asked if I'd go along, in case there were technical questions they couldn't answer. I thought it might be fun. So here I was.

No-one left the auditorium. As for me, I don't think my jaw closed for the next two hours. We saw a lot of footage of the wild chimpanzees in Gombe National Park. We saw them getting all excited and then setting off through the trees and along the forest floor, in search of red colobus monkeys. There seemed to be a division of effort; some gave chase and others laid ambush. Whatever the game plan was, it was certainly effective. We heard the screams of the monkeys as the chimps tore them apart, and there were some pretty stomach-churning scenes of chimps feasting on monkey limbs. Other speakers explored the relationship between this predatory behaviour and the social status of males within chimpanzee society, and the insights all this might provide into the hunting patterns of early hominids. *Not to mention modern man,* I thought.

One of the speakers was Dr Richard Gainsville. He was at Washington, D.C. and he had an international reputation for his work on the evolution of primate behaviour. I'd come across his name before, but I hadn't realized he was English. He was a tall, rangy, fair-haired, guy, and the way he was dressed it was like he couldn't wait to get back into the bush. He raised a lot of questions about how the roles of individual animals in the hunt were assigned, and how it affected their share in the spoils and their subsequent access to females.

"These animals can't know in advance where the colobus are going to be and how they're going to react. So how do they coordinate the attack? Colobus are wary, so they probably can't use much in the way of sound cues—they'd just spook their prey. We do know that chimpanzees use a whole variety of facial expressions and postures to communicate, so perhaps visual cues like these play a part. Of course it would be really nice to know what signals actually do pass between the animals, but they're moving fast, on the ground and in the trees, along totally unpredictable routes, so I'm afraid that's an impossibility."

In the coffee break after the session I found myself standing near Richard Gainsville, so I bit the bullet.

"Dr Gainsville? I enjoyed your talk."

He gave me a quick smile and nod, but his eyes were moving and it looked like he would move off at any moment, so I continued quickly.

"That problem you mentioned about monitoring visual cues passing between the chimps. It could be done, you know."

Suddenly he was all attention. "Oh, really?" he said. "How?"

It was noisy in the coffee area so I could only give him a brief outline. When I'd finished he looked at me silently for a moment, chewing his lip. Then he just said, "Where can I get hold of you?"

There was a list of attendees and contact details in the back of the conference programme. I put a ring round my own entry, tore the page out and handed it to him. He stuffed it into his conference bag and then someone else spirited him away.

To be honest I wasn't expecting him to come back to me. Either he'd let the idea drop or he'd follow it up with one of his own people. But two weeks later he phoned me and invited me down to Washington.

He took the time to show me round the department, introducing me to staff as we encountered them in offices and labs. He'd put a hand on my shoulder and say "Ben here's from the Goodfellow. He's an electronics wiz". I was warming to this guy.

After the tour we went back to his office, where some chairs were grouped around a low table. Two members of his research group joined us. Tina Bertheler was a postdoctoral fellow who'd originally graduated in psychology. She was quite handsome in a leonine kind of way, and she wore her honey-blond hair tied tightly back. Consuela Perez (her real name was a lot longer than that) was a biologist from Cuba. She was raven-haired and dark-skinned, and she spoke English with a voice like gravel. She was doing a Ph.D. And then a mature but athletic-looking guy came through the open door. Richard got up and greeted him warmly.

"This is Mark Pelham," Richard said, after he'd introduced the three of us to him. "Mark's an Associate Professor with Chris Stebbens. He and Chris have been to Africa—how many times, Mark?"

"Seven trips in all. For a while it seemed like I was living there."

"Apart from Chris himself I don't think there's anyone in the world who knows more than Mark about these animals, and the whole set-up out there." He indicated a seat to Mark and sat down himself. "Now, Ben, why don't you kick off by fleshing out this idea of yours."

I'd given the whole thing more thought since I'd received Richard's phone call, so I was prepared for this.

"Well, basically, the idea is to fit each of the key animals with an instrumented collar. We build in a miniature GPS location system, a radio transmitter, a microphone and a very small video camera. The camera has to see what the animal's seeing, so we fit it with a lens that gives it the identical field of view. It's not conventional video, by the way; it has to be of the security type."

"What's the difference?" asked Tina.

"In conventional video, successive frames are interlaced. In a security camera each frame is complete. That way all the pictures can be synchronized to a fraction of a second at the receiving end. So if two animals look at each other you can play it back frame by frame and see exactly which one is signalling and which one is reacting. I designed a system something like that for captive marmosets."

Consuela's dark eyes were wide. "This could be done?"

"Oh yes. The technology's all available. The only thing is, you have to get permission to attach the collars. I thought that might be a problem."

"It is," Richard said, "but maybe not an insuperable one. I talked to Chris about it. We were already setting up a joint field trip for next year. He can't come himself but he's agreed that Mark should join us. And he thinks we might just get official sanction to use the instrumentation. Mark, I think you've got some questions about that."

"Well, first off, how big would this collar have to be?"

"Not much bigger than one of the commercial collars people use for tracking animals the size of—what?—koalas, foxes? The camera and the circuitry can be packed into a really small volume; the main size and weight is going to come from the battery. So it depends on what operating life you need."

Richard said, "We can't spend longer than two months out there."

"No problem, then. We can use the smaller battery size so long as we keep the collars switched off until they're fitted. That way you'll get the full operating life."

Mark nodded thoughtfully. "There's still a problem. We'd have to tranquillize the chimps to attach the collars and that might change their behaviour. And just wearing the collars might alter their position in the hierarchy."

"This type of collar's been used a lot for radio tracking," said Richard. "It doesn't usually affect social status."

"I know, but these are sophisticated animals and we're looking at a highly evolved behaviour. There's a definite risk of coming away empty-handed."

"Yes, but Mark, think about the data we could get if it worked! It would be mind-blowing! I think we'll just have to take the chance. We'll monitor the animals carefully, of course, before and after. If there's a problem, then as you say, we'll have to abandon the project."

"Sorry, but that's not all. You can't just leave the animals behind with the collars on; the authorities won't sit still for that. These are supposed to be wild animals. And they won't be happy about us tranking them again either."

There was a bit of a silence. Then I remembered something. "Um, there is a way around that," I said. "You can fit the collars with radio-operated release systems. Before we leave we just send out the signal and the collars drop off."

Mark and Richard looked at each other and grinned. "Nice one," Richard said.

Mark added, "The collars will still be transmitting their positions, won't they? I suppose we could go out and retrieve them?"

"You could if you wanted to. It would only be worth it if there's some operating life left. Once the batteries are flat you can't use them any more."

Richard looked round the table. "Anyone see any other problems?"

I did. "Look, I think we need to be clear about this. Quite apart from the collars there'll be a fair amount of equipment on the receiving side. Antennae to erect, receivers to tune, video channels, audio channels, video recorders, power generator... Someone's got to be trained to set all that up."

"Why, Ben," said Richard, in what seemed like genuine surprise. "I assumed you'd be coming with us."

I blinked and swallowed hard. My heart beat fast. I'd never been to Africa.

"Erm, I'm not sure my boss would be too happy about that."

"Oh, don't worry. I'll talk to him. I'm sure we can arrange a temporary Leave of Absence."

And he did. I suppose I shouldn't have been surprised, because I already knew how persuasive Richard could be. The prospect of being tied into the two most famous primate biology research groups in the world must have been a fair incentive, not to mention the money that would be flowing into the Institute for the instrumentation I was developing. But freeing me up for the work was one thing; Richard and Mark must have pulled all the stops out to get the project approved by the National Parks Authority and the Ministry. Chris Stebbens used his contacts as well and helped to smooth the way. I gather it was the radio-release collars that finally swung it. We got permission to attach collars to five key animals in the troupe. We'd take two more collars in case of accidents or failures.

I had to put together a budget, of course, but money wasn't really a problem. Richard was well-connected: he had grants from the U.S. Government, World Wildlife Fund, National Geographic, and even a nature TV channel that wanted first refusal on any exceptional footage that made it into the public domain. With that kind of support there wasn't any point in re-inventing the wheel, especially as time was short. The collars had to be robust, reliable, and weatherproof and the release mechanisms had to be totally dependable. I did the sensible thing and went to a company that specialises in this type of kit. They were interested and very helpful. I was allowed to purchase the collars with GPS, transmitter, and radio-release fitted but not encapsulated. I added the video and sound systems and then they took each collar and embedded everything except the camera lens in black resin to make it waterproof and, we hoped, chimpanzee-proof. After that I was kept pretty busy purchasing all the rest of the equipment, connecting it up and testing it. Finally everything had to be packed carefully and sent on ahead by air freight.

The crates were a bit large so we unpacked them to fit the stuff into the two trailers (we had two vehicles in case of breakdowns). It didn't take us that long but it still brought me out in a sweat, working in that climate. Finally we hit the road. Richard and Mark drove the Land Rovers and Tina, Consuela and I rode in one or the other. At the final village we were met by two rangers, who led us in, helped us set up camp, and made sure we had everything we needed. We got a fire going and offered to share our meal with them, but the light was fading and they wanted to get back. Before they left I set up our transmitter and we checked that we could communicate with them by radio, just in case of problems. We weren't anticipating any; Mark knew the terrain very well and actually so did Richard.

Next day we put what we needed into backpacks and headed deep into the jungle. It was hot and humid, and the insects were a pain, but I was so excited I hardly noticed. Mark was fantastic; he led us in without any hesitation. We heard the chimps before we saw them. We spent all day observing them through binoculars, maintaining complete silence and concealment. We had a book, put together from previous trips, with pen sketches to identify individuals in the troupe. A chimpanzee's facial creases are as characteristic as a fingerprint. From time to time Mark would point to an animal and then to a picture, helping Tina and Consuela to identify the animals, particularly the males. They repeated this exercise over the next few days, getting a baseline for the chimp's behaviour and checking that the social hierarchy hadn't changed since the last visit. After the first foray I stayed back at the camp, setting up the equipment tent. The next time we went out together I had the collars in my backpack, and Mark was carrying a dart gun.

They'd identified all five of our target animals: Leo, Phoenix, Aaron, Hector and Joseph. The idea was to wait until one of them strayed from the rest of the troupe, which they did when they were foraging; then we'd dart him and fit the collar. That was the theory. Tina loaded the syringes but Mark and Richard were very anxious about overdoing it so she was conservative with the dose. The first time we tried it, the dart brought the animal down, but it started to recover before we'd finished. Even in this half-paralysed condition it was unbelievably strong; it took four of us to control it while Richard fitted the collar. I was so scared I almost forgot to actuate the transmitter. After that first experience we upped the dose somewhat. It took several days but we eventually had all five animals wearing collars. Richard, Tina and Consuela continued to watch the colony for any changes in their behaviour while Mark and I set up the intermediate receiving stations a good distance away. There were three of these stations, because you can get a lot of dropouts and multipath interference in a forest environment. The stations would combine the signals and relay them on another frequency band to my equipment tent. Once all that was in place the equipment was pretty much operational.

Richard was satisfied that there weren't any significant changes in behaviour. He said the chimps were interested in the new neckwear at first but after a while they completely ignored it. With that established we didn't have to go into the jungle at all; we could do all the monitoring from the equipment tent.

Two days later we recorded an attack.

I'd set up a series of split-screen displays to show the outputs from all five video cameras. On a larger screen I'd used the GPS fixes to display the location of each chimp as a coloured dot on a map of the terrain. On another screen I had a rolling set of traces that carried the signals from the microphones. The pictures made me a bit dizzy if I looked at them for long; it was like watching five really bad home movies at once. Still, it was interesting when the chimps were active; you'd get glimpses of them running up trees and shaking branches, that sort of thing. But then, I'm just an engineer so I probably wasn't noticing a fraction of what was going on. The biologists were absolutely fascinated and recorded a lot of material. Tina was particularly good at it; she'd watch the monitors for hours, making notes all the time. What they were really hoping to see was a particular grouping and level of activity that always occurred just before one of the killing sprees. And suddenly there it was. Tina started the videotape rolling and in the next couple of hours we watched the whole attack develop, from beginning to gruesome end. There was enough material to analyse for the next year. Our spirits were sky high. Everyone was shouting and hugging each other, Richard broke out a few bottles of beer, and we had ourselves a party. It was just as well we were so far away or the chimps would have heard the racket.

Our euphoria was short-lived.

We were busy monitoring for another attack when a call came through on the radio. It was one of the rangers. He told us that three white people had set up camp not far from us. They had camera equipment and guns. The rangers had gone to have a word with them but their permits seemed to be in order so there was nothing they could do except warn us. He gave us a map reference.

Richard decided he should go and talk to the newcomers. The others were busy monitoring so I said I'd go with him, although I'm a bit nervous about guns.

We were met by an unsmiling guy dressed in a khaki hat, shirt and shorts, with a hunting rifle hooked casually over his shoulder. Richard explained that there was an important project in progress, and told him how a valuable scientific resource and years of patient work could be jeopardized by any intrusion into the chimpanzees' territory.

He looked at us for some time. He seemed to be chewing something. Then he spoke.

"Basically, piss off."

We were taken aback. By now a man and a woman had appeared outside their tent and were watching what was going on. Although they were a good distance away it sounded like they were speaking to each other in German. Richard speaks German. He asked if he could have a word with them.

"No, I'm not going to allow you to do that. Look, man. I'm a hunter and tracker—that's my living, right? It used to be a good living, too. I took a lot of parties out here, and we shot a lot of big game. Not any more. Wimps like you put paid to that with your bloody conservation nonsense. So don't expect me to listen to your scientific crap because I couldn't give a shit. If some folk want me to take them where they can photograph monkeys, and they're prepared to pay good money, I'm going to take them. Got it?"

"Photographing monkeys?"

"Yes."

"So what's the rifle for?"

"Self-defence."

"Self-defence."

"Yeah, self-defence."

"If you use that gun I'll have you arrested."

"I'm quivering with terror, man."

"How the hell did you get permission to come here?"

"None of your bloody business. Now I've said it once and I won't say it again. Piss off."

He unhitched the rifle. We left.

The others were dismayed when we told them. We agreed that all we could do was continue the operation and hope to hell we could record at least one more attack before the chimps' territory was violated. Richard got on the radio to people he knew to see if this party could be stopped, but he didn't hold out much hope of prompt action. Somewhere along the line palms had been greased.

We were out of luck; they blundered in the next day. They saw the chimps and the chimps saw them. We know that because we saw the three of them on the chimps' collar cameras. The man and his wife, if that's who she was, were filming away, highly excited. But not as excited as the chimps. The GPS fixes were moving all over the place, and the cameras would record a blur, then the picture would freeze suddenly with a view of the human intruders from yet another angle. Then they'd be off again.

We decided to pack up. The project was hopelessly compromised. We couldn't expect normal behaviour from this troupe for months, maybe years. Everyone was very depressed. It would take a while to dismantle the three receiving stations so we decided to make a start the following day.

Next morning Tina called us back just as we were about to start out. She'd been determined to monitor and record right up to the last moment and now she'd seen something. We followed her into the equipment tent.

"They're grouping, and there's a lot of display activity. I'm sure they're warming up for a hunt."

Mark looked at the monitors carefully. "They don't usually do it this early in the day," he said.

"I know, but I started the tapes, just in case."

We watched, riveted to the screens for maybe an hour. The coloured dots on the GPS monitor had all moved off. The cameras registered branches and leaves as the chimps moved slowly through the jungle, and once in a while we'd get a glimpse of a dark, furry shape as they looked round at each other. Were they signalling? I couldn't tell.

They were moving so quietly that the sound traces were almost flat; the microphones weren't registering anything above the background noises of the jungle. From time to time a bird would screech or a distant monkey would whoop and that was easy enough to identify because you'd see a blip on all five traces at once. But suddenly just one of the traces started to wobble; Phoenix's mic was picking up something. I switched that channel through to the loudspeaker.

"*...Aufnahmen bei diesem Licht...*"

"*Schau! ...da oben!*"

"*Wo? Ich sehe nichts.*"

"*Leise! Er ist auf dem dicken Ast—links von den beiden Schlingpflanzen die da runterhängen!*"

"*Wo...? Oh, ja! Schön!*"

We looked at each other in disbelief. Tina said, "Oh...my...God!"

"Maybe they're just curious..." said Consuela weakly.

"Not a chance," said Mark grimly. "That's an attack formation—I've seen enough of them to know. Our friends there are being stalked. Did you catch what they said, Richard?"

"Not all of it, but they've seen something. I think they've spotted one of the chimps."

"Which one?" Consuela asked.

Mark pointed to the red dot on the GPS display. "I think it must be Leo. He hasn't moved for several minutes. They could be filming him."

Tina breathed out. "Thank God for that."

"Er, it isn't necessarily a good sign."

"Mark? What do you mean?"

"I've seen a tactic like this once before. One of the big males, like Leo, shows himself. The monkeys get all agitated, of course, but he doesn't seem to be interested, and so long as they can see him, and he's outside of their flight distance, they feel safe enough. What they don't see is the others moving into position."

"We must warn them," said Consuela.

"That's impossible," said Richard. "They're much too far away. We can't do a bloody thing."

Tina buried her face in her hands. "I can't look."

We held our breath. The dots had stopped moving, and the cameras still revealed nothing but leaves and branches, and then suddenly it all changed and the screens briefly showed the two tourists and the hunter guide from five different angles. And then all hell broke loose.

The attack was swift and efficient. I don't think the hunter even had the time to get the rifle off his shoulder. As expected, the tagged chimps were at the centre of the action, so we got a ringside view, which was a lot more than any of us would have wanted. I won't try to describe the images that flashed in front of us. Let's just say that it was an object lesson in the fragility of the human body and the immense strength of adult male chimpanzees. The loudspeaker was still through to Phoenix's mic, and the screams chilled us to the marrow before I managed to cut it off. Then the troupe dined out.

Tina left the tent in a hurry and was very ill outside. Consuela just sat there, shivering. Mark said, "Christ." Richard and I stared into each other's white faces.

We spent the rest of the day packing up the equipment. The mood was sombre; we said little. We released the collars. Although they still had a lot of operating life left there was no way we were going in to retrieve them. We decided to get to the village, spend the night there and set off in the morning.

Richard reported the incident on his radio before we left. The authorities were very concerned. In fact they were so concerned that not long after reaching the village we found ourselves host to a helicopter full of militia. They held us at gunpoint, swarmed all over our stuff, distributed our equipment all over the ground, and found and confiscated our precious videotapes. Then another helicopter flew in and an immaculately dressed civilian got out. The platoon leader saluted him smartly and handed him the tapes, and there was a brief exchange in a language I didn't recognise, let alone understand. The man strolled over to us.

It was still warm and humid and what with that and the stress the sweat was rolling down the inside of my shirt, so I was wondering how this gentleman could look so cool in his creaseless dark grey suit, silk shirt and tie. He introduced himself in perfect English.

"Good evening," he said pleasantly. "My name is Oscar Obindagabe and I am here on behalf of the Department of Wild Life and Tourism. Which one of you is Dr Gainsville?"

Richard stepped forward. Mr Obindagabe nodded and, still pleasantly, said, "You and your colleagues are all under arrest on suspicion of the murder of Mr Friedrich Gunther and two foreign tourists whose names have yet to be established."

There was a shocked silence. Then Richard spluttered, "What the hell are you talking about? I told you what happened…"

"Yes, yes, Dr Gainsville. And I believe you. I believe you, but the Court will not. Not after these tapes," he held them up, " have been destroyed. It will be clear that these people disrupted the study that you and your companions had been planning for some time, and that you were so incensed by this that you killed them." He turned to the platoon leader and jerked his head.

That's how we found ourselves sitting on the floor of a hut, handcuffed to each other by our ankles, with a murder charge hanging over our heads like a big black cloud. Two hours passed and we said barely a word. I leaned against the wall of the hut, feeling the prickle of the rushes through my shirt. Various lines of thought were crowding my mind. How the hell could we extract ourselves from this situation? Escape was impossible: even if we weren't handcuffed there was an armed guard at the door to the hut. Every now and then he would come in and look us over. He'd unslung his automatic weapon and he looked like it wouldn't take much for him to use it. We needed legal representation; would we be allowed to get it? Would they let us contact the Embassy? How the hell did an innocent research project turn into a murder trial? Why are they trying to pin it on us? Is this Obindagabe the guy who took the bribe from the hunter? In my agitated state each line of thought would nudge the other out of the way, until I was going round in circles.

The armed guard stepped inside the door again, followed this time by Mr Obindagabe and the platoon leader. Obindagabe looked at us in silence for a few moments, then he turned to Richard with a condescending smile.

"I want you to understand the position, Dr Gainsville. We are a poor country..."

I remember thinking, as I looked at this smooth operator, that the poverty he spoke of was not all that evenly distributed.

"...We cooperate with researchers such as yourselves because it is necessary for our image with certain international organizations. But you do not bring significant money into this country. Tourism, on the other hand, is a major source of revenue. And an incident such as this could be very bad for tourism. That is my difficulty, you see. If we let you go back to your country we will have very bad publicity. On the other hand if we bring the five of you to trial there will be interventions by lawyers and your State Department and the publicity will be even worse. I am almost led to the conclusion that it would be better if you," he paused for effect, "disappeared, rather like the unfortunate Mr Gunther and his friends."

The word was hanging in the air. *Dees-ah-peayahd.* My mouth was dry. Richard cleared his throat. *Tell him, Richard,* I thought. *Tell him the whole thing's preposterous. Demand that we are allowed to contact our Embassy immediately...*

"Now, Mr Obindagabe, if we are sensible about this, the disappearance of five internationally known scientists is likely to attract even more notice than that of a hunter and two tourists. On the other hand I understand what you are saying. I have been thinking myself that it might be in all our best interests if this matter went unreported."

I looked at Richard in amazement. He was as cool as a cucumber. Obindagabe gave another of his Cheshire Cat smiles.

"Now that is a very interesting suggestion, Dr Gainsville. I wonder, could you perhaps enlarge on it a little?"

Richard turned slightly so that he was talking to us as much as to Mr Obindagabe, and there was a strange firmness in his voice. "We've all been through a very traumatic experience. Reporting the events would mean reliving that experience again and again, to police, lawyers, media. I don't think any of us want that."

We took the cue and shook our heads vigorously.

Obindagabe smiled. "Do go on," he said.

"Secondly, we've enjoyed good relations with this country. We've been allowed access to a unique scientific resource. We wouldn't want any actions of ours to jeopardise that in the future."

"Go on."

"Finally, there are the tapes. They constitute the only evidence that Mr Gunther and his companions were killed by the chimpanzees. If we returned to our country and reported these events we could, in the absence of this evidence, be laying ourselves open to the very same charges as we are facing here."

Mr Obindagabe applauded delightedly. "Capital, Dr Gainsville, capital! I find that a most convincing argument. Your American media are very vigilant. It would not take very long at all for suspicions like that to be raised."

Yeah, with your generous help, I thought.

His smile vanished. "Are you all in agreement with Dr Gainsville's analysis?" he asked.

We nodded in unison.

"So you will leave this country now and swear, each one of you, that you will not reveal anything of the unfortunate events that you have witnessed here?"

We nodded again.

"And you appreciate the serious consequences that would follow if any of you attempted to depart from this agreement?"

We nodded. Obindagabe said something to the platoon leader, who came forward and released the handcuffs. We got unsteadily to our feet.

"Thank you, Mr Obindagabe," said Richard calmly. "There's just one more thing. The first videotape has nothing incriminating on it. But it does contain priceless scientific data. Could that one be returned to us?"

Obindagabe closed his eyes and shook his head slowly. "I think it would be best for all concerned if there were no suggestion that equipment of that nature had been successfully deployed at the very time that the unfortunate Mr Gunther and his companions disappeared."

Oh, well, Richard, nice try.

So that's why you won't be reading about this in your newspapers. Chris Stebbens came over to meet us on our return, but all we could tell him was that the chimps seemed to have become peculiarly aggressive, and that they should be very careful if they were planning another field trip. In Richard's report to the grant agencies he had to say that attachment of the collars disturbed the chimpanzees' behaviour to such an extent that we were unable to make useful observations. We assume that the military disposed of the tourists' tent and belongings. As for any other evidence—well, the chimps did that for them.

Except that somewhere on the floor of that forest there must still be a hunting rifle and an expensive pair of video cameras. But I wouldn't advise you to go looking for them. It can be murder in the jungle.

৪০ଓ

Footnote: The author acknowledges with thanks the assistance of Dr Rainer Abel with the German conversation.

Joanne

He hadn't met Joanne before. That didn't surprise him; in an establishment of this size there were a lot of staff you never got around to meeting. But here she was, standing hesitantly in his office.

"Sorry to interrupt you. I've brought the notes you requested from Medical Records. Graham Thomas."

She was a tall, handsome girl, with mousey-blond hair and pretty hazel eyes. She wasn't overweight but she was ample in the hips. His practised eye suggested that she would look better for the loss of about twenty pounds.

His secretary held out her hand and took the manila pocket file.

"Thanks very much, Joanne," she said. "We've been waiting for that."

The girl nodded, smiled uncertainly in his direction, and left.

"Who was that?" he asked.

"Graham Thomas. Facial burns. He was referred to you by Dr Savindra."

"No, I mean the girl."

She flashed him a quick glance. "That's Joanne. Joanne...I think it's Joanne Phillips. Works in Medical Records."

It wasn't difficult to find out more about someone who worked in the hospital if you were resourceful, and he was nothing if not resourceful. By the end of the day he knew that she had been working at the hospital for a little over a year, that she had qualified straight from school as a Medical Secretary and that she had additional library and computer skills. She was twenty, unmarried and lived in a flat in town.

She hadn't met Malcom before. That wasn't surprising; the Medical Records Office was located in the basement and you didn't often get to meet medical staff, least of all surgeons, who spend a lot of their time in theatre or out-patients. He just happened to be in the office when she knocked and went in. His diary was open on the desk so he was probably talking to his secretary about his appointments. She was sensitive enough to catch the flash of annoyance that crossed his face at the interruption—and to notice that his expression had softened by the time she left. He looked to be in his mid-thirties, very lean and fit; he probably went running. She liked his blue eyes and curly hair. The girls in the office would probably go all silly over him. Well, he was quite attractive.

She would have liked to say something more, but what was the point? A man like that wouldn't give her a second thought. She looked him up just the same. Malcom Shepherd, thirty-six, Department of Plastic and Reconstructive Surgery, qualified Cambridge, trained Manchester, Cardiff, Louisville, Kentucky, four years as Senior Registrar at University College, appointed Consultant here three years ago. That much was on open file; she didn't have access to more personal information.

He waited until his secretary was out of the office before he telephoned her in Medical Records.

"Joanne? Malcom Shepherd here. I've been going through these notes on Graham Thomas. I think there's something missing."

"Oh, I'm sorry. I'm sure I brought the whole file. What do you think is missing?"

"Do you think you could come up and take a look?"

It was a pretext, of course. The only thing that was missing was the invitation to have dinner with him. She was clearly taken aback. Then she recovered her composure and smiled shyly. She was busy that evening, but possibly later in the week...? He made a date for Friday evening.

He was well established now and he could entertain a young lady in a manner that would have been unthinkable in his student days. He picked her up in his Porsche 911 and they drove out to an expensive country-house restaurant. The evening was a success. Initially she was in awe of him, but he was easy to talk to and gradually she relaxed. He saw her to the door of her flat, told her politely how much he'd enjoyed the evening and that he hoped they could do it again soon. She thanked him for a lovely evening and said she'd enjoyed it too.

They saw each other more often. He took her to the best restaurants and tipped heavily so that when they returned they were remembered and given a big hallo. She loved the theatre so he booked a box, with drinks delivered in the interval. They went to auctions and visited stately homes. They managed to get away for a week's holiday and went walking in the Lake District. It was around that time that they decided it wasn't necessary to book separate rooms.

Six months after he'd seen her in his office for the first time, he proposed.

He explained that he had a lot to offer her. He was earning a good salary, plus the income from a growing private practice. He had a lovely house, which he'd bought mainly as an investment, but it was really too large for him on his own, and it needed a woman's touch.

She was overwhelmed but happy. She knew she was no match for him in intelligence and education, yet he seemed to want her. She wondered what the other girls in the office would say. Some of them had been taken out by doctors, but usually it wasn't with marriage in mind. They discussed the age difference, decided it didn't matter, and she accepted him.

They both enjoyed walking in the countryside so they booked a walking tour in Provence for their honeymoon. Each day a van would take their luggage on, leaving them to walk and find their way to the next stop. They did between eight and fifteen miles a day.

"God, I'm ravenous," she said, at the end of a particularly strenuous day. "I think I'll have the whole menu."

"Let's both have the sole Provençale," he said.

She looked up from the menu, a little surprised. "The duck looks nice, Malcom," she said.

"Very fatty. I think you should get your Body-Mass-Index down a bit if you can."

She looked at him in hurt surprise. "Malcom Shepherd! Are you saying I'm fat?"

"No," he laughed, "Not fat. But you know you're at greater risk of heart disease and diabetes at the moment. You can eat plenty, but you just need to be careful of what you eat. I'll show you. Look."

He went through the menu with her, and she ended up with a melon starter, followed by the fish and roasted Mediterranean vegetables. They had wine but no dessert. Then they strolled around town and he bought some beautiful local fruit at a stall, which they had when they got back to the hotel room.

"You can have as much fruit as you like," he said, "but not within an hour of eating the main course. It has to do with insulin metabolism. You'll get the hang of it."

Reluctantly she went along with it. She knew he meant it for her own good and who, after all, was better placed to know what was good for her? She certainly wasn't hungry and by the end of the first week she realized, while dressing for dinner one evening, that her dress was slipping around her. She resolved to keep up the diet, and two months after returning from Provence she was pleased to find that she'd lost twenty pounds. She felt better for it. She looked good and she had more energy than ever.

She wondered if all husbands were as attentive to her needs as he was. It was as if she was so precious to him that he couldn't bear anything to be wrong with her. One day she had a bad headache. He insisted on taking her blood pressure.

"Your blood pressure's okay," he announced.

"Of course it is. It's only a headache, Malcom. It'll pass."

"All the same... When did you last have your eyes tested?"

"Ages ago. Malcom, I don't want to wear glasses..."

"You don't have to wear glasses, you can have contact lenses if you need them. I think we'll set up an appointment for you, just in case."

The optician found some astigmatism, mainly in one eye. At Malcom's suggestion she had the contact lenses made up with a tint. It took a bit of getting used to, not just the lenses but seeing those dark brown eyes gazing out of the mirror at her, but Malcom said she looked great.

Malcom worked hard. He operated on his private patients at another hospital, where he had a list most Saturdays. A lot of it was cosmetic surgery. The secretary there looked after his billings but he checked the accounts meticulously, and he gave the same close attention to the statements from Joanne's bank and the credit card account he'd arranged for her. One Sunday she took a cup of tea to him in the study, where he was checking bills and writing cheques at an antique bureau he used for the purpose. She took pity on him.

"Malcom, why don't you let me do some of that? It's only financial paperwork. I could look after it for you."

"No, no, I prefer to do it myself."

"But you work hard enough as it is."

"Just leave it alone, will you?"

He relented a little when he saw the way she recoiled at the unaccustomed sharpness of his tone. "Look, I'd only be asking you all the time whether you'd done this or dealt with that. It's better this way. Just let me have the receipts for anything you spend. I'll look after the rest. I can manage."

She didn't make the offer again.

They'd been married for five months when her birthday came around. He bought her flowers and presented her with a pearl necklace. She was thrilled.

Then he told her where they were going to have dinner.

"We'll eat at Radley Hall, and I've booked a suite for afterwards so we can stay over. We'll come back tomorrow."

"Radley Hall? That costs a fortune! Can we afford it?"

"Of course we can. That's the reason I have a private practice, my love, so we can enjoy some of the good things of life! Oh, and I thought you might like to spoil yourself first."

He handed her an envelope, which she opened with keen anticipation. Inside she found a voucher for one of the better beauty salons in town. It would pay for a facial, a manicure, hair styling and…

"Oh, that's so thoughtful of you, darling." She leaned across the table and kissed him, and then continued to read down the list. "What's this bit…? I don't normally have my hair coloured."

"I know. I thought you might fancy a change."

She looked a little crestfallen. "Don't you like my hair the colour it is?"

"Yes, of course I do, but let's face it, it's a bit—what shall I say?—in between. You're not a blonde and you're not a brunette. This would be more definite. Why don't you try it for a change? If you don't like it you can always let it grow out."

She was dying to have the facial and all the other treatments, so she decided to go along with it. When she came home she posed in the doorway with one hand behind her head and said: "How do I look?"

"Wow, you look terrific! It really suits you. Super style too. Did you enjoy yourself?"

She crossed over to him and put her arms round his neck. "Mmmm. Pure luxury," she whispered into his ear.

"Good, I'm glad. We've got time for a drink if you want one. I'm driving so I'll just have a tonic. Then we'd better get dressed."

As the wife of a consultant surgeon she had other, more social, events to go to. The Annual Ball of the College of Plastic Surgeons was a black tie affair and he seemed particularly anxious to make an impression. She accompanied him in a long, black, off-one-shoulder dress, which he had insisted on choosing with her, her hair piled high, in a style he'd discussed personally with her hairdresser. She wished he would leave the responsibility for these decisions to her, but she knew by now how much he liked to be in control and she'd learned to live with it. And as she examined the effect in the mirror before they left, smoothing the silky material of the dress over her flat stomach, she had to admit that, whatever his faults, he knew what was right for her. She felt good and she looked good.

There were a lot of people at the Ball. He introduced her to various colleagues and College officials, and then a man crossed the floor to see him, towing his wife too quickly behind him.

"Malcom, haven't seen you in years!" He turned to Joanne, tilting his head on one side, and then to her astonishment took her by the shoulders and planted a kiss on her cheek. "Hello, my dear, as lovely as always."

Malcom stiffened. "Sorry, Deryk, I don't think you've met Joanne. Joanne, this is Deryk and his wife, Lisa."

Deryk was flustered. "Sorry, sorry. Come to think of it, I thought I'd heard that… Yes, well, sorry. My mistake."

As soon as they'd left, Joanne turned to Malcom.

"You know him well?"

"Deryk and I were at Cardiff together."

"But I haven't met him before, have I?"

Malcom was still scanning the room for people he knew. "Not that I know of. Why?"

"He seemed to think he knew me."

"Oh, he gets people mixed up. Clumsy fellow, always was."

She smiled and said nothing. The explanation was less than convincing but it didn't bother her. *He's a good looking guy, my husband,* she thought. *It would be surprising if there weren't a few old flames around. Well, tough luck, girls. I've got him now.*

Two weeks later, he surprised her at breakfast.

"Darling, there's something I should mention. Please don't take it the wrong way. Promise?"

Her voice rose in panic. "My God, Malcom, what is it?"

"Don't get excited. It's nothing serious, really. Um, there's no easy way of saying this. You're snoring quite a lot."

Her face fell. "Oh, how awful! Oh God, I'm so sorry. Oh, I feel dreadful. What do you want me to do? Shall I sleep in the other room?" She was breathing rapidly and her eyes had filled with tears.

He got up quickly and put his arm round her shoulders. "Now, now. Take it easy. The snoring itself doesn't bother me. Honestly. I just thought I ought to take a look at your nasopharyx, in case something's amiss."

After repeated assurances she lay down on the bed and he used a fibre optic

instrument to examine her nasal cavity and her throat. He straightened up and
helped her into a sitting position.

"Well, it's as I expected. You have a deviated septum, and a slight prolapse of
the soft palate. It's not serious at the moment, but it's worth getting something
done about it. If it got worse you could end up with obstructive sleep apnoea.
You don't want that."

She was close to tears again. "Should I see an E.N.T. man?" she asked.

"No, no need for that. It's only a minor procedure. Bob Garston can do it for
you at the clinic. I'm a colleague so he won't even charge us for it."

Bob Garston was a little surprised when his senior colleague, Malcom
Shepherd, came into the anteroom, gowned, gloved and masked.

"Hi, Bob. How's the patient?"

"Out like a light. We were just going to take her into theatre. Do you want
to watch?"

"No, actually I thought I'd do this one, if it's all right with you, Bob."

"Are you sure? I mean, is that okay ethically?"

"Yeah, she signed a consent form. I've got another case later so I had to come
in anyway. I can easily fit this in and actually I'd feel better about it, if you
don't mind."

"Well, okay, suit yourself. I've got a pretty full list, so I could do with a little
help. But I'll stay if you want."

"Who's assisting? Greg?" He looked around and a gloved, masked and
gowned figure nodded to him. "Greg will do fine. Go on, you buzz off."

Before they started the operation he explained what they were going to do,
mainly for the benefit of Greg, the theatre nurse and the anaesthetist.

"The palate isn't serious. The main thing is to deal with the deviated septum.
Then we can straighten up the nose and we'll do one or two other little cosmetic bits while we're at it."

The procedure took a lot longer than any of the others had anticipated.
Finally Joanne was transferred to a trolley, and taken to the recovery room.
Malcom stayed to do a second operation—his scheduled case—and then went
to see her. All six beds in the recovery room were now occupied; Bob had filled
the other four. The nurse was attending to the latest arrival and for a moment
Malcom was left alone with his wife. He glanced through the notes and charts
hanging on a clipboard on the end of the bed. Heart rate, temperature, blood
pressure, respiration; all stable. She was doing fine. The airway had come out

half an hour ago and she was just sleeping off the anaesthetic. He bent over her face, which was largely obscured by bandages and dressings, smoothed the brown hair back from her forehead and whispered something. Under the bandages her eyelids fluttered.

She hadn't gone back to work. After the bandages had come off she couldn't bear to show her bruised and swollen face outside of the house. Malcom was attentive but matter-of-fact.

"I know it looks a bit bad at the moment, dear, but it's quite normal. You're doing fine. It's the way the tissues drain. You have to expect the swelling over the bridge of the nose and the black eyes. It'll resolve. Just give it time. Believe me, I know."

It took some weeks for the swelling and bruising to subside and over this period she became increasingly aware that her appearance had changed. Her eyes looked larger and they were slightly tilted up at the corners. The nose— she used a second mirror to look at her nose in profile—was now small and straight, where her old nose had been a little broader and rounder. She found herself looking into the mirror expecting to see one thing and seeing quite another. It upset her deeply. She was sure all this had nothing to do with a deviated septum. He'd deliberately changed her appearance, and without her knowledge or permission. Why?

She knew it was no good confronting him with it. He'd only come out with some highly plausible medical exigency for what he'd done and she'd get no-where. So she waited for her opportunity. Before long it came. Malcom was attending a conference in Utrecht. He offered to take her with him but she said she didn't feel up to it. He would be away for a week.

As soon as she heard the car leave she started to go through the house sys-tematically. The drawers of the bureau were locked but she knew where to find the key. She went through drawer after drawer, examining papers, bills, ac-counts, tax returns, guarantees, investments, correspondence, but she found no clue. All she learned was that this was a man who couldn't bear to throw anything away, even documents that were clearly out of date. She was driven by the certainty that he was hiding something from her. Her searching became more desperate, more frenzied. She looked in cupboards, under the beds, and in drawers of old clothes, and still she found nothing. She stood in the middle of their bedroom, breathing hard, trying to think. And then, quite slowly, she raised her eyes to the ceiling.

There was a small library ladder in the study. She placed it on a table so that she could reach the trap door into the loft. She dislodged the trap door and slid it to one side. Then she got her head and shoulders up through the aperture and cast a torch around. On a wooden beam adjacent to the trap door was a modern plastic light switch. She flicked it on and hauled herself into a loft space that was now illuminated by two bare light bulbs. It was cold and it smelt damp and musty. The only sounds were odd gurglings from a lagged water tank close to the eaves. She moved carefully along the bare rafters, shining the torch into the hard shadows cast by the light bulbs. There was a lot of junk, empty picture frames, chairs without seats, rolls of carpet bound with rope, some chests. Everything was covered with a thick layer of dust. Then she noticed a cardboard box sealed with polyester tape. That had to be more recent than the rest of this stuff. She peeled off the tape, opened the box, and her heart stopped.

There was something indefinably different about Joanne when she came back into the house. She did everything with deliberation and quiet resolve. She had a bath and shampooed her hair, rinsing out the dust and cobwebs. She put on a nightdress and a dressing gown, for it was late now, made herself a mug of cocoa and sat down in an armchair to go over what she had learned today and what she had to do tomorrow.

It had been a shock, looking into that box and seeing her own face gazing calmly out at her. How long had she waited for the pounding of her heart to subside? How long before she'd turned back to the box, her torch reflecting from the glass that protected the photograph in its heavy wooden frame? How long before she'd lifted that photograph, placed it to one side, and started to examine the contents of the box?

The joint British passport, old-style, in English and French.

Name of bearer Nom du titulaire	Mr Malcom Shepherd
Accompanied by spouse Accompagné de son épouse	Sandra Danielle Shepherd
National status Nationalité	BRITISH CITIZEN

She turned the page.

2   **DESCRIPTION**   *SIGNALEMENT*

	Bearer Titulaire	**Spouse** Epouse
Occupation Profession	Surgeon	Secretary
Place of birth Lieu de naissance	London	Worcester
Date of birth Date de naissance	2 Aug 1966	27 May 1961
Height Taille	1.83 m	1.78 m
Distinguishing marks Signes particuliers	-	-

And on the facing page, below the colour photograph of Malcom, Mrs Sandra Shepherd, with her dark brown hair, tilting dark brown eyes, and straight nose. Mrs Sandra Shepherd, in whose image Joanne now knew she had been fashioned.

She flicked the page over.

This passport expires   Ce passport expire le

10 AUG 2003

PASSPORT OFFICE 10 AUG 1993 PETERBOROUGH

Deeper in the box: a driver's licence, birth certificate, marriage certificate, library tickets, theatre programmes. Photographs, lots of photographs, loose in paper wallets. Malcom tending a barbecue, Sandra on the beach, Malcom and Sandra, Sandra and Malcom... A large photograph, taken professionally on some formal occasion: Malcom in his black tie, Sandra looking stunning in a long, black, off-one-shoulder dress, with her brown hair piled high... A diploma, hard to read now because she is looking through tears: "The Governing Body of the Bristol College of Further Education has conferred the Diploma in Medical Secretarial Studies on Sandra D. Jameson, who has completed a course of studies approved by the Association of Medical Secretaries, Practice Administrators & Receptionists Ltd (AMSPAR)". A wedding invitation: "Mr and Mrs David Shepherd invite you to join them in celebrating the marriage of their son Malcom to Sandra, only child of the late Mr and Mrs Arthur Jameson... Saturday, 25th July 1992, Ceremony 12.30 am, and afterwards at the Banqueting Suite, Old Crompton Hall..." An album with padded white leather covers, the words "Our Wedding" embossed in gold on the front cover. A happy Malcom with his radiant bride, outside the church, dancing with her, cutting the cake... Still there is the unanswered question in her mind: what happened to her? And finally the large manila envelope, lying against the side of the box where she hadn't seen it before. Correspondence with an insurance company, The Scottish Permanent Life Assurance Society. A letter "...in full and final settlement..." A copy of a Death Certificate, dated 10th August 1997. "Mrs Sandra Shepherd. Cause of death: peritoneal haemorrhage secondary to ruptured ectopic pregnancy." An unreadable signature... And suddenly, as if it had taken this shock to jerk it out of her dormant memory, she remembers what it was that he whispered when she was in a state of delirious half-sleep after the operation. "Now," he had breathed. "Now, Sandra, my only love, you can live again."

She lifted her feet onto a chair, took a sip of cocoa, leaned her head back on the armchair and closed her eyes. *They must have met when he was in Cardiff. He would have been an SHO or a Registrar. She was probably working as a medical secretary at the same hospital. That fellow at the Ball—what was his name, Deryk?—knew both of them. No wonder he took me for Sandra. And that was before Malcom's final deft touches.*

He and Sandra had been married just five years. I can feel sorry for her, being snuffed out like that when she had so much to live for. Shouldn't I feel sorry for him? No. He deceived me. He doesn't love me, he never loved me. For him I was just a piece of putty, of approximately the right size and shape to be remodelled into a replica of his beloved Sandra. Well, I'm not a piece of putty. I have my own feelings, my own memories, my own skills, my own wants, my own regrets, and, dammitall, I had my own features until he stole them from me.

It's five years since she died and he's still carrying the torch. Did he really love her that much? No, he's not capable of love. He killed his own wife by impregnating her. That wasn't supposed to happen. He doesn't like it when things don't go according to plan. I'm just his way of getting back in control.
That isn't a very charitable thought, Joanne.
I know, I'm not in a very charitable mood.

The man at the branch of the Scottish Permanent Life Assurance Society in town was confused, as well he might be. He was looking from the computer screen to her and back to the computer screen.

"The records are quite clear, madam. Mrs Sandra Shepherd died in 1997 and we paid out on her life cover. It was a substantial amount; she was only young when she passed away."

"Well as you see, Mr Warburton, I didn't pass away. Far from it; I'm very much alive. He tried to get rid of me but it didn't work."

"But it says here that we had sight of the Death Certificate."

"He's a doctor, isn't he? How difficult do you think it would be for him to forge it?"

"Well, if what you say is true this is a very serious case of fraud. We will be obliged to notify the police."

"That's entirely in your hands. I just thought you should know."

When Malcom came back from Utrecht, a letter from the Scottish Permanent Life Assurance Society was already awaiting him on the bureau in his study. He came into the room, waving the letter.

"What the hell have you been playing at, Joanne? Are you out of your tiny mind?"

"Not at all. I know what you've been doing, Malcom, and the game is up. I found the box in the loft."

"You did what? What business have you to go rummaging around in my private..."

"Oh, pipe down, Malcom. I knew something was going on. I had every right to find out. And I did. You wanted me to be Sandra. You put me through that hellish operation just so that you could have her back. Well, all right. Here I am. I'm Sandra. I'm alive. Only in that case you shouldn't have collected my life insurance."

"You're barmy. You'll have to tell them what you've done. They're accusing me of fraud. They're taking proceedings. I could be arrested."

"Oh, you will be arrested, Malcom. But the police may not press the fraud charges if they think they can make the murder charge stick."

"What? What are you drivelling about? Murder who?"

"Why you murdered Joanne, Malcom."

"You're crazy. You're Joanne."

"No, I'm not, I'm Sandra. You just don't get it, do you, Malcom? I look like Sandra and I have all the documents I need to prove I am Sandra. For God's sake, even my passport is still valid! So if I'm Sandra, where's Joanne? She hasn't been seen at work. You were supposed to have married her, but she's not here, is she? You must have murdered her, Malcom."

Malcom had gone white. "You're Joanne, you're not Sandra. I can prove it. Sandra died. She was..."

"Cremated, yes. I saw the Cremation Certificate. You do like to keep everything don't you, Malcom? That means there's no remains. That's unfortunate. It could have been anyone inside that coffin when it was committed. Or no-one at all. And DNA samples aren't going to help either. There's nobody to compare me with. Sandra was an only child, and both her parents had already passed on when you married her. Don't you remember? That's why your Mum and Dad had to host the wedding. Well, well. I can't hang around here. I'm leaving for a secret address. The police will know where to find me, but you, I'm afraid, will not. Goodbye, Malcom."

As she walked down the path to the waiting taxi his anguished cry followed her:

"SANDRA....!"

ဆဝ ಛ

The Plasmid

Ron Heskisson is one of those unfortunate individuals who can never do things by halves.

I met him for the first time when we got involved in setting up a course for undergraduate students in biological sciences. The course was called: 'Structure and function: a modern synthesis'. I covered the microanatomy and he covered the biochemistry. Because our departments are housed in different buildings I would arrange to go over to his room or he would come over to mine and we would work on the course for a few hours at a time. Ron would come up with lots of ideas and we would bat them back and forth, discarding a lot and refining others. After that it tended to be me who worked on the finer details. Nobody asked us to operate in that way; we just recognized that we had strengths in different areas.

At the end of the course the students had to hand in questionnaires saying what they thought of it. It seemed to have gone down pretty well on the whole. The free comments about Ron's lectures were interesting. Students tend not to be inhibited by niceties like a sensitive regard for people's feelings. Some wrote 'Couldn't understand what he was on about', 'Total chaos', 'Lost him at the beginning and never caught up again'. Others reacted very differently. 'Exciting, I could feel my brain expanding. This is what university should be about'. 'Brilliant. I'd love to do a research project in his lab'.

Ron was that sort of person: he tended to polarize views. Some of his colleagues liked the fact that they could rely on him to give an offbeat view of things; rather more of his colleagues thought he was perfectly potty. I never met any that had no opinion one way or the other. As for me, I liked him. He was lively and stimulating and original. Although he was never short of ideas of his own he was open to my ideas too and he could take criticism. I enjoyed working on the course with him and by the time it was over we had become good friends.

We decided it might be fun to meet up for dinner one evening at a local Chinese restaurant, and bring our wives along. The evening was a great success. He introduced his wife Julie to my wife Viv, and after that you couldn't get the two girls apart. Viv quite liked Ron, but she really took to Julie. It was a little unusual for her; although Viv is socially skilled she doesn't normally go out of her way to seek out company. But after that evening the four of us started to meet quite regularly, usually at one another's houses.

Ron gets enthusiasms. In fact he gets more enthusiasms than Toad of Toad Hall. Shortly before I met him I believe he'd taken up the piano. He practised like a demon and drove Julie up the wall with scales and arpeggios. Then quite suddenly he gave it up. If he can't be the best, or at least unique in some way, he's no longer interested. By the time the four of us were getting together socially he'd taken up painting. It wasn't enough for Ron just to paint; he wanted to make his own pigments. He thought he could distinguish himself from the pack by using his knowledge of chemistry. He'd had the idea that if he painted in fluorescent dyes he could get the picture to change colour by illuminating it with light of different wavelengths. He was going to establish a completely new movement in modern art. Of course as soon as he started putting a brush to paper he found that it was a bit more difficult than he'd thought. He tried reading a few books and amateur painting magazines, but it didn't help. Then he noticed that there were courses advertised in the backs of the magazines. So he chose a residential course somewhere in the Lake District and took Julie and their two-and-a-half-year-old, Kieron, on a painting holiday. During the day he would get some tuition with the class, and Julie and Kieron would be left to fill their day however they pleased. As summer vacations go it actually suited Julie down to the ground. Ron had had many enthusiasms before, but this one had the merit of taking her to a very pretty guest house, set in lovely scenery, and she and Ron got to spend every evening together. During the day she would play with Kieron and take him for short walks. He would often fall asleep in the push-chair and then she would find a convenient bench with a nice view and read one of the several books she'd brought with her. She came back contented, relaxed and pregnant.

When they came over and broke the news to us I think Viv may have felt a bit envious, because we don't have any children of our own, but there was nothing half-hearted about her happiness for them, especially as Julie was positively radiant.

"The only thing is," Julie said, her voice still husky with excitement, "we're going to have to move. We'll never manage in the present house. It's much too small for a growing family."

"Didn't I see a 'For Sale' notice on one of the houses in Mulberry Close?" Viv said to me. I shrugged my shoulders; I hadn't seen it, but Viv drives out that way and the question was rhetorical anyway; you could be very sure she'd seen it. "It's only a couple of roads over on the same estate as this," she explained to Ron and Julie.

Julie looked round at Ron. "I say...that would be good, wouldn't it, Ronnie? We'd be living close by! I do love this location. You're just on the edge of town, so it's easy to get out into the countryside. I've always liked this house, too— would it be like this house?"

"I don't know if it's the same design. Same contractors probably, because it's part of the same estate. Tell you what: I'll show you where it is on the map and you can pass it by on your way home. Then you can give the Estate Agent a ring tomorrow and arrange a viewing. Steve, have you got a map?"

That's how they came to buy the house in Mulberry Close. Of course we went and looked at it with them, even before they'd moved in. It wasn't identical to ours, but it was similar in many ways. There had been one owner and he'd focused a good deal of attention on the house, which was therefore in good decorative order. The garden was another matter. If you were listing words to describe the previous owner, 'plantsman' would come fairly low down the list. The front garden was paved; the back garden was a rectangle of lawn that extended right to the fence. It was crying out for someone to devote a little time and imagination to it. The siren song was irresistible to Ron.

"I've taken up gardening," he announced when we visited them for the first time after the move. I wasn't all that surprised. Their previous house had been a nice modern terrace with a communal area at the back. This was maintained by a team of groundsmen. He hadn't ever had responsibility for his own little plot before and I could see how that would appeal to him.

"What about painting?" I enquired, knowing as soon as I'd asked how entirely pointless the question was.

"Painting? Ah, painting's very conventional really! Gardening is painting with a living canvas!"

"He's bought a small library of books, subscribed to three gardening magazines, and we watch every TV programme that was ever made about gardens," said the ever-patient Julie. She tried to say it in a neutral way but we knew exactly what she meant.

"Well," I said, trying to remain buoyant, "what are you going to grow, Ron?" I must say I was thinking 'vegetables'. I could see Ron growing vegetables. He'd be able to sell the idea to Julie, as it would cut down on grocery bills. At the same time he could experiment with different varieties, and maybe even grow some giant ones.

I'd underestimated him. Totally.

"Dahlias!" he declared triumphantly.

"Dahlias," I said.

"Yes, dahlias."

"Er, dahlias, and…"

"No, just dahlias."

I saw the look of concern, bordering on alarm, on Viv's face. It was directed to Julie, whose answering expression had all the eloquence of raising her eyes to the heavens, without actually raising her eyes to the heavens. Viv and I take a modest interest in gardening, but the notion of monoculture in a suburban plot about six by five metres wasn't one I had encountered before.

"Why dahlias, Ron?"

"Well you see dahlias have been declining in popularity in recent years, but for no good reason. There's a vast number of types, every size, shape and colour you can think of. The catalogues are fantastic. I'm going to specialise in the spiky ones. I've joined the National Dahlia Society. I'm going to enter competitions."

"Ron, I hate to be the one to break the news, but they only flower from about August onwards. You'll have nothing to look at the rest of year."

He paused and thought, but only for a moment. "Ah, but that's the advantage, you see. I can keep the beds completely free of weeds right up to the moment that the dahlias start sprouting. Weeds take all the goodness out of the soil. When the dahlias come up they'll be in the ideal environment."

Viv's face was an absolute picture. Fortunately she was standing behind Ron. We took our drinks across to the patio doors and looked out at the garden. I don't want to sound unkind to Ron, but in his case resolution is not always translated into action. However, on this occasion he'd clearly made a start. Even though the light was failing a bit you could see that he'd removed a strip of grass about a metre and a half wide along the back fence and down the right-hand side to form an L-shaped bed.

"See," continued Ron enthusiastically, "that direction's south, so these two sides will get the most sun. It may not look much, but I've done a lot of work on it. It was really compacted and full of stones and bits of brick and broken glass. I've dug it down two spits and sieved the lot."

"What's the soil like?"

"Quite heavy. Unfortunately it's dreadfully impoverished by the grass. I've tested it, of course. pH is a bit low and it's very deficient in nitrogen, especially for dahlias. It'll take a lot of improving. Dahlias are greedy feeders. I had a look at stuff like mulches, composts, soil improvers, and slow release fertilizers in the garden centre. Do you know what it would cost for an area like this?"

"Prohibitive?" I hazarded, helpfully.

"Absolutely. I had to find another way. I've been composting the grass cuttings and some kitchen waste but it takes too long. So I've been bringing home the ammonia solution left over from the separations we're doing at the lab. There are litres of it. Seemed a shame to pour it down the sink when it can do some good here. Actually it has corrected the acidity nicely and put a bit of nitrogen into the soil at the same time. It's too soluble really but some of the nitrogen ought to get trapped, and I can always add more next year, nearer to planting time."

"I thought you had very strict controls on stuff going out of your lab." Viv was following the conversation so I turned to her to explain. "He runs a GM lab."

"What's GM?" asked Viv.

"Genetic Modification."

"Oh, that GM."

Ron enlarged on it a little. "Yes, we're developing some new plasmids for inserting genes into a whole variety of organisms."

"Well, couldn't this ammonia that you're dumping on the soil still contain some plasmid?" I asked.

"It's a distant possibility, I suppose, but it wouldn't matter. It wouldn't last long on soil. In the lab all the glassware and instruments have to be really clean—not just clean but baked—otherwise enzymes that are just floating around in the environment break down the DNA. You know, there's an awful lot of rubbish talked about the spread of GM crops and stuff. People panic and go over the top. It's not so easy to introduce new genes into DNA. I should know. The risks just aren't that great."

"Well, I hope you're right."

I remember feeling distinctly uneasy about what he was doing but I'm not going to claim second sight. None of us could have anticipated the sequence of events that had already been set in motion.

A week later Ron and Julie came round to have dinner with us. There was never a shortage of things to talk about with Ron and Julie, and it wasn't until we'd finished the main course that I happened to ask Ron how the garden was going.

Julie responded before he could. "Oh, don't get him on that subject."

I thought Viv was very tactful. She said to Julie: "I'll go and get the dessert. Do you want to give me a hand?"

As they went into the kitchen I poured a little more wine into Ron's glass and said: "Why, is there a problem?"

"Cheers, nice red, this. Cats and dogs are the problem, Steve, bloody cats and dogs. Dozens of them, all over the bloody beds. At first I thought they were using it as a latrine. I wouldn't have minded that, it would help to enrich the soil. But it's nothing like that. They just come and sniff and rub their noses and paws in it. I don't know what they're up to. I could tolerate one or two, but it seems like the whole neighbourhood's animals are in my garden. And our cat's out there with them."

"That's strange. I've heard of cats getting attracted to grass and catmint and some other plants, but it's hard to see what they'd find attractive in…well, I mean there aren't any plants. Not yet, anyway." It was hard to be delicate about Ron's barren beds. "Dogs are trained to hunt for truffles, of course. Maybe you've got truffles," I ventured. I wasn't being serious, but he took it at face value.

"Not after I dug it all over like that, no. And there's another problem—the white stuff. It wasn't there to start with, but it's been spreading and now it's all over the bed."

"What, like crystals?" I asked. I was thinking of the quantity of ammonia salts he'd been chucking onto the bed.

"No, it's not crystalline. It's more like a thin layer of wool. It seems to be growing. Some sort of fungus, I think. You don't think that's what attracting the cats and dogs do you?"

"Could be. I've no idea. I've never heard of anything like that."

The examination period was over and we had the last lot of papers in from the course. They had to be double-marked. What that amounts to is that Ron had to mark them, and then I had to mark each question again independently, not knowing what mark he'd assigned. As usual, Central Examinations Office took ages to collect the papers and check them against the registered students, so by the time the papers came out to us we had about one day in which to do all the marking and hand in the marks. We agreed that I would go round to his house to pick up the papers he'd marked; then I could make a start that evening. I found him in a very agitated state, holding a fairly well charged glass of whisky. At first I thought it was the tight deadline. The pile of papers was ready on his desk, though, tied round like a parcel with some coarse twine. He put three fingers on it.

"You'd better be especially careful when you're checking the last few," he said. "I was a bit distracted."

"Is something the matter? Is Julie okay?"

"Yeah, no, Julie's fine. Damnedest thing. Have a drink?"

I declined, but we sat down and he continued.

"I'm working at my desk, over there. You know, we're going to use the small bedroom as a study but we haven't redecorated it yet so I'm working in a corner of the lounge. Julie is busy in the kitchen so she leaves Kieron here, playing on the floor. He's talking to himself, the way they do. You know, when you're concentrating you tend to shut these things out. But gradually it's starting to permeate what he's saying. He's saying 'Clever pussy, clever pussy' over and over again.

"So I look round. Kieron's got some plastic bricks scattered around and the cat is picking them up and putting them down. Steve—the fucking animal is picking them up properly with fingers on one side and thumb on the other! It's a pussy cat, f'r Chrissake, and it's got an opposable thumb!"

I'd never heard him swear like that. He must have been really shaken. I suppose I was concerned for him, because I wasn't really taking in the full implications of what he was telling me.

"Then the bloody cat looks up and sees I'm watching it. The look it gives me, Steve—I'm not kidding, it sent the chills right through me."

"What sort of look?"

"Oh, I can't describe it. A searing look. Pure, undiluted hatred. And then it scats. That was an hour ago. We haven't seen it since. It's always here in the evening. Normally goes to sleep on Julie's lap or mine. Julie's upset, she was fond of that cat."

Walking home, with the stack of exam papers under my arm, I started to wonder if Ron hadn't exaggerated a little. Did he really see an opposable thumb? A cat only has four proper digits on the front paws; the remaining one is much shorter and laid further back, the so-called dew claw. Couldn't it be that its claws were long and it was just gripping between the digits and the dew claw? He could have been wrong about the look, too—it was probably a trick of the light. And as for disappearing, well it had only been gone an hour. Maybe it would come back and all would be well. We had a cat once, and it used to go insane at ten o'clock every night. You could set your watch by it. It would be sleeping peacefully one moment and the next thing it was racing around the room and trying to climb the curtains. Then it would look at you with wild eyes and ears flat against its head. Cats are a bit bonkers that way. Turning it over in my mind like this, I was able to come up with a rational explanation for what had happened. Although Ron was clearly agitated by the incident, I dismissed it. I didn't even mention it to Viv. But something happened the following evening that made me change my mind.

I was reading a journal in my study. I usually fancy a cup of tea around nine or half-past so I went downstairs. I found Viv sitting in the lounge, knitting and reading at the same time. I've always admired the way she does that, and I say that as someone who would need their entire concentration just to finish one row without dropping stitches or otherwise making a complete pig's breakfast of it.

"I've put the kettle on, Viv, fancy a cuppa?"

"Please. Can you close the curtains while you're up, dear? The nights must be drawing in."

I knew what she meant. As in Ron's house, most of the end wall of the lounge is taken up by a pair of sliding glass patio doors. It affords a nice view onto our garden (such as it is) during the day. But as soon as it gets dark it looks like a black hole, so it was definitely time to draw the curtains. I always check that the doors are latched properly before I do that. That's how I found myself eye to eye with a very large dog.

Viv looked up frowning, wondering why I'd sat down so suddenly without closing the curtains or making the tea. When she saw my face she put down her book and her knitting and came over in a hurry.

"What on earth's the matter? Are you all right, Steve? Steve? Are you feeling all right? God, you haven't half lost your colour."

"I'm okay, Viv. Really. Just a bit shaken. Be a dear, would you, and make the tea? And put about ten spoonfuls of sugar in mine. Then I'll tell you what happened."

She hurried off. I think she was glad to occupy herself with something, although no doubt piqued that I'd been so mysterious. But I needed to gather my wits. And I needed that hot, sweet tea. It tasted wonderful. She was waiting for me to explain.

"Sorry, Viv, I got a bit of a shock. When I went to check the latch on the door there was a big dog there, up on its hind legs, pulling the handle down, trying to get in."

Viv's eyebrows said 'Is that all?'. And not just her eyebrows.

"Is that all? Goodness, I thought you'd had a heart attack or something. Dogs can be clever like that. People train them to prop their paws on a handle and pull it down to open the door. It's a party trick. It was probably only doing what it was taught to do."

"No, you don't understand. It wasn't just leaning its paws on the handle. It was actually gripping the handle, between fingers and thumb. It was a dog, Viv, and it was using an opposable thumb."

Her mouth puckered on one side. "Steve, I know you got a fright, and I'm sorry about that, but the light's terrible out there. Don't you think it just looked like that for the moment?"

"No, I don't. Because Ron told me their cat had developed an opposable thumb and I didn't believe him either. But I do now."

"Their cat's gone missing. Julie 'phoned to find out if I'd seen it."

"That's right, it took off as soon as it saw Ron watching it. But it gave him a hate-filled look first. The exact same thing happened to me. I don't know what shook me more: the opposable thumb or that look of sheer malevolence in its eyes. God, it froze my blood."

Viv went and checked the latch, and then she drew the curtains. "Well there's nothing there now. Drink your tea and you'll feel better."

But I didn't feel better. And I felt still worse after I'd spoken to Ron the following day. We'd met with the Course Convenor to agree the final marks. When we finished we went back to his room. He was very excited; he clearly had something to tell me.

"Wait till you hear this, Steve. You know what I said about the opposable thumb on our cat? You didn't believe me, did you?"

"No, to be honest, I didn't believe you at the time. I do now, though."

"Oh?"

I told him about the dog. He nodded grimly. "Well, listen to this. Next door but one from us there's this couple, Mr and Mrs Coxall. Nice people. Invited us in for a coffee almost as soon as we'd moved in. Anyway, yesterday I got back from work and Julie told me she saw police cars outside their house in the morning. So I said 'What's up?' and she said 'I don't know' so I said 'Let's go and find out, then' and she said 'You go, I'll look after Kieron'. So I did."

He was barely pausing for breath. "Slow up, Ron. Take your time."

"Okay. Mrs Coxall was there on her own. I could see she was pretty agitated. I said I didn't want to appear nosy, but I'd heard she'd had a problem and wondered if I could do anything to help. She was very grateful. Seems she was in

London overnight, with her husband. He was going to stay on for a day or two to visit some business clients so she'd come back on her own that morning. She didn't notice anything wrong at first, but when she took the dirty washing into the utility room she found it had been broken into."

"Doesn't she have a burglar alarm?"

"Yes, but it hadn't gone off because there aren't any sensors in the utility room. Nothing of value there, you see. Normally it would pick up an intruder when they moved into the rest of the house, but whoever it was hadn't moved into the rest of the house—they hadn't gone anywhere except the utility room. That's interesting for a start-off, isn't it?"

"Yes, it is. Go on."

"She has a couple of cats, at least she did have until last week," he tilted his head at me and said slowly, underlining the words, "when they disappeared suddenly. Okay?"

"Okay."

He was back to speed. "That was where she fed her cats, in that utility room. So she took me through and showed me. The room was as she found it, she'd been too upset to do anything about it. A cupboard was open. All the cat food had been taken out, and packets had been opened and food was strewn all over the floor. Hell of a mess."

"Vandals?"

"Yes, if vandals can come and go via the cat flap. There weren't any broken windows or forced doors, and nothing was taken. Only food all over the floor."

"Well, she must have had a few stray cats in."

"That's exactly what the police said. Apparently they could hardly keep the smiles off their faces. She heard them laughing as they went down the path to their cars. She felt totally humiliated. So I said to her very gently 'And you don't you think that's the explanation?' and she said 'No, I don't. I'll tell you why. The cupboard door doesn't latch properly. My husband's not much of a handyman so he's never fixed it. It's a nuisance if it swings open because it can catch me when I'm carrying the washing in and out. So I always lock it and I leave the key in the lock.'" Ron raised his eyebrows enquiringly at me.

"Maybe she forgot, or didn't turn it completely?"

"I thought that. She swears she didn't. She hasn't opened it for a week anyway. That was the last time she saw her cats. There's another thing. She buys those sealed sachets of cat food for her cats. She showed me the way they'd been opened. If it had been just ordinary stray cats you might have expected them to be scratched or clawed open, but they weren't. They'd been peeled open." Ron used his thumb and fingers of both hands in a precision grip to illustrate the point, but I knew what he was saying. "She was pretty mad with the CID. They wouldn't even come out and fingerprint."

"Well, I suppose you can't blame them really..."

"Yeah, but there's more. Listen to this. I helped her clear up the mess, because it was beginning to get pretty smelly in there. As we're finishing off she says to me: 'There's something funny going on round here'. So I say 'What makes you say that?' Then she tells me about the people who live at the back of her—you know, their gardens back on to one another. They got to know each other because when her pussies were little they used to climb over the fence and then miaow like crazy because they couldn't get back. They used to have to go round and fetch them. Well, she thought whoever it was that broke in might have made off over the fence into their garden so she asked these people if they'd seen anything. They hadn't, but they said they'd had a break-in themselves!"

"Another break-in? What happened?"

"Apparently a window was smashed. They were in bed so they came downstairs as soon as they heard the noise. There wasn't a sign of anyone. They looked into the garden but it was dark outside and the light was on so they weren't going to see anything. The hole in the window looked too small even for a teenager to get through and there were still jagged bits of glass in the frame. Again there was a lot of mess but nothing had been taken. They found a lawn edging tool outside. It looked like that was what had been used to smash the window. They recognized the tool. It was from their own shed. The shed door is normally locked, but they only keep a few garden tools in there so for convenience they normally leave the key in the lock."

Ron looked at me. "It's the animals. It has to be." I was shaking my head in disbelief, so he persisted. "Okay, take her neighbour. How did they get in through such a small hole? Why was nothing taken? Why a lawn edging tool? Why not something heavier, like a spade?"

"Ron, it's one thing to have an opposable thumb. But what you're talking about implies tool-using and planning in advance. That's something only the great apes, including us, can do."

"I've been wondering about that. We always associate increasing intelligence with the use of tools. But tool-handling is made possible by the opposable thumb. Maybe it's a package—a high-level gene that controls both the development of the opposable thumb and the intelligence to use it. It's not out of the question. Look at the development of flight in birds. That required feathers, lightweight construction and all sorts of motor skills. It's difficult to see how that could develop a bit at a time. Much more likely to be a single mutation that causes a leap forward in a new direction. What do they call it: punctate evolution? The new gene doesn't kill the animal, in fact it makes it easier for it to survive, so it passes it onto its progeny. Hey presto! Natural selection."

"Where did they get this high-level gene from then, Ron?"

He looked at me. He knew very well what I was driving at.

"You can't be sure."

"It's circumstantial, I'll grant you. But you've got to say that it's highly suggestive. You dump your ammonia with the plasmid in it. A week later there are hordes of cats and dogs grubbing around, apparently attracted to this woolly stuff on the ground. And then this series of incidents. Highly suggestive."

"The bugger of it is, I haven't the first clue what it is they've picked up. If I could isolate that gene I could make my reputation."

"You could always analyze the white stuff."

"No I can't. Didn't I tell you? I meant to collect some, but it's gone now, disappeared. It was after that thunderstorm we had a few days back. The next morning I looked out the window and it wasn't there any more."

"And have the animals been grovelling in the beds since it disappeared?"

"No, actually."

"You see, it was the white stuff they were after." We were quietly thoughtful for a few moments. Then I heaved a sigh and stood up. "I don't know. I don't like the sound of it at all. Ron, I hate to say this, but I think you've started something. And I think we're at the beginning of it, not the end."

It was Julie who'd spotted the piece in the local paper. Ron cut it out and showed it to me. His expression was grim.

Pensioner found dead

82-year-old widow Mary Jeeves was found dead by a neighbour at her home in West Thornton on Tuesday. Police are treating the death as suspicious. Mrs Jeeves was one of the pillars of Cat Rescue, the organization that finds homes for unwanted cats. Her work earned her the nickname of 'The Cat Lady' with local children, who used to bring her stray cats. "There was a lot of commotion," said neighbour Sam Wellchetts, "so we called round to see if she was all right. She never answered so we went back for the key and let ourselves in. We had a key because we used to feed the cats when she was away." Mr and Mrs Wellchetts found the pensioner lying on the floor and alerted the emergency services, but she was already dead. "There was a lot of mess but no sign of a break-in that we could see. The windows weren't broken and the doors were still locked. Bit of a mystery really. It's a shame, though. She was a nice old lady." Detective-Inspector Colin Gifford said "I'm afraid this has all the hallmarks of a vicious and unprovoked attack on a defenceless old lady. We will spare no effort in bringing the perpetrators of this cowardly crime to justice."

"I'll tell you, Steve, I'm fitting mortise locks to all the doors and windows. I told Julie not to leave Kieron unsupervised in the garden. Not even for a moment. She said what do I take her for, she never does anyway."

"You'll have to go to the police and tell them, Ron. I mean, even now there might be another explanation but they need to know what's going on."

"They'll think I'm pots."

"I'll come with you."

The sergeant on the desk was not being helpful. "DI Gifford's very busy right now. Would you like to tell me what this is about, Mister...?"

Ron was getting impatient. "Doctor. Doctor Heskisson. I've told you, it's about the Mary Jeeves case. Look, with all due respect what I have to say is quite complicated. If I explain it to you I'm only going to have to explain it all over again to DI Gifford. It will save valuable time if I can talk to him."

Eventually we were allowed to see the DI. He listened patiently for a while, but it was a mistake to let Ron try to explain something like that to him. Ron has many talents, but diplomacy isn't one of them. He spent a lot of time on how people could be murdered by cats with opposable thumbs and I think the DI was having a real struggle to keep from rolling his eyes. Eventually he managed to interrupt the flow.

"What did you say you did for a living, sir?"

"I'm a University Lecturer."

It looked like the DI might lose the struggle.

"Well now, you're entitled to your theories, sir, but if you don't mind I think we'll just get on with the investigation in our own way. And if I might give you a word of advice, sir. I wouldn't go round repeating what you said to me just now. Someone might get the wrong idea, if you know what I mean. Now if you'll excuse me I really am very busy..."

"But you don't understand..."

"Come on, Ron. He's right. Let them do it their way."

Outside the station Ron turned on me.

"What did you mean 'He's right'?"

"Couldn't you see the expression on his face? We weren't getting anywhere, except closer to getting ourselves committed. You did try, Ron, but you have to agree it is a pretty far-fetched idea. I didn't believe it myself until I saw that dog with my own eyes. He's only doing his job. You're going to need more evidence if you're going to convince him, eye-witnesses, that sort of thing."

"More deaths, you mean."

Ron's house was slightly nearer so we went back there. Julie made us some coffee and left us to it.

I'd never seen Ron looking so down. Not just down; he looked trapped. "We can't just give up. We've got to do something," he muttered.

"I agree. Let's try to delineate the problem. How many animals do you think are involved?"

"I don't know. When they were in the garden night after night it looked like dozens, but maybe some of the same ones were coming back again so it's very hard to tell."

"And the white stuff has all gone."

"Yes, it was only there for about a week in all. If that was responsible there won't be any new contacts."

"I think we can be pretty sure the white stuff was responsible. We're very lucky it didn't spread. Right now we've got a local problem. It could have gone all over the country.'

Ron's eyes widened at the thought. "What can we do?"

"Well, one thing we could do is set traps that only they can operate with their modified paws."

"Okay. Then what?"

"Then we have to kill them."

"Are you mad? These are people's pets!"

"They're not cuddly animals any more, Ron. They are rabid, psychopathic killers."

"Yes, but the owners aren't going to believe that. They'll just see it as two sadists killing their pets. We'll be arrested. A conviction wouldn't look good on the CV, Steve, especially when you're just getting ready to apply for a Senior Lectureship."

"I suppose so. I don't know. I'm out of ideas at the moment. Let's sleep on it."

"Okay. Look, I've got to go to Bristol tomorrow. Biochemical Society meeting. One of my students is presenting so I have to go."

"Will Julie be all right?"

"I'm taking her and Kieron with. I wouldn't normally but I'm not taking any chances. She's got some family somewhere round there. They'll probably get together. It'll be a break for her; she's been a bit tired lately. We'll be back on Sunday. All right if I touch base with you Monday?"

"Sure. I don't suppose much will happen between now and then."

I've no idea why I said that.

As it happened, Viv was going to be away too. She'd arranged to spend a longish weekend with her mother, arriving on Friday. She and her mother drive each other nuts, but she always forgets that when she's making these arrangements. She would certainly be glad to get back on Sunday. The car was booked in for a service later that morning so I ran her to the station first.

We'd only just turned the corner out of our road when I noticed three dogs, trotting along the pavement. Ordinarily I wouldn't pay much attention to that but I was sensitized by what had happened during the last few days. Even as I looked another dog crossed the road to join them. Then the group of four was joined by two more, who emerged from an alley between the houses. You accept that three dogs might hang around together, but six seems altogether more threatening. It certainly was to me, in my present frame of mind.

"That's an unwelcome development," I muttered under my breath.

Viv has excellent hearing, and never more so than when a comment is intended to be inaudible to her.

"What's so unusual? Dogs do that; they're pack animals."

"Maybe."

I dropped Viv off at the station and took the car to the garage. They 'phoned me at work early in the afternoon. I needed a new accumulator and there wasn't one in stock. Of course. They could get one and fit it the next day. I agreed. I hadn't been aware that there was the slightest thing wrong with the alternator but I had to believe them. They are, after all, paid to know these things and I didn't want to get stuck somewhere with a car that wouldn't start, least of all on Sunday when I was due to pick up Viv from the station. I would just have to go home by bus. As Viv was away I decided to work late and eat at the theatre café, which is close to the University.

There's a bus stop at the edge of the estate, and it isn't all that far to walk home from there. At nine-thirty it was beginning to get dark. I encountered the dogs as I turned into my road. There were about eight or nine of them, maybe ten yards away, standing right across the road and both pavements and all looking in my direction. It was as if they were waiting for me.

I was rooted to the spot, debating what on earth I could do. The street was quiet, unnaturally quiet. There was a rustle and I heard the irregular tapping of their dry pawpads as they started to come towards me. They weren't just advancing in a line; the ones on the far pavement were moving a little more quickly. In a few moments I would be surrounded. Now there was a new noise: a low, throaty growling that seemed to be coming from every direction. One or two of the dogs had peeled back their lips and were showing their teeth, their ears flattened against their heads. I thought: *If I carry on walking they'll attack me, of that I'm certain. If I turn and run they'll come after me. I'm no match for one dog, let alone that many.* I was trying to back slowly away, clutching my brief case, my only weapon, in front of me. The dogs kept coming. I was breathing hard and beginning to sweat. Suddenly I heard a car engine.

As the headlights swept round the corner and illuminated the glass marbles of the dog's eyes I don't know who was more surprised, the driver or the dogs. He slowed up and as he did so I waved and hurried towards him. I thought the dogs might make a last-ditch attempt to get me, but I think they were baffled for the moment by the headlights. I opened the passenger door.

"I live at number sixteen. Could you possibly drop me off? I'm scared of dogs," I stammered out.

"Sure, hop in."

"Most grateful." I got in, closed the door firmly, and melted into the passenger seat. It felt unbelievable secure inside that car.

We moved off but the dogs were standing their ground. The driver swore softly and started to accelerate. A gap appeared in the line of dogs as they moved slowly and reluctantly out of the way.

"I'd be intimidated by that little lot too," said the driver. "What on earth's got into them?"

"I've no idea," I said.

I was lying. I knew very well what had got into them. Something that enabled them to plan intelligently and use tools. And unfortunately whatever it was had also unmasked their most primitive aggressive instincts.

I must admit that before I went out the following morning I took a good look up and down the street from my bedroom window. Normally I wouldn't think twice about walking to the newsagent on the corner, especially on a fine day like this, but I don't mind telling you that on this occasion I would have taken the car if it had been there. But the car was at the garage and it wouldn't be ready until three o'clock, so I had no choice. I always buy a national paper on Saturday, but I wanted to go through the local paper as well, to see if any more incidents had been reported.

When I reached the newsagent I noticed a pram parked outside. In it was a sleeping baby accompanied by several bags of groceries. As I registered this, a pretty young girl came out of the newsagent's carrying a couple of magazines, which she tossed in with the baby. She looked to be about sixteen, rather young to be the mother of the baby. She caught my eye so I smiled and she smiled back and said "Bonjour", released the brake and set off with the pram. *Problem solved*, I thought. *A French, or possibly Belgian, au pair. Perhaps she's from a country district where they can afford to be a bit more casual about leaving babies unattended.*

I bought the papers and, suppressing my usual habit of scanning the headlines as I walked home, folded the papers resolutely under my arm and kept my eyes open. To my relief there were no dogs around, just a black cat trotting along the opposite pavement. *Cats are so elegant,* I thought, tip-toeing along like little ballerinas. *Except that this cat seems a little heavy-footed...* I thought of the opposable thumb and a chill ran through my veins. I didn't slacken my pace, but watched it carefully. It was moving along the edge of the pavement, close to a low wall, and then it jumped effortlessly up onto the wall and over into the front garden, its tail disappearing last. I crossed the road and approached cautiously to see where it had gone.

By the front door was the pram I'd seen earlier. The bags of groceries had gone; no doubt the au pair was unloading them inside. I couldn't actually see the baby but I knew it was in there all right—I knew because of the cat. It was on the lawn, and its whole manner had changed. It was in the hunting posture, low in the grass, walking stealthily towards the pram, ears flattened against its head. It reached the pram, measured the distance carefully, crouched and jumped up.

I was horrified. I stepped quickly and quietly over the wall, and crossed the lawn but before I could get to it the cat had lunged towards the baby. Gripping the sides of the pram with its hind paws it had reached forwards with its front paws and clamped them around the baby's throat.

I had no time to think. Coming up behind the cat I grabbed it by the loose skin at the scruff of the neck and further down on its back. It went limp for a moment, obeying the built-in reflex that enables a kitten to be picked up by its mother. But as soon as I'd lifted it clear of the pram it started to flail with its back paws, trying to slash at me. It was incredibly strong and I knew I couldn't hold it for long. I turned and simply ran it into the wall of the house as hard as I could. Then I carried the limp bag of black fur back to the front of the garden and looked up and down the road. Fortunately no-one had seen me. I knew I couldn't afford to be caught with it; my explanation would get the same reception as the DI had given Ron on Thursday evening. So I tossed the lifeless body into the gutter. People would think it was a road casualty. In my urgency I'd dropped the papers on the lawn. Now I picked up them up, but hesitated for a moment. Should I say something to the au pair about leaving the baby out? The chances were that she was on her own and I would only alarm her, especially if she had problems understanding English. Reluctantly I decided against, stepped over the wall, and walked home.

Now I really did know how Mary Jeeves had died. I'd saved a baby's life but I didn't feel proud of myself.

I scanned the local paper but there was nothing in it of note. In the afternoon I went down to the garage. The car wasn't quite ready, so I sat in the waiting-room and had a look at a copy of the previous day's local paper, which I hadn't seen. Inside, in a column of short news items, something caught my eye.

Pylon pussies get a shock

Five cats were electrocuted when they tried to climb a pylon in the Lampton district yesterday. A spokesman for the RSPCA Animal Centre at Trebor, which attended the incident, said that cats do not normally try to climb pylons because the metalwork is too slippery for them. They would not be suggesting modifications to pylon design because the event was so unusual.

I smiled bleakly. Metalwork wouldn't be too slippery for a cat with an opposable thumb on forepaws and hindpaws. The item gave me an idea. They would have taken the carcasses back to the Animal Centre. Perhaps someone looked at them and noticed the paws. It wouldn't be much, but it would be good to have at least some independent evidence.

When the garage finally parted with my car, and I had parted with a large cheque, I drove straight to Trebor and went into the RSPCA Animal Centre. The waiting room was full of strangely quiet animals and their owners. I didn't feel threatened. Lampton is the next district to West Thornton, where we live, and both would lie in the catchment area for this hospital, but it was miles away. Also, if an animal was still with its owner the chances were that it hadn't been exposed. I went to the desk and told them I was looking into some unusual incidents involving animals. Could they tell me anything more about the pylon incident in which the cats were killed? The receptionist referred me to one of the vets and we spoke quietly at the end of the counter. I told him who I was and apologized for bothering him, because he was clearly pushed for time. I told him I had an interest in animal behaviour, which was certainly true, and mentioned the pylon incident.

"The paper exaggerated. It wasn't five cats, it was three."

"That's still pretty unusual, isn't it?"

"Very. I've never seen one do it, let alone three. I've no idea how they got up there."

"Were the animals examined when they were brought in?"

"Just a minute." He went over to a filing drawer in the reception area and came back with a slim folder. "Doesn't look like it. Nothing in the notes. I'm not surprised. The bodies were very charred and the animals were obviously dead so we would've disposed of them as soon as possible. You know, we're busy enough round here dealing with the live ones."

"Well, thanks, anyway. Sorry to take up your time." I was turning to leave when I had another thought. "Have you had any other strange incidents like that? Just in the last week or so."

He looked a bit desperate, and I couldn't blame him. "Look, I'm tied up. Angela?" He was calling to a nurse who was just delivering a cardboard box to a customer. Loud miaows were emanating from the box. It reminded me of the incident this morning, and I felt quite uncomfortable. "Angela, do you have a moment to go through the records with this gentleman?" He lowered his voice. "Unusual D.O.A.s in the last week or so."

"What, like the cats up the pylons?"

"We've just covered that one. See if there are any others." He disappeared before I could thank him.

Angela was clearly busy too, but she pulled a sheaf of folders from the drawer and went through them quickly with me.

"Here's one. I remember this. It was a dog. It got onto a balcony on the fourth floor of a block of flats. A woman was in the lounge and when she saw it she banged on the glass doors. The dog took off and fell to the ground. She was quite upset. She said she got a fright and she wasn't thinking when she banged on the doors. The odd thing was how it got on to the balcony. The woman said there was no way it could have come through the flat. There are some large trees close by. The residents wanted them felled. They'd been complaining to the agent that a burglar could climb a tree, leap over onto the roof and come down a drainpipe to a balcony. She wrinkled her nose at me and shook her head. "A dog couldn't do that, now, could it?"

"No, of course it couldn't," I said.

Yes, it bloody well could, I thought. It seemed incredible, but I was getting quite used to the incredible.

"Did anyone examine the dog when it was brought in?"

"No, it was a mess. No collar, no microchip, so it was just bagged and disposed of."

She was already leafing rapidly through the other folders. "This might be one. Another dog. This one was killed by a car."

"Nothing unusual about that, is there?"

"Just the driver's story. He brought it in. He was pretty shaken. He said it jumped out and reared up on its hind legs as if it was trying to stop him."

"Interesting. Had he been drinking?"

"I don't think so." She lowered her voice. "They don't generally bring in the animals if they're over the limit."

She closed the last folder. "There aren't any others."

"Angela, I'm most grateful for your time. Sorry to bother you when you're so busy."

"No problem."

Thinking about it on the drive back I wondered if the animals were becoming a little intoxicated with their new capabilities. There were certainly five here that had over-reached themselves, and these were just the ones that had been brought to the Animal Centre. I found myself guiltily hoping there were a whole lot more.

I made doubly sure that all the doors and windows were locked before I poured myself a beer, went into the lounge, and drew the curtains. I was thinking: *This is Ron's problem, not yours, you know, so why do you have to get in so deep?* I supplied the answer myself. *Come on, it's no good thinking that way. It's everyone's problem now. Ron's in Bristol, and Viv's at her mother's, and you have to do what you can, like it or not.*

Viv had 'phoned a bit earlier. I told her I missed her. She laughed and said she'd only been gone one day, but it was true. Apart from anything else, Viv is a really practical, down-to-earth person; it would have been good to discuss things with her. On second thoughts, I didn't think I could tell her about this morning's incident with the cat. What with that and the dogs last night and everything else I felt tense and ill at ease. Perhaps that was it: if Viv had been around, things would have seemed more normal, more settled. I heaved a long sigh as I dropped into the armchair. It was the first time I'd relaxed all day. And then I switched on the TV to watch the evening news.

I watched the national news without much interest. Then the local news came on and I watched that without much interest. And then the last item came on and I jerked upright in my chair.

"A young boy had a narrow escape today after being attacked in Thornton Park by a group of cats." The newsreader pronounced "cats" with a little separation, to give it emphasis, but if he thought it was a humorous item he was keeping his face commendably neutral. "Some teenagers playing football nearby heard his screams and came to the rescue. Craig Hawley reports."

The report had been filmed in the park. The interviewer was bending over a nine-year-old boy, who was speaking into his microphone. The youngster had a strong regional accent. He was saying "There were loads of them, all grabbin' at me clothes and pullin' me down." The interviewer, flicking the mic briefly back to himself said: "You mean clawing at you?" "No!" exclaimed the boy. "They were grabbin' me, like this!" and he grabbed the hem of the unfortunate interviewer's jacket between finger and thumb and tugged hard. "And then they got me down and they was squeezin' me throat." He lifted his chin and pointed. His throat was covered with scratches and small red bruises.

The interviewer straightened up to address the camera. He looked distinctly uncomfortable. He seemed uncertain whether to play the item for laughs. "Well," he said, "it isn't often that you hear of cats ganging up on a child. Being mobbed by pussy cats sounds a bit like being hit with a pillow, but obviously this little boy has had a terrifying experience. He may be a little confused about the details but he can count himself lucky that the bravery of these local lads saved him from injury. Craig Hawley, Channel News, Thornton Park." As he was signing off, the camera was panning round to finish on a group of teenagers, all of whom were grinning hugely and jostling each other to get into the picture.

I went straight to the 'phone and spoke to the desk sergeant at the police station.

"This is Dr Ingman. Can you tell me when I could have a word with DI Gifford?"

"Just a moment, sir. I think I have a note here. Ah, no, this was for a Dr Heskisson."

"That's right. Dr Heskisson is my colleague. We came to see the DI on Thursday."

"Ah, right then. Could you give me a contact number? I'll get back to you in the next ten minutes."

To my slight surprise he did.

"DI Gifford was hoping you'd call." *Hoping? Had he made a mistake?* "He says he'd like to meet both of you at the station at nine o'clock tomorrow, if that's convenient."

"Dr Heskisson is out of town, I'm afraid, but I'll be there."

The DI took me straight back into his office. It was a small office and every available horizontal surface had a stack of paperwork on it, including the chair, which he cleared for me to sit down.

"Thanks for coming," he said.

I lost no time. "Did you see the item on the news about the little boy in Thornton Park?"

"Better than that: I went and had a look at him. The marks on his throat exactly matched the marks we found on Mary Reeves. I'd been puzzled by that. Never seen anything quite like it."

I was taken aback. I had been ready to spell it all out, but he was way ahead of me. "We tried to warn you…"

"I know, and I wasn't listening. But I'm listening now. What are we up against here? Your friend had some story about a disposable thumb."

"Opposable. That's only part of it." I was anxious not to identify myself too closely with Ron's arguments, which had found so little favour on the previous occasion. "You have to think of these animals as infected."

"What, like rabies?"

"Yes, like rabies, but a hundred times worse. Look, let me explain it this way. Humans have been domesticating animals for thousands of years. Initially it was done for some good reason—you know, cows for milk and meat, cats to control rats and mice, dogs for guarding, hunting and retrieving, that sort of thing. In the modern world some animals—cats and dogs particularly—have graduated to a more privileged status. They're not expected to work for a living; we keep them for companionship. The relationship between owner and pet is a strange one. It can get so close that people forget that it's only a thin veneer. Underneath it all, the cat or the dog is a wild animal. You only have to watch a cat tracking a bird to realize that. What this infection seems to do is to strip off that veneer. The animals become extremely aggressive towards people. And they revert to instinctive behaviours. In the case of dogs they roam and cooperate in large packs."

"Like wild dogs and wolves, you mean? Yeah, that fits. The patrol cars have reported seeing large groups of dogs."

"I had the bad luck to encounter a pack of them myself on Thursday night when I was walking home. They'd spread out right across the road. If I hadn't been able to flag a car down I think I would have become another item on your caseload."

"Did you report it?"

"No. I should have, I know. Quite honestly I was so relieved to get home and bolt the door behind me that I didn't think of it. But even if I had it wouldn't have been very convincing, would it? 'There are eight or nine dogs in our road.' You know, so what? You had to be there to feel the threat."

DI Gifford nodded. He picked up a slim folder. Despite the apparent confusion of his office he seemed to know just where to find things. "There's a case here." He looked up at me. "This is just between us, understood?"

"Understood. It won't go any further."

"We went out to a 999 call on Friday. This woman is cooking in her kitchen when the window smashes and suddenly the room's filled with snarling dogs. She shows amazing presence of mind. She grabs a drum of ground pepper and starts throwing it at them. That confuses them. They back off in a hurry and scram. My chaps were a bit puzzled about how they broke the window so I dropped by. There wasn't any sign of a tool, just a lot of broken glass. But the window glass had broken inwards, so I wondered what the glass was doing outside. It was from a milk bottle. If it was thrown at the window it would have gone through with the rest of the glass, so it must have been held in the hand to smash the window and then dropped. I thought some kids had smashed the window and the dogs came in afterwards. I mean there's no way dogs could do that, is there?"

"Well," I said, "these animals are doing unusually intelligent things."

"Yes, but how the hell could a dog pick up a milk bottle?"

We looked at each other. I held out my hand, palm upwards, and rotated the thumb over the fingers two or three times.

His eyes narrowed. "The opposable thumb. Christ. It's a bit of a lethal combination, isn't it?"

"It certainly is. There's another thing. Pack-hunting animals will often select the weakest victims to attack. You know, wolves prefer to go for a baby caribou, or a sick one that can't run as fast as the others. There are some signs of that happening here. I think the old and the young are especially vulnerable. Like Mary Jeeves, and the little boy in the park." I was about to mention the business of the baby in the pram too, but I thought better of it.

"See what you mean. But now you mention it, they don't really fit with your theory, do they? I mean, cats aren't pack animals."

"That's an interesting point. I puzzled about it too. You're right: lionesses will hunt and cooperate as a group, but most other members of the cat family are solitary hunters. I think the answer lies in Mary Jeeves. She rescued strays. She probably had at least twenty or thirty cats in there. It was a ready-made pack. Then they turned on her and killed her. I'd like to bet it was the same group that attacked the kid in the park. They've got used to working together."

He nodded thoughtfully. "Yeah, could be. Well, the bottom line is, of course, what to do about it? I've seen enough to know we can't leave these furry assassins wandering around. We could ask the RSPCA to round them up. They're used to handling animals and getting them out of weird places."

"I wouldn't feel comfortable with that. Their top priority is animal welfare. They'd try to catch them all, and then they'd want to get them checked over and rehomed. Ordinarily I wouldn't have any quarrel with that, but these animals are different. They're dangerous and they're smart. Even if they don't evade capture they're bound to escape, and the problem will be there all over again."

"Well, what else is there?"

"Kill them."

"What?"

"Kill them. Leaflet the area. Tell people there's been an outbreak of a deadly form of rabies. Any cats or dogs found on the streets will be culled. And then go round shooting every animal you see."

"We can't do that; we don't have the authority. We'd have to go through channels. Report it to DEFRA."

"DEFRA… Remind me."

"Department for Environment, Food and Rural Affairs. They've got an Animal Health and Welfare remit. They'd send down Ministry vets to take a look at the situation and advise."

"That could take months! More people could get killed."

"Well, I'm sorry, that's democracy. There'd be one unholy row if we did what you're suggesting. We could…"

His mobile rang. He drew it from a pouch on his belt. "Where? Okay, I'm on my way." He clicked off the 'phone and turned to me. "There's been another incident involving animals. Might be useful if you came with me."

The driver put the sirens and flashing lights on and we drove at high speed. I felt a ridiculous sense of privilege riding in the back with the DI. A few minutes later we pulled up in the local shopping centre. A uniformed officer led us into the maze of corridors between the shops. Some other officers were holding back a small crowd.

Gifford said to me: "Stay here for the moment. I just want to suss it out." Five minutes later he came back. "Trust me, doc, you don't want to see this. There are witnesses, though. Come on, we can go and talk to them." As we walked he said: "Lot of homeless people kip down in here, in the doorways— bit of a cardboard city. This poor bugger was attacked by dogs. The others saw it. Here they are."

There were five of them, sitting up against a wall, hands in pockets or wrapped around their arms. All were thin and grimy, and dressed in many layers of dirty rags. There was a strong odour of unwashed bodies. They kept glancing furtively at the two officers who had been left to keep an eye on them. It was understandable. They were probably more used to being moved on by the police than being asked to cooperate as witnesses. Gifford dropped to a crouch to talk to them at eye level. "Now lads, there's been a nasty killing here. All we want from you is to tell us what you saw. First off, who was he?"

One of the men seemed more ready to talk than the others. "Norm," he said. "We jost called him Norm."

"So what happened to Norm?"

"Must've been a dozen dogs came up the alley, surr. Seemed t'be lookin' fer trouble. Norm was jost gettin' up and they went for him. Ach, it was horrible. We were shout'n at 'em but 'tweren't no use."

"Have you seen these dogs before?"

"Seen them around, aye. But not in here before."

"How long've they been around?"

"Not long, a week or so. Norm's dog was with 'em."

"He had a dog?"

One of the others answered. "All the time. Porter, 'e called him. Dark brown job with white patch over one eye. 'e worshipped that dog. When 'e didn't 'ave enough to eat hisself he'd always give the dog first. It took off about a week back, and I seen it in there with the rest of 'em, tearin' him to pieces. There's gratitude for yer."

Neither of us spoke on the way back to station. I had to go and pick up Viv so I took my leave there.

"I'll get in touch with DEFRA," Gifford said. "In the meantime I'll ask my chaps to look out for any incidents involving animals, small or large, and report them to me. We'll get a bit of a dossier together."

"Do you think I could have your mobile number? Just in case I see something that could be useful to you. It'll save me explaining to the desk and going through all the usual palaver."

"Sure." He tore a page from his notebook, wrote the number on it, and handed it over. "Don't worry, Doc. We'll get it sorted. Thanks for your help."

On Monday I brought Ron up to date on developments. As I expected, he was chagrined to have missed all the action, but pleased to learn about DI Gifford's change of heart. Like me, though, he wondered how long it would take to get some official action.

Things seemed to have gone quiet. The next day a short article appeared in the local newspaper about the street person who had been killed by dogs. It was accompanied by a piece on the general dangers of sleeping rough. I showed it to Viv.

"I would have thought they would try for a news black-out on that," I said. "Those dogs are still on the loose. It could cause a bit of a panic."

"They probably couldn't keep a lid on it," she said. "Too many witnesses. I expect his friends in cardboard city got some nice handouts from the Press boys."

There was another item about some dogs that had been killed by a train. The driver had seen a pack of dogs running along the line instants before he ploughed into them. Two or three had been killed. The local hunt strenuously denied that the dogs belonged to them.

In the afternoon, Ron 'phoned me in the Department. He was a little breathless.

"Steve, are you tied up right now?"

"No, you're all right. What's the problem?"

"Julie's just 'phoned. She's down at Grangemouth Road. She went to pick Kieron up from play school. She's still there. Seems like there's an animal problem."

"I'm coming. Who else knows?"

"Well, Viv's in the picture. Julie 'phoned her first to ask her what she should do. Viv said to contact us. When I spoke to Julie I told her not to do anything before we arrived."

"Smart man. Okay. I think we should take one car, don't you? Let's go in yours."

Ron had a four-wheel drive with bull-bars in the front. It was the kind of vehicle I wanted to be in if there was going to be any trouble.

On the way, Ron provided some more details. "She always goes at this time. So do the other mums and dads—mostly mums, actually. The principal insists on them all coming at the same time, otherwise one kid gets his mummy and the others all start yelling the place down because they want their mummies too. Some of the mums pick up each other's children too; that's all right because the kids know them. So all the mums are in there, pulling small arms through coat sleeves and admiring those terrible crayon drawings the kids do, and then someone notices that the playground's filling up with dogs and cats. And the bloody animals are sitting there waiting."

I was trying to visualize the situation. "I suppose the playground's fenced?"

"Oh yes. It's got wire netting about six or seven feet high all round, to stop the kids climbing out. Or maybe it's to stop people climbing in."

"What about the gate?"

"They keep the gate locked during the day. During the good weather they like the kids to play in the open air as much as possible. I know that because Mrs Warbright told us when we first went down there to see if it was any good for Kieron. Mrs Warbright runs the place. Julie's into fresh air so that was one of the things she liked about it. Later on in the afternoon they take the children inside. I think that's when they unlock the gates, so the mums can come and fetch their little darlings."

I wasn't taken in by his jaunty manner. He was biting his lip furiously the whole journey and his gear-changing was nothing to write home about either.

"Can we drive through the gates?"

"Only if both are open. It'd be wide enough then."

When we arrived we could see that only the right-hand gate was open. Looking carefully at it through the windscreen, I thought I could make out a bolt securing the left-hand gate to the ground. There were animals in the playground and also a few behind us on the road, and none of them looked friendly. But one of us was going to have to get out to open that gate.

"I'll go," I said, and opened the passenger door before Ron could react.

My heart was banging in my ears. I moved forward as swiftly as I could and went to lift the bolt on the inside of the closed gate. As I did so I heard the most ferocious growl. Looking to the right I saw that the open gate was actually being held back by a Rotweiler, who was sitting against it. Presumably the gate was sprung and it may have taken several of them to push it open. This animal was making sure it stayed open for the rest. And the show of teeth confirmed that I was in his territory. I withdrew sharply. I thought for a moment, then tried to reach through the gate from the outside, biting my lip, fumbling for the bolt. The dog growled again. He couldn't see me, but he could almost certainly see my hand. I got ready to snatch it back in an instant if he attacked. I found the bolt. It was reluctant to move. I prised as hard as I could with my fingertips, grazing the other knuckles against the bars. Growl. I think he would have had a go at me by now if he hadn't been focused on the need to keep the gate back. My efforts had attracted attention from the playground, and several other dogs were moving towards me. Time was running out. I tried working the bolt back and forth. It squeaked, and the Rotweiler snarled and lunged. I whipped my hand back. Thank God the dog wasn't following through the attack; he was still keeping the gate back. But two things had happened: my finger was bleeding from a skinned knuckle and the wretched bolt had lifted. I reached in recklessly and slammed it round to stop it dropping back. Then I turned to the car.

I had left the passenger door open so that I could get back inside quickly, but now to my horror I saw that one of the dogs from the road was half way in. Ron seemed to be making futile attempts to beat it off with a road atlas. I stepped up quickly and slammed the door into the dog's hindquarters as hard as I could. The animal yelped with surprise and pain and backed off. Without hesitation I drew the door back, jumped in and slammed it shut.

"Well done, chap." Ron licked his lips. He was breathless and sweating. He edged the 4WD forward, nudging the left-hand gate open with the bull-bars. "I'm going to drive round to the left and back the car up to the entrance. Then we can get out of the back doors straight into the school."

We sounded the horn just before clambering into the back of the vehicle, and Mrs Warbright was there, opening the door for us. I was glad to see that she locked it again as soon as we were inside the building. It was quite crowded and noisy in the front room, with about a dozen mothers and twenty or thirty children, aged from about two to five. The mothers were mostly talking to each other, although the children hadn't noticed that, judging from the excitement with which they were retelling their day. As soon as she saw Ron, Julie came hurrying over with Kieron, and I noticed that Viv was with her.

"That was nice of you, Viv," I said.

"The poor girl sounded so shaken," she said. "The least I could do was to come down and offer moral support. There were about a dozen dogs and a few cats then and it was scary enough. Look at it now."

We crossed to the windows, which overlooked the playground.

"Jesus."

I'd only had a restricted view of the playground from the gate, and after that we were entirely focused on getting into the building. Now that I had a full view I could see the scale of the problem. There had to be forty or fifty dogs and about twenty or thirty cats out there.

"How did you get in, Viv?"

"Very quickly."

"But there was a Rotweiler on the gate."

"Then I'm glad I didn't see him."

I nodded. She had a lot of guts, Viv. The animals were prowling relentlessly back and forth in the playground, casting baleful glares in the direction of the school. There was a feeling of contained energy about them. A few more cats and dogs hurried in through the gate.

A dog sat down, raised its muzzle and howled and another followed suit. *Was that a summons?* I wondered. Under my breath I muttered: "Problem or opportunity?"

"What do you mean?" Viv's hearing was acute as ever.

"Hang on, you'll see in a moment. Can you see where Mrs Warbright is?"

"She's over there."

I crossed the room and spoke to Mrs Warbright. "I'm going to summon help. Obviously nobody must leave the building at the moment."

"Obviously. I would have called the police before now but Mrs Ingman insisted we waited for you." Her manner was a bit starchy, but she was probably frightened too.

"I've got a hot-line to the right sort of help," I said, in a confidential whisper, aware at the same time that my attempt at charm had gone absolutely nowhere.

I spent some time on the 'phone to DI Gifford, describing the layout, the number of mothers and children, the numbers of cats and dogs, even the position of the Rotweiler. Then it was a matter of waiting.

Half an hour later we heard the sirens cut off as the police cars entered Grangemouth Road. A Land Rover and a van banged through the gate and stopped just inside. From the back of the van two police jumped out carrying riot shields and sticks. A third ran behind them and locked both halves of the gate. Then they jumped back in and brought the vehicles round to the entrance door. I went to let them in but Mrs Warbright was already there. The DI had been as good as his word. First to come in was a five-man armed response unit carrying automatic weapons. They were followed by DI Gifford, who flashed a grin at me. He obviously relished action. Finally the two-man rearguard, still wielding their riot shields and sticks, backed through the door. They made quite a stir as they entered the front room.

Gifford said to me out of the corner of his mouth. "Sorry it took a while. I had to summon up the swat squad and brief them."

"Nice entrance. We're glad to see you." I took him over to the window so that he could see the problem for himself.

"Creepy, isn't it, the way they're circling quietly around," he said. "How can we be sure these aren't just ordinary cats and dogs."

"If they were normal they'd be chasing each other, wouldn't they? And look at the way they walk. Flat-footed."

"The opposable thumb?"

"That's right."

"And you think they're all here?"

"Can't guarantee, but I can't imagine there are many more than this. Something's attracted them all here. Maybe one of them spotted the children playing earlier in the day and called the others. If their instinct is to isolate one or two vulnerable animals out of a herd, twenty or thirty children must be an overwhelming stimulus to them. My feeling is that you've got the whole damned problem here in one big cage."

He nodded and gave a quick grimace. "I'll talk to the mums."

Gifford was about six-foot-four and had a voice to match. He had no difficulty in getting their attention.

"Now, boys and girls. I'm Detective-Inspector Colin Gifford. First of all I want to say that Mrs Warbright has done exactly the right thing in keeping you all here." I glanced at Mrs Warbright who was flushing importantly. "Those aren't ordinary animals out there." I thought: *How much is he going to tell them?* "They are carrying a very nasty disease, a sort of rabies. A bite from one could be very dangerous. They're going to have to be put down anyway, but in the interests of the children's safety and your own we're going to have to do it here and now. Now I know that isn't very pleasant, but it's a job that has to be done. The situation is all under control. I just want you to clear this room now. Mrs Warbright will lead you into the rooms at the back. It'll be a bit crowded but it shouldn't be for long. You'll hear quite a bit of noise, and then when it's perfectly safe to leave we'll come and get you. Any questions?"

There weren't, so Mrs Warbright started to herd her flock into the back. I noticed Julie, Ron and Kieron among them. The marksmen took up positions by the windows.

"Doc," he said to me. "I think you'd better go in the back too. I don't want any civilians caught up in this."

"Right you are," I said to him. "Before I go could I make a quick suggestion?"

"Yup."

"Those windows aren't that high off the ground. When you open them you could get some animals jumping in here. It would be an idea to station one or two people to cover the back of the room."

"Will do." He was already taking ear protectors out of his pocket.

I joined the others in the back. One of the girls had started up a sing-song to take the kids' minds off what was happening. By now all the other mums had joined in. The children were looking at them in astonishment. It sounded awful and it was a thoroughly good idea. After a few moments the sound of their singing was almost drowned by the chatter of automatic gunfire. I could see the mums looking sideways at each other but they carried on. It was all over in a few minutes.

Another few minutes passed and then Gifford appeared at the door and the singing died abruptly. "All right, boys and girls," he said. "You can come out now. My officers and Mrs Wainright will conduct you to the gate. Thank you for being so cooperative."

They all filed out. I noticed that the van had now been moved to the left of the gate, blocking the view into the playground. It was a deft touch. We watched the mothers and children file out to the gate. We could still hear the piping voices of the children chattering happily to the mothers, who were trying hard to pay attention to them. I went back inside with Viv, Ron and Julie. Ron was still carrying the wide-eyed Kieron. I went into the front room and looked out onto the playground, which was now a scene of carnage. Two of the officers were going round with automatic pistols, finishing off anything that was still moving.

Gifford came up behind me. "That is one of the saddest things I've ever had to do in my whole life."

"I have to hand it to you, DI. That operation was managed expertly from beginning to end. Will you get much flak for this?"

"I don't care if I do. What we were talking about before, that needed to go through proper channels. This was different. It's my job to protect the public. Sometimes that requires an on-the-spot decision. I'm prepared to defend it. The safety of those kids came first."

"I'd be more than happy to back you. You know, in case someone tries to rubbish the stuff about the animals."

"Thanks, but I think it'll speak for itself. Mary Reeves and the kid in the park ties it up for the cats, and poor old Norm for the dogs. I don't think there'll be any trouble."

We all shook hands and left. Ron dropped Julie and Kieron off and took me back to the University to pick up my car. He was unusually quiet, no doubt reflecting on all that had happened. He had been fortunate to emerge from this relatively unscathed. I was fairly certain that what he had done had breached Genetic Manipulation Advisory Board guidelines. If that had come to light his lab would have been closed down immediately. He might then have faced further prosecution. It would be hard to demonstrate a direct connection between his error of judgment and the disastrous changes in the animals—we weren't even sure of it ourselves—but even so he would be feeling the weight of responsibility for the deaths of two people and so many animals. It was a heavy burden to bear for someone who just wanted to grow nice dahlias.

It had been a traumatic time and we all tried to put it behind us. For the moment we stopped seeing each other. Nothing was said; it just seemed to be a matter of mutual consent. However, the course for the new academic year was running and that brought me into contact with Ron again in February. There was no awkwardness; we simply picked up where we'd left off. I was glad; I realized that life had been a little dull without him. Then in late March Julie went into confinement and Viv and I visited her in hospital. All had gone well and it was another little boy—they named him Paul—and everyone was very happy. To my mild surprise, Viv said the little pink mass of wrinkles was very beautiful, which may just have been Viv being tactful but perhaps it had tapped her innate maternal instincts. Viv invited them over when things had got a bit more settled and in this way we picked up the threads again socially.

Then we had some news of our own. To our utter astonishment and delight, after we'd long given up hope, Viv was pregnant. The girls chattered happily on the 'phone, and Julie said she had a lot of things to lend her, so they invited us over for tea on Sunday.

It hit us as soon as we'd gone into the lounge. The garden was totally transformed. It looked ten times as large as it actually was. There was a water feature, curved paths, grasses and bamboos, dwarf conifers and heathers, and a small patio area. Even the hard outline of the fences was already starting to dissolve behind ceanothus, pyracanthas, clematis and climbing roses. My jaw had dropped so low I thought I would have to winch it up.

Viv recovered first. "I say, the garden looks fantastic! You've done absolute wonders, Ron."

I was confused. "I thought you said you were going to specialize in dahlias."

"Oh, it's not my handiwork, it's Julie's. I gave up gardening last year after, well, you know. But Julie took over. She did the design and had a chap come in to do the landscaping, and another chap to lay the electricity cables for the water feature and another chap to lay the patio. After that we were in and out of garden centres every weekend. It's cost me a fortune."

"It's beginning to look nice, isn't it?" said Julie. "It gives me a lot of pleasure. I'm out there every day. It's ever such good exercise. I put on a bit of weight having Paul, so this will help me get it off."

We tore our eyes away from the vista only to find them riveted to a spectacular display of dried flowers and grasses that was fairly exploding from a shallow vase on the sideboard.

Viv gasped again. "Julie, that's gorgeous."

"Thank you. I think it works quite well. I joined the local garden society. They've been running a course in flower arranging, so I thought I'd go along. It's great fun. Now, let's get some tea. Viv, do you want to give me a hand?"

As the girls went out I turned back to the garden, taking in more details, such as a small raised gravelled area with miniature alpines adjacent to the patio.

"It's so lovely, so tranquil," I breathed. "She's really got a talent." Then turning to Ron: "What about you, Ron? Have you taken up a new hobby?"

"Me? Hobby? Who's got time for hobbies? In the day, I'm at work, Kieron's at play school, and she's taken the baby with her, rushing around to friends, swapping cuttings and the like. Then it seems like every evening there's something else: garden society, flower arranging, and God knows what-all, so I have to stay at home and look after the children. Come the weekend we're off to a garden centre or visiting some famous garden to see if anyone else does it better. I can't think what's got into her, can you?"

"I really can't imagine, Ron, I really can't imagine."

⁔℃